The Gingerbread House

Lesley Summer is a foundling with a gold band in her hair—gipsy's gold. They say she cannot speak, only repeat that her name is Honey; yet she reads what is written over the arched door of the orphanage: 'Count Your Blessings.' She can learn that the Matron rules with other words: 'In here, Im's the law.'

There are mists from the past in the confusion of her mind—a nightmare, a memory of a scream and a far-off splash that chokes it short deep down in the ground. Yet there is Mr. Barleydrop, who gives sweets to crocodiles. There is Jonah Rohan, who opens the gate and lets her go free. Then at last there is Ireland, where she discovers 'Tinker', a dog as broken as herself, and surely with the same nobility.

A mystery surrounds her, and the solution of it makes compulsive reading down to the last word. This is a truly magnificent novel, that Alice Dwyer-Joyce's thousands of fans will read with joy.

By the same author

Price of Inheritance
The Silent Lady
Doctor Ross of Harton
The Story of Doctor Esmond Ross
Verdict of Doctor Ross
Dial Emergency for Doctor Ross
Don't Cage Me Wild
For I Have Lived Today
Message for Doctor Ross
Cry the Soft Rain
Reach for the Shadows
The Rainbow Glass
The Brass Islands
Prescription for Melissa
The Moonlit Way
The Strolling Players
The Diamond Cage
The Master of Jethart

Alice Dwyer-Joyce

The Gingerbread House

ST. MARTIN'S PRESS
NEW YORK

ROBERT HALE LIMITED
LONDON

© *Alice Dwyer-Joyce 1977*
First published in the United States of America 1977

All rights reserved. For
information write:

St. Martin's Press, Inc.
175 Fifth Avenue
New York, N.Y. 10010

Library of Congress Catalog 76–28072

First published in Great Britain 1977

ISBN 0 7091 5785 1

Robert Hale Limited
Clerkenwell House
Clerkenwell Green
London EC1R 0HT

Printed in Great Britain by
Clarke, Doble & Brendon Ltd.
Plymouth

To my father,
John Peacocke Myles,
I dedicate this story.

Chapter One

"IN HERE, IM'S THE LAW"

"Count your blessings."

The policeman read out the writing on the curved scroll over the front door of the grey stone house, as he reached for the bell pull.

"Cor! That's a rich one. That is."

There was a clang-clanging from somewhere far within and I looked up at him and was cheered a bit that he winked at me. The woman wardress, who stood at the other side of me, had a hard face. She muttered to herself that the bell had an empty sound to it . . . almost as empty as our stomachs were after the journey. She doubted that those inside would offer us even a cup of tea.

Then the door opened a crack and two eyes peered out. "Missis is expecting you."

The door was open fully now and a small girl stood on the mat, looking at us out of the anxiety of her face.

Time was spaced out as dreams are. There was a lady behind a desk with a book open in front of her and the policeman was putting down a parcel for her safe keeping, or so he told her.

"So here you are at last? We had quite given you up," she smiled but there was no warmth in her.

The policeman was telling her how sorry he was that we were late but it had been a hard place to find, the Female Orphan House.

7

My hair was loose down my back held by an Alice in Wonderland band. The wardress had combed it out very carefully, but now it must be plaited or sheared off short. I had got used to having my head examined by many different eyes.

"She's clean. It can be plaited."

"Lesley Summer," the woman behind the desk said and I thought it time that I told them my real name.

"My name is Honey."

Somebody explained that that was all I said, but it was a treat to have me say anything and it was no good discussing the child in front of her. I was to go to the playroom. The dream faded or maybe, the reality. Over the next five years, I learned about reality the hard way, the reality of being a foundling with no kith and kin, with no person who had any real interest in me, with nobody to fight my battles for me but my own self. It was a time when Female Orphan Houses were called just that and not Mayfields, or Ferndale, or Holly Lodge. There were no pink and blue and clover and red and green doors . . . no house-mothers in pastel nylon dresses, and there was very little smiling. It was a grim struggle to keep out of trouble and constantly there was trouble brewing like a teapot on the hob of the range. It came from the matron, from the "misses", from the bigger girls. The place was a hen run and there was a pecking order to it and that first day, I was the smallest, weakest, most vulnerable chick.

"Missis" lifted a bell from her desk and rang it twice and the child, who had opened the door to us, appeared at a run, bobbing a curtsey to the policeman and to the room in general.

"Take Lesley Summer to the playroom, Betsey. Lesley, say good-bye to the constable and to the wardress and thank them for taking such good care of you."

I put my hand out to the wardress, but she did not see it. The policeman lifted me up into his arms and I felt the scrub of his face against mine, remembered and forgot the scrub of a man's face against my face from another life, forgot it, quick as I remembered it.

"Thank you for having me."

The children were in the playroom, all alike in grey dresses and flowered aprons. They crowded round me, running like hens to flung corn.

"Betsey is my name," whispered the girl, who held my hand. "Don't show them you're frit."

I held her hand like a drowning man clutching at a spar.

"Her name is Lesley Summer. She come with a policeman and a jail woman. Best not harm her or the jail woman will take you to clink."

"My name is Honey."

A big girl thrust her face up close to mine, her arms akimbo.

"And mine is Lady Caroline Vere de Vere. That's why I talk so posh like."

"Is it a workhouse?" I whispered and Betsey told me it was the same sort of thing.

"It's a place for female girls, what nobody don't want."

"Am I to stay here for ever?"

There was a terror that possessed me as bad as any nightmare, but I was awake and it was no dream. I began to learn where my travels had landed me. I had ended up in a pit as deep as . . . as deep as . . . as deep as . . . I did not know what. There was a gauze that blocked out my thoughts. Yet after a time, they told me that there was an escape from this grey stone house, where on wet days, the furniture and the walls ran with moisture from the damp. The big girls were mostly taken out as domestic helps eventually. That was why we must all learn to sew and knit and scrub and polish . . . blacklead the stoves. We must see to it that we knew how to set a fire so that it lit with one match. We must avoid at all costs the temptation to sweep dust under the rag rugs.

9

There was better hope for a bright girl, but I was classed as being far from that. I could not remember. They all said that, said that I could be as bright as a button, if I wanted to try. Nobody realised how hard I tried, but I could never sort the dream from the reality. I had no hope of being good at lessons. If I had been, there might be a chance of my becoming a counter hand in a shop, to slice out a yard of calico or snip ribbon. For that honour, you must know pounds, shillings and pence and do sums in your head like lightning, for the change.

I tried to count my blessings, was reminded to do it every time I came in through the front door, or played in the asphalt yard. Betsey was a blessing without price. I had a roof over my head and a bed to sleep in and I remembered a time I had had neither, and made up the balance of living with laughter, but here was no laughter, or if there was, it was tight-rationed.

That first day, Betsey took me into the playroom and introduced me to the inmates and presently a big girl took charge of me and brought me upstairs to a long room with latticed windows at each end of it and a ceiling that sloped to meet the walls. She had stopped at a cupboard on the landing, measured me with her eye, collected some clothes. Now she brought me to a bed, in a line of white coverleted beds, black enamelled, with mattresses very thin and a blanket no warmer than a blanket could be and retain its name.

"One blanket, pair of sheets, one pillowslip and see to it that nobody takes a fancy to the blanket and pinches it off'n your cot. It's bleedin' cold here in the hard days . . . and Mrs. Creek will flay you if you've a blanket lost . . . not but what it wouldn't be your fault . . . and call her "Missis" or "Ma'am" every time you speak to her, after every sentence if you're obliged to . . . keeps her happy, if we all bow and scrape. Just for now, I've got to get the clothes off your back to put in mothballs. So strip off, right to the skin. I have your new clobber here and I'm almost sure to be right as to sizes. If I'm not, it don't matter none . . . a hem here or a tuck there. Don't look so scared. We've all been through it and we're all in the same bowl of porage in this establishment and much good may it do us!"

I took off my head scarf first and folded it and put it on the white coverlet. Then I undressed, right down to my skin and stood there, shivering for all that it was summer.

"I'm supposed to see that you take a bath, but you're clean. Just tell Missis you've had one if she asks you. You don't want a cold bath in a rusty hip bath and we'll have to carry up jugs of water and the dirty water downstairs again. It's in regulations, but regulations was made to be bust wide. Else we wouldn't survive in this merciful home for poor orphan female children, would we?"

I put on the cotton vest and the long black stockings, the white knickers, that reached to elastic knees, the white petticoat and the grey dress on top.

My companion eyed me without enthusiasm.

"There's more to it than that. You have a wool vest in winter and a grey wool cardigan . . . but for heaven's sake, you gone and forgot your liberty bodice. How do you hope to keep your stockings up without it?"

She was examining the silk stuff of my discarded dress and her fingers played with the bells on the collar. She went over the head scarf and touched the gold rings on its border one by one.

"You must have come from a real posh place. How happen you landed up in jug?"

It was a long story and I knew maybe a tenth of it. The rest of it was behind the muffed glass of my memory.

"I can't remember. It was always summer and there were tents and caravans and gallopers that went round and round,

11

and music . . . loud music . . . and so many people . . . I don't remember. I wasn't unhappy . . . only lonely . . . used to think it was a funny thing to be lonely with the whole place packed chock full of people . . . and all of them happy."

I was dressed in the uniform of the Female Orphan House and my liberty bodice was now in correct position, though it signified no liberty for me, only four suspenders that held my black stockings in position and was fastened with a row of buttons down the front.

"You've a lot to say for a girl that don't talk much," my companion said and I looked at her out of black sad eyes.

"I was a dummy," I said and no more than that, while she looked at me in such amazement, that I had to go on.

"I didn't talk at all, one time."

"Oh, well! it takes all sorts, and you're half sharp."

She wheeled away no longer interested in me or my problems.

"Well, there you are then, all fitted out in fashion and mind you keep your stuff tidy. You have a change of every stitch you've got on, in the bottom drawer in that chest there . . . put it there myself just now, and if you can use marking ink, you're to write your name on every last bit of it. Don't lose nothing neither, or there'll be murder done. Do you know how to mark clothes and that? Oh, no! I couldn't hope for it. Get some from Missis, and a nib. I'll do it for you later. I ain't got enough toil to fill my days, without helping some of God's holy orphans, what can't help theirselves. . . ."

There was a clang-clang of a bell downstairs and she drew in her breath.

"Run fast as you can. If we're late for dinner, we'll cop it."

The dining room was a long space with a scrubbed deal table, set with place after place of bowl and spoon and chair. At the head of it, stood Mrs. Creek, who had admitted me to the Home. There was a ladle in her hand and on the table in front of her, a tureen. I wondered how I knew what a tureen was and imagined that it came from the land of dreams and imagination. I was hustled into a chair and found Betsey beside me and was glad, remembered the kindness of her hoarse voice.

"We pass the empty bowls along and they come back full, and each girl has her day's turn to give out the bread."

There was a girl, my own size, engaged in the task, going from place to place. She had a large wicker basket of cut bread and she lifted out a piece at a time and put it on the table beside each spoon. The bowls went round and were duly filled and came back to their owners and a silence fell and the whole room held its breath.

"For what the blessed Lord hath given us, in His great bounty, make us truly thankful," Mrs. Creek's voice said and I wondered if she were in a hurry to get off to her own room for kidneys and bacon, but where such a thought came from, I did not know. There was a smell of frying kidneys and bacon, strong in our noses, but no such luxury in sight.

I watched the other girls and did what they did . . . lifted my spoon and dipped it into my bowl, ate it hunger-quickly, the barley and lentils and peas and carrots. It was watery but who was I to complain, who had gone without food many a time? Again, came the dream, the nightmare, and I pushed it away from me. It was comforting to sop the bread up in the watery gravy and it was gone too soon.

"Half an hour in the yard now and then back to lessons," said Betsey at my side.

There was some bread left in the basket and the big girls grabbed it, as we walked past on the way to the door.

"Waste not, want not," whispered Betsey in my ear. "But the big ones always nab what's left."

Then in the play yard, they were all about me, like vultures about a dying animal. Who was I? What crime had I done

13

to land me in jail? Had I no people? It must have been something awful to end up in clink. Come on and tell them.

I was rescued by one of the bigger girls. Missis said I was to have my hair done right. I had been "queening it round" in a gilt Alice in Wonderland band, but now this was discarded and left in Mrs. Creek's office on her desk.

"You should have had your hair done when you changed out of your own clothes," said the big girl savagely and plaited my hair too tightly to pay me back for what was no sin of omission on my part.

"You're as black as a crow and your eyes are like currants," she said and asked me why I couldn't plait my own hair.

"I can," I said and then she demanded why I hadn't. Did I want to get them all into hot water with "Missis"?

"Where's your ribbons then?"

"I only have that band."

She tut-tutted at me and did not like me one bit, searched round in her pocket and came up with a bootlace, bit it in two with her teeth.

"This 'ull have to serve then. I daresay you're used to tying your raven locks up with bootlaces."

She gave me a vicious little shove in the back in the direction of the play-ground.

"Now see you keep your hair tidy at all times. It's got to be fine-combed every Friday and washed out proper once a fortnight. Else you'll get a smacked bum. . . ."

She sighed as a bell rang clangourously.

"There! I've spent my free time, plaiting your head. Go along to the school-room with you. You'll be in the bottom class."

There were fifty or sixty girls in the school and the number varied little and they all worked out their lessons in the same room, with its floorboards bare and its windows so high that there was no chance of looking at the world outside. There

14

were desks of dark wood and two girls sat at each desk and shared the depths of its interior. There was a blackboard at each end of the room and little knots of girls, under monitresses, big girls, who had attained the honour of teaching the little ones, who needed to be "brought on". It seemed that I was one of these. I had not spoken much so I was not able to read. It was time I started to learn. Yet I knew I had read "Count your blessings," to myself over the school gates, before the policeman had pronounced the words aloud. I had been able to read them and knew what it meant, had presently counted Betsey as one of my blessings and I knew what blessings were, knew there were very few of them in this "Female Orphan House". There was a secret world that I inhabited where nobody came but myself . . . and now I was bottom of the whole school, under the tutilage of the girl who had dressed me in orphan garb and who now was given the task of teaching me my letters.

"A, B, C, D, E, F," she said. "Come on, now. It's no good twisting your hands together like a widow mourning for her mate. You've got to get it off and learn to read proper and it don't make the slightest difference to me if you open them big saucer black eyes at me and beg me to take pity on you. I ain't got an ounce of pity in my whole body and if I had, I wouldn't dole it out to the ones like you. You come from jail and you must ha' done something to ha' landed up there in the first place. . . ."

Something came floating into my mind from the secret world and before I could stop my mouth, I said it out to her.

"The ram, the bull, the heavenly twins. . . . The sign of the ram is the first sign in the Zodiac. Mars, the God of War is its ruler and the Sun is exalted therein. In the Tarot, it refers to the card called the Emperor. . . ."

"The girl's cracked!" exclaimed my monitress and she said it so loudly that the mistress of the class looked over at her

15

and asked her what was wrong.

"Come on, for pity's sake, stop your clown-act. Get on the alphabet and leave the ram alone. Don't draw Miss down on us, or you'll learn better."

"A, B, C, D, E, F, G, H, I, J, K."

"You know them all, you sneaking little brat. When I get you outside, I'll teach you to make a monkey out of me."

In the mists of the past, there had been a man's laugh and a voice.

"I can't make a monkey out of you. You're a monkey already . . . my baby, but you'll not get your way with me this time."

My mind was a clear crystal pool and the thoughts swam in it like fish and I could see every scale on every one of them. Then, as if a cloud moved low in the sky and reflected on the surface of the pool, the water would turn into milk and the fish would be gone and nothing to see but white opacity and my head felt dull and full of sawdust. It happened to me all the time and I was very familiar with the exasperation I caused. I knew that my eyes were empty, looking into the far distance of nothing, but I could not see what was in the dream . . . and my head ached with trying to remember.

That day, the big girl, who had been my monitress cornered me against a brick wall in the play yard.

"What's all the talk about rams and bulls and twins and that? I ain't heard nothing like it. What was you talking about?"

I looked up at the slated gables of the house. The lozenged windows were pretty and made the place like a giant's cottage.

I shivered and shook my head, told her that I could not remember what I had said.

"You may have been a dummy before, but you're a daffy now," she said and slapped me hard across the face.

"Maybe that'll bring your senses back to you, but you had

16

bells on your dress collar and rings on your head cloth. You told me that you were somewhere with caravans and gallopers, that went round and round. It's my opinion you're a gyppo child. Is that it?"

I shook my head and told her that I could not remember and she asked me if I wanted another crack on the side of my face to help me.

I clasped my hands to beg her for mercy and she looked at me scornfully.

"Cor! You've even forgotten what I said to you just now. It ain't no good looking for pity. I told you. I ain't got a pinch of pity in my whole body, no more than anybody else here."

She slapped me again and I cringed away from her, with my face in my hands.

"I haven't forgotten. You helped me change my clothes and you gave me a bootlace for my hair. You were kind to me. . . ."

She tired of her bullying at that and turned away.

"You're dumb when it suits you and daffy when it suits you. I'll thank you not to be daffy with me, if I gets the job of teaching you to read. I daresay you'll shake your wits out in a week or two. The first five years is the worst in here and that's a true word, sure as my name is Sal."

Maybe the first five days were the worst. I do not know. It was a hard life by any standard. The house looked bleak enough from the outside for all its gables and pretty latticed windows, but inside, there was real harshness. My friendship with Betsey was a small bright candle, which lit the darkness of every day. Without her, I think I might have died from the loneliness, loneliness again in a crowded place and I had known that before.

We got up in the dark of the morning and washed at a tin basin on our lockers. At bedtime, we each carried up a jug of water and in the winter it had congealed into ice or near ice by the next day. There was a prison atmosphere about the Orphan House, as we carried down our slops to spill them into the drain in the yard. We walked in line one behind the other and a big girl stood to watch us pass and check that our clothes were on properly and that our hair was neat.

In the dining room, we stood at our places for "family prayers" and they were read out by Mrs. Creek or by one of the mistresses. Then came the passing of the bowls in a regimented line, that turned a right angle at every corner of the table and came back to its owner with porage. On my first morning, I asked Betsey in a whisper what it was.

"It's porage and you'd best sup it all up. There ain't nothing else now and there ain't nothing more till dinner."

I dipped my spoon into it and it had no likeness to porage. Porage was crisp with brown sugar and luscious with cream and there had been a plate with a jester painted on the bottom of it. You ate the porage and at last, you saw the jester, maybe his cap and bells, maybe his pointed toes and you finished it up so that you could see his picture and not because your stomach was twisted with hunger. Then there was a boiled egg and toast and marmalade, but as soon as I thought of it, it was all gone again, like fog before the sun and I was back at the scrubbed boards of the table in the Orphan House and the taste of the gruel was mean in my mouth and Betsey's whisper hoarse in my ear.

"My! You polished that up quick, but don't go asking for more. There ain't never no more."

I felt the blankness of my eyes and thought of somebody called Oliver Twist. He had found himself in a similar situation to mine and he had asked for more. He had walked the length of the room and his voice had been as thin as himself. I had cried at the story for it was only a story. It was not true, just something somebody had made up. "Oliver Twist Asks for More . . ." and there was a man in a braided uniform with

18

a cane in his hand. . . . Perhaps I had known him somewhere in another life, but it was only a fairy tale like Hansel and Gretel. It was like the dream that I had again and again, the dream of the Gingerbread House. Even as I dreamt it, I knew it was a dream, but this in no way detracted from its horror. I knew it was just the story of Hansel and Gretel, but how could I ever have got mixed up with it? I knew well that I should not be frightened, nor terrified, for terrified I was every time I dreamt it. I knew that I would wake up soon and be safe in my bed, but first I must play out the dream and it had different forms, each one more frightening than the last. There was this house and it was not just any house. It was a place built to entice children from their homes and from their mothers and fathers. It had a brown thatched roof with wide eaves, but the roof was not straw. It was made of gingerbread. Hungry children might see it or find it in the deep parts of the forest and break off a piece of it, because they were starving. There was a window at each side of the door and the glass was sugar, sweet to eat, with small lozenge panes set out with criss-cross icing. The walls were gingerbread too and the sills of the windows, white painted with icing, like the latticed windows. There were flowers growing by the front wall, hollyhocks that crept up to reach the eaves, but they had stems of green angelica. The flowers were pink and white, busy with the humming of late bees, for the sun was low in the sky and soon, it would be night, when the bats fly and tangle in your hair. I knew the dream so well, but there were changing forms of it. The front door should be polished bright, but in the nightmare, there was moss growing on it and part of it rotted away. The doorstep, which should be as white as snow, in the dream, was grey with dirt and neglect and the people had all gone away. I am so familiar with this dream, that I know what will happen next . . . how the door will creak-groan open and how I will creep inside, where the ghosts are, the ghosts of

19

furniture hidden away beneath white sheets, but who is to say it is only a chair there or a chesterfield, or a table and not wicked malignant spirits, who clutch at you with horny hands? The sheets are moving and it is only the draught from the open door. You must hold tight to the fact that it is only the draught moving the white sheets and not hands reaching for you. There is somebody in the attic behind the dormer windows. You could see the windows from outside before ever you went in, pretty latticed windows, but now there is a board that creaks in the ceiling where the attic is. The nightmare turns this way and that and it is as familiar as my own face in the glass. I have somebody with me and I do not like her much, but surely she will protect me from harm? A spider's web floats across my face and a thick-legged spider runs down my bare arm and I scream and she laughs. "Hansel and Gretel," she says. "Look at the bread all gone mouldy on the table. There's nobody living here now." Somebody has set a place at the table with a knife as big as a carver and I know it is a "King's Pattern" knife, but whose house it is, I do not know . . . never in any of the dreams. I think sometimes, that I must ask whose house it is, but then I forget to ask, just pick up the knife and look at the handle and see the hound engraved there, a fine graceful hound-dog, small and well-proportioned, with his head held proudly and his fore feet crossed one over the other. It's from "home", I imagine, but where home is, I have no idea. I have no home and we have come to this awful place. It is a cottage in a forest, where a charcoal burner might live, a cottage from Grimm's fairytales, but it has fallen to desolation. It is Hansel and Gretel all over again and I never want to hear that story any more, but there is an oven in the kitchen. The witch wants to roast Gretel in the oven. There is a pot to boil Hansel into stew and he is in a cage till he gets fat. He held a bone out to the witch through the bars every day to let her feel how thin he was and she waited day after day, but one day, she would wait no more. Then the nightmare is gone and the cottage vanished with the mists and I am in the garden, breaking off the cups of the hollyhocks and finding them just hollyhock cups and not pink and white icing sugar. The stems are not made of angelica and they are hard and like fibre to break and the witch will not be pleased, that I have broken one of her holly-hocks. Then the nightmarish quality is back a hundred times worse than before. The oven is not in the kitchen. It is in the garden and it should have a wood door set flat over it to keep people away. The grass is up to my eyes and I can see nothing, only the oven open in the ground and I am more full of terror than ever before. It is no ordinary oven. I know it, even before she shows me. It is a shaft in the ground . . . an old evil well, not used for a hundred years. It is maybe three feet across and there are cobwebs to show it is not used now, yards of grey chiffon cobwebs. Nobody comes to this place any more, only the ghosts under the sheets of the furniture. There is no sound except the croaking of frogs and the whisper of the wind in the trees that indeed, it must be a forest or maybe the sea. They are all about me, the faceless ones, in the long grass, bending down to me to whisper to me to run . . . run . . . run. . . . The rose bush puts out her thorns to catch at me. I can hear the tear of my silk dress in the silence of the night and I am held, but not by the rose. The witch has my hands in hers and she is going to put me into the oven. In mercy, I know it is only a dream that I have dreamed a score of times. There is a white dead face at the window, but it is only the moon shining in the glass. There are drowned people at the bottom of the shaft, but this is not possible. It has been dried up for twenty years and maybe it goes right down to the centre of the earth, where there are fairy people and a land of hap-piness. I slip and fall and the world whirls to nothingness and I am free. I run and run and there are those that chase after

21

me, but this is the common stuff of night terrors. I run for a hundred miles and wake up out of breath with the breath caught in my throat and the panic thumping in my chest . . . and of course, it is just another nightmare and I am done with it, for it is time to get up, yet it pursues me out into the day, even when it is summer light. It turns my sun to gloom and my happiness to sorrow. Again and again, it comes, no matter where I am. It turns itself on like a magic lantern on the foot of my bed. For all that I recognise it as a phantom thing of no importance, it possesses the power to stretch after me into my waking hours . . . and cloud my sky to unhappiness and forebodings of evil to come. . . .

Oliver Twist is no part of it. It is part of me and Oliver Twist was a story that somebody read to me . . . something to do with the brush of a man's face against my cheek.

"There now, Honey! We'll have no more of Oliver. You're far too young to be made unhappy by the adventures of a poor orphan boy, so I'll tell you the end of it. He found a happy home and he lived there ever after, as happy as anybody in this world can possibly be. He never had to be hungry any more. In fact, they gave him rather too much to eat and he had to watch his figure . . . and if you eat any more marshmallows you're going to have to watch yours too, no matter how delicious they are toasted in front of the fire . . . and don't give them to the dogs, either, even if they do slaver with desire."

Last night, I had not dreamed the dream, yet the Orphan House had a quality about it that suggested the after-dream gloom.

I had finished my porage and then there was a walk, two by two, through the town, with our hands clasped in front of us and a "Miss" at the tail of the crocodile to see that we did not laugh or otherwise misbehave ourselves. People looked at us as we went by and sometimes there was pity in their eyes, but mostly they cared nothing for us. We were well looked after and fed and perhaps they paid for it in their taxes. They had fulfilled any duty they owed us. They owed *us* nothing.

Maybe some of the shopkeepers' wives gave more attention to the older girls, to work out whether one of them might be worth consideration for hire, put to help with the housework. There might be a strong lassie, approaching the age of escape from the Female Orphan House. It was as well to assess her beforehand to see how much work she had in her. "Never choose a girl with a long back," they said among themselves. "They've no work in them. Low sized and strong and not too much fat on them. Fat shows they gorge their selves. . . ."

That first day in the "crocodile", I had no knowledge of such things, but I collected it later, with the information that the best job of all was with a shopkeeper's wife, where the food was good. They had to eat up the unsold produce of the industry below stairs in the shop, so a grocer's was choice or maybe a butcher's. A genteel household was the devil, for there was the pecking order all over again, of the servants' hall, where the most you might become was a scullery maid. In that sort of place, you had every servant in the house as your better, not to speak of your employers, who had far less say in your happiness than the house-keeper or the butler or the cook.

Still, let me go back again to that first walk, with Betsey at my side and my hand in hers till "Miss" told us it was not allowed to hold hands . . . and Betsey filled me in on the rules of the Home for Female Orphans.

When we got back, there would be "domestic training". It was very important that I try to do my best, even if my lessons were not "much cop". There was the whole house to clean down and we did it between us "on shifts". There was a notice board in the hall, where there was a thing called "the duty list". Duties started early in the morning, but I had missed

23

the first part of it.

This week, my name would not be included, but presumably somebody would tell me what I was supposed to do. It was simple enough. Next week, it would be written clear where I was to be at every work hour of every day and what my duty would be. This morning, while our dormitory had still slept, there had been girls, who scrubbed the stone staircase and dusted its iron-railed banisters, girls who started off the laundry in the wash room to boil, before the rinsing of it later on and the ironing and the folding, for we took in the town's washing against our charge on the rates and that was fit and proper. Throughout the day, domestic training went on and on and on, with cooking and dishing up and washing up and drying up and stacking away and with scrubbing, stoking stoves, cleaning and polishing and blackleading. There was no minute to call your own, but it was all for your own good, or so Betsey told me. If you worked hard, you got a good job later and maybe one day, your prince would come and you might get married. There might be a shop assistant or a messenger boy, though "messenger boys was rather young". Then you could set up home and have a baby and maybe two or three and start your working cycle all over again.

"Maybe *you* wouldn't want your own cottage. The girls say you're a Romany lassie and that you lived rough, before they took you to jail. A gyppo don't ever want a roof over his head."

"I can't remember it, Betsey, only in bits, here and there. If I could, I'd tell you. It's not nice, not knowing who you are. Lesley Summer! Now! That's not right for a start. My name is . . . was . . . 'Honey'. . . ."

"That's not a proper name. That can't be right. Honey What? I'd stop telling them your name is 'Honey', for it only makes them wild, like that posh accent of yours does, for

24

sometimes you talk like a lady. Surely you must know it for yourself. There's a mystery about you, if ever there was a mystery about anybody. Maybe, you're a kind of a changeling."

She looked sideways with her eyes crinkling with laughter.

"That'd explain why they called you Summer. It happens on Mid-summer's night, or Mid-summer's eve, a changeling is born—a fairy child."

"They called me Lesley Summer."

"It's all the same, stupid! One swallow don't make a summer, and one summer don't make nothing that I know of, but if a woman was to have a baby on Mid-summer's night or eve, whichever it is, she's got to watch out. The fairies come and steal her child away and they goes and puts a fairy child in the cot and they takes the real child back to fairyland and that's the last anybody sees of it ever."

I walked along beside her and did not listen to much more that she said, for she was back in the realm of fairy tales and I did not like Grimm's stories nor yet Hans Anderson's. Hans Anderson's name popped in and out of my mind, but Grimm . . . the brothers Grimm. I knew it well from somewhere. "Rapunzel, Rapunzel. Let down your hair. Rapunzel, Rapunzel. Lass dein Haar hereunter," and Frau Holle and Die sieben Raben and Sneewittchen and the Fox and the Goose, the Golden Goose too . . . and Der goldene Vogel . . . and in German, all nouns had capital letters, whether proper or common. . . .

"So if you have a baby on Mid-summer's night or eve, and it's in its cradle, you hot a poker up in the fire and you run at the baby and shove the poker into its face. You don't try to harm it, but the little people aren't to know nothing about that. They think you're trying to kill their fairy child and they whisk it away and put your own kid back in the cot again. I don't know if it's a fact, but an old Irish woman onst told

25

it me."

She looked at me and sighed at the blankness of my eyes.

"She told me the fairy child is a thing called 'a changeling'. Strikes me you're the likeliest changeling I ever come across."

We were walking along the main street of a small town, that stood at the foot of a hill about half a mile from the Orphan House. The Baker's shop was a torment to our stomachs, and the Grocer's not much better. As for the Sweetshop window, it cannot have failed to fill our mouths with the moisture of longing, with its chocolate bars and the jars of boiled sweets and the boxes of striped peppermint rock.

The man of the shop was fat and jolly and more a white apron, and a gold chain across his waistcoat. He smiled at us as we went by and told us it was a fine day for young ladies and he handed a big bag of sweets to the mistress at the end of the line. It might have been better if he had let us help ourselves as we went by. We never saw the contents of the bag, though we smelt peppermint on "Missis's" breath for a few days. It was to happen so often down the time I stayed in the place. We were never lucky, but always we thanked him politely and nobody complained. There was no place for the lodging of complaints. There was no Court of Appeal, we were totally without help of any kind and totally at the mercy of "Missis", who had no mercy.

That day, I looked forward to eating the sweets when we got home but still the names kept echoing in my head. There had been Rumpelstilzchen. . . .

"Ach, wie gut ist, dass neimand weiss,
Dass ich Rumpelstilzchen heiss!"

Betsey's mouth was at my ear as we moved along the street. I had said the two lines aloud and she was more surprised at at me than ever.

26

"And what's that when it's at home?"

Still I shook my head, for I did not know myself what it meant or where it had come from.

"There's a mystery about you . . . more mystery than ever I know's of, for you're no gyppo kid and I doubt you're even English. Funny that girl said in the room that you maybe was Lady Caroline Vere de Vere, with that posh way you go on Missis and the others think you're not all there and it's on the cards they 'ont keep you at the House. Missis told somebody that she don't think you'd be employable, whatever she meant by that. I reckon she meant too daft to do any sort of job. I ain't very big and I ain't very clever, but I know better than they do. There's something all about you . . . bright and clever and happy, as the sun maybe, if you had the chanst . . . and one time you had the chanst, but you ain't got it now. Remind me to read your cup when tea comes, if there's enough leaves. I'll tell you what's to come, maybe a dark handsome prince on a white horse . . . or a letter from over the water."

"I can read fortunes in a tea cup," I told her and she grinned at that and told me that pigs could fly.

"You turn the cup over on the saucer and then spin it three times round, so that the tea drips run into the saucer and take the tears away."

She put back her head and looked up at the sky and for all the sorry place she found herself, she was a natural clown. I found myself smiling, when I had thought never to smile again, but now she was frowning and pursing up her mouth, shaking her head.

"If you're all that good at fortunes, tell me when we'll get them sweets the man give us just now," she demanded.

"After tea, I should think, so we won't spoil our appetites."

When I listened to my own voice, it did sound different to the voice of the Female Orphan School, yet I knew there were times when I said "ain't" and "nuthing" and broke every grammar rule in the book. I was a mystery right enough, perhaps two girls shut up together in one body and both of them in prison for something they had never done.

"We won't never have any appetite spoilt while we're in the House and don't you never think it, Miss Mystery Bag. We won't never get even one of them sweets either, so don't go watering your mouth with the thought of it. Ain't you see the notice in Missis's room behind her desk?"

There was a parchment there, framed in black and written in old-fashioned writing with a quill pen, Betsey told me. The double s's were spelt like f's and it was not all that easy to make out, but if you could read properly you could understand it. I read it myself a day or so later and it was headed Zachary Myles's Trust Fund for the Inmates of the Female Orphan House.

It seemed that there had been a kind man by that name and he had made a trust fund fifty years before. It had left enough money to provide each one of the inmates with three pence every week to spend "on some frivolous item, which might delight her sad heart".

It was turned face to the wall and I turned it about as I dusted it and Mrs. Creek came quietly up behind me and found me studying it.

She had no idea I knew what was written on it, but she read it aloud to me, checked that I had dusted it and then she slapped it back with its glass against the light green of the painted wall.

Betsey had told me that Missis had pinched the money for her own ends and no orphan had ever seen a penny piece of it, since she had been "Missis" and indeed Mrs. Creek judged herself and found herself guilty.

"Frivolous item to delight her sad heart, indeed!" she said. "There are laws and regulations for the respectable folk out-

28

side these walls. . . ."

Her hand splayed itself against the brown boarding on the back of the notice and I saw that her thumb nail was short where she had bitten it.

"Laws and regulations are for the respectable folk outside," she repeated and looked down at me.

She had a sharp way of talking that betrayed her cruelty and her meanness.

"In here, Im's the law."

That was the law by which I was to live for a long time, but I knew it well already. Had not Betsey told me all about it on my first crocodile walk between the little shops in the town at the bottom of the hill?

"In here, Im's the law."

Chapter Two

DR. ZACHARY MYLES

For year after year, I followed the course of life in the Female Orphan House. My background was the stone staircase, the iron banisters, the wooden wainscot with the light green painted walls above, the walls, that dripped slow tears on a damp day, the drab dormitory, the cheerless rooms. I got up early and filled in my stint of domestic training. I knew well what it was to scrub down the long flights of stone stairs, with fifteen steps to each, my hands cold-chilblained in the winter, the washing-soda a torment. How often I had tried to light the kitchen stove, which turned into an old enemy at the sight of me. The paper was damp or the wood green. So often, before the day was light, the fire dimmed and sulked and sighed out at last with a puff of grey smoke. It had to be raked and re-set and maybe an old candle end offered up to the God of Fire. Then suddenly, it would catch and the kindling would sparkle and the coal begin to glow at the edges and the chimney to purr in its throat. Then the top would warm and the bars become gapped with flames . . . that brought back the life to my hands, to my face, to my body, so that almost I knelt down in front of its blackleaded ovens and worshipped it. It was pleasant to polish the shining parts with emery paper, till they reflected the light, but the fire had to be just bright and glowing too, to toast the bread to take upstairs with Missis's morning pot of tea. There was the floor to be brushed and scrubbed and the table set out. There was so much to do and so little time to do it in and if the fire went out first match, everything else was done at racing speed, yet with the thought of the eyes, that would search out shoddy work later on.

They kept me on in the Orphan House after a meeting one day of the Board of Governors, all good men and true, from the town at the bottom of the hill. They sat in committee round a table in Missis's room and I stood in front of them for judgement as to whether I was "educationally subnormal" or not. I did not speak much and I could not read, as far as they knew. They had not heard the conversations, that passed between Betsey and myself. They had not heard the stories I told in the dormitory at night, for I was in great demand as a story-teller and as time went by, I learned how to stem despair in the heart of the younger children. There was another land, where I could bring them, where Snow White lived and Robinson Crusoe and Alice in Wonderland.

"She does her domestic training well, I'll give her that," Mrs. Creek addressed the Board and her Second-in-command, echoed her last words, as she habitually did with "give her that".

The Second-in-command was Miss Frith and she was as tall and thin as Missis was short and stumpy. Her hair was greasy and black and tight-drawn back from her head, to make her face more like a hatchet than it was. She stood behind Missis's shoulder and frowned down the table to where I waited for sentence.

"If Summer is to go for a kitchen maid when we're done with her, it doesn't matter much if she's able to read *The Times* or make up poems," said Missis and Miss Frith echoed "make up poems."

"She can do plain cooking already and she's clean and she's a worker. I'll give her that too."

". . . give her that too," said Miss Frith.

31

The man who sold sweets whose name was Mr. Barley-drop, was on the Board. I wondered what would happen if I found courage to tell him what became of all the sweets he fed to crocodiles passing his shop.

He smiled at me, as I thought it, and I smiled back at him, for after all, it was the thought that counted and it was not his fault that he was not such a benefactor of orphans, as he believed.

"I say give the lassie a chance," he said, "Let her stay on another year or two, see how she makes out with the sums and that. As long as she knows that two and two make four, she'll get by, if she can cook a good breakfast."

He nodded at the parchment framed on the wall above Mrs. Creek's head, turned right ways out as it always was on Board Meeting days, or when visitors came.

"Zachary Myles, that penned that paper there, he understood the worth of a good breakfast. You'll none of you, remember him now, but my old father was always talking about him . . . went round in a high dog cart with yellow wheels, he did, not my old father, but Dr. Zachary. Real good doctor he was and he took an interest in this place. Before he came, they used to hire out the girls to work to hoe fields and that, 'most as soon as they could walk. He put a stop to it sharpish."

He nodded to a desk by the wall.

"That's his desk over there, left it in his will to the Female Orphan House to stand in the Matron's office as it does today. Funny how things survive, but not people."

We all looked at the familiar desk with its three shelves above with coloured delph plates. Underneath at the bottom were two deep drawers and above that the shelf where "Missis" did the accounts. Above the desk part were pigeon holes and small drawers and in the centre of all, a tiny cupboard with a door with a keyhole. There was a pillar each side of it and

I always thought it a magic Alice in Wonderland place, where one might lock secrets away, where they would never be found. Now I know the whole piece was a secretaire "of fabulous quality" as the catalogues would say. It was made at the end of the seventeen hundreds and it was made by a craftsman, with the drawers sliding on silk runners, so smoothly they moved, and every part fitting every other part with precision.

"That there piece of furniture is worth hundreds today . . . no knowing what they would bid for it, con-*know*-shers."

There was no calling to order of the Board of Governors and Mr. Barleydrop went on and on, while we listened with interest, all but the young doctor, who did the parish practice. He had talked to me the day before here in Missis's room in her presence, with Miss Frith as well, so that I hardly opened my mouth to him. He had been called to give evidence upon my health, but today he seemed very tired. He sat with his eyes closed most of the time and probably he had heard the Seller-of-peppermint-sticks on the subject of Zachary Myles so often at such gatherings, that he was bored by it. Still, his lack of attention by-passed Mr. Barleydrop, who seemed to have made a study of the Myles family.

"Old Zachary had a son," he told us, "Called him Malachai. Malachai became a doctor too, but he went to Ireland for his degree, to study . . . to a place called Trinity College. Malachai took a shine to the place and he never came back here. Zachary had a daughter too and she went off to Ireland to some God-forsaken place, to keep house for Malachai. Malachai never wed, but the daughter did. Her name was Mary. She took up with a doctor called Rohan and they had two children, a boy and a girl . . . grandchildren for Zachary, but the names were lost. Rohan they were, of course, not Myles. They're still alive to this day, but they're getting on. The nephew . . . Malachai's nephew didn't take to doctoring.

It's strange the way life works out. He took to being a pharmaceutical chemist. They say his son is to be a doctor, is studying at it now, so it came back to the medical profession in the end. It were in their blood, that and the biblical names . . . never met up with so many biblical names. They had a weakness for the Bible. Somebody told me the other day that the young chap's christened Jonah . . . Zachary's great grandson, the lad, who'll soon be qualified. . . ."

The local doctor maybe had had enough of family history. More likely he had had enough of the meeting. He opened his eyes and looked round the table with no affection for anybody he saw.

"I hope he doesn't come back here and squat down on my patch. I just hope he stays in the whale's belly, this God-forsaken what's-his-biblical-name, Jonah Rohan. I've settled in here and I like the Fens. It's handy being near my Alma Mater, but not too near. Still a college dinner is a college dinner, but for pity's sake let's get on. We came here today to discuss this girl and I've looked into the situation with regards to her. She's no material for a home for the mentally disturbed. She's what they're beginning to think of as withdrawn into herself. She's like a snail and she's safe in her shell. Presently, if we give her time, she'll come out of it. She's a pretty child and as strong as a filly foal. Don't let's put waxed paper on her and tie her away in a jar in vinegar to become a pickled cabbage."

I had lost all idea of what he was talking about. I had thought him careless, but I was almost certainly quite wrong.

"Give her a little tender loving care. It's all she wants, but she's crying out for it."

He looked at Mrs. Creek, as if he liked her no more than I did and I thought he knew well that tender loving care was in short supply in the establishment. Still there was a carelessness about him. He had saved me from the mental home,

34

but that was as far as he would go. He had no intention to try to alter the characteristics of the Female Orphan House staff. Perhaps he was not old enough or established enough to prevail against such experts as the staff or against other members of the board. Mr. Barleydrop had hardly paid him any attention whatever. His thoughts were still back with the old doctor and his biblically-named family, and he had got the subject launched again.

"As I said, Dr. Zachary was a great man for a good breakfast," he started off. "My dad once told me that the old chap gave the Orphanage a hen house, paid for it out of his own pocket in gold guineas, and for four dozen pullets on the point of lay . . . or was it four score? I don't recall exactly for it was a powerful long time past. Maybe it was four score . . . pullets, not guineas. Each girl was to have a fresh laid egg for her breakfast every morning. I never forgot what my dad told me . . . Zachary said . . . and mind you he got very eccentric as he grew older, but he said, if his wishes weren't carried out, he'd wring the hen's necks . . . else he'd wring the Matron's, always had a laugh on his lips. They loved him, the town's folk did, but it's all long ago now. There's a tombstone in the churchyard with Beloved Physician carved out on it, but nobody bothers about it any more. . . ."

"Let's get on with the matters in hand," said Mrs. Creek politely and her Second-in-command, echoed "matters in hand."

The doctor opened his eyes again and said it was decided that the child stayed on and he smiled at me.

"See to it that you set yourself knowing that two and two make four . . . as Barleydrop said, if you add them up that is. If you put them down side by side, they make twenty-two. . . ."

I was down in the town by myself posting a letter for Mrs. Creek, the next week, when I remembered the meeting and I went along to the churchyard and looked up at the church with its velveteen roof of old tiles. After a while, I found the grave of Zachary Myles and did not realise, that day, how closely he and I were to be linked together.

IN GRATEFUL MEMORY OF ZACHARY MYLES
DOCTOR OF THIS TOWN FOR FIFTY YEARS
THE BELOVED PHYSICIAN
SUFFER THE LITTLE CHILDREN TO COME UNTO ME
ERECTED BY HIS SORROWING SON

The stone was a granite block with a polished face and I remembered that they had said in the meeting how things survive, when people have gone. This stone was made to stand for eternity by the look of it, for the weather had not eaten it away, as it had the limestone blocks all about. Only the soft moss had invaded the lettering and I picked at it with my finger, till I had made his name clear and sharp again. Then I wondered if the moss was not a soft comforting thing to have to keep your name safe against the rain and the wind. I remembered the "three pence every week for every orphan girl to buy some frivolous thing to delight her sad heart" and in some strange way, I was sorry that I had not been born earlier or that he had been born later, so that we could have met, one with the other.

I stayed on in the Female Orphan House and followed the pattern set out for work, but I never made much progress, not in the eyes of my teachers. They did not know that I stored up every fact they taught me. I knew the answer to every question they asked, but I never spoke the answer aloud. I thirsted after knowledge like a man lost in the desert for three days. There were books on a shelf in one of the rooms, sets of Dickens and Shakespeare . . . Brontë, Trollope, Galsworthy— the classics of English literature. Nobody seemed to want to read them, but I borrowed them, one by one, in secret and read them under the bedclothes at night, by the light of a

36

candle in a jam jar, at great risk to the whole institution. In the summer, I escaped for an hour or two and read them in the fields in the long grass, like a leveret in a form. Sometimes, I went to the church and leaned back against Zachary's granite memorial and one day, Mr. Barleydrop found me there. I hid the book under my pinafore, before he saw that I was doing what he might think was wasting my time.

"I'm glad to see that you've took an interest in the doctor. If he's anywhere about that he can understand such things, he'll be pleased to think that one of his orphan girls was so kind as to visit his tomb. . . ."

I was confused about the Myles family, for Mr. Barleydrop had made it sound complicated at the meeting of the Board that day. I had a jumbled idea of names from the Old Testament and I knew that the stone had been erected by his sorrowing son. I squinted my eyes against the bright light and looked up at Mr. Barleydrop.

"His sorrowing son," I said and ran my finger along the line at the bottom of the memorial.

He did not note the fact that I might be able to read after all. He was launched on his favourite topic.

"There's more wrote under that," he said and got a length of stick to beat the grass down and reveal more engraving.

"And by many of the parishioners, who were his patients and will never forget him. . . ."

He remembered that I could not read and he read it out for me and then told me that "never" was a long day.

"Six months," he declared. "I give the public six months and the forgetting begins and in no time at all, there's nobody who even recalls your name. If I was to die today, there'd be another man in my shop and soon there'd be no child in the whole village that would recall poor old Barleydrop."

"I'll never forget you, Mr. Barleydrop," I told him with sincerity. "You don't forget people, so people won't forget you, for you're a good man."

I had rarely spoken two words in sequence and he was moved by my eloquence and after a bit, he started on the Myles family again.

"Malachai was the son and there was a daughter too, called Mary."

I listened very carefully to every word he told me and I drew a picture of it in my head. Malachai had gone to Ireland and lived there, practising as a doctor. Malachai had never married, but Mary had marrid a doctor called John Rohan. Mary and John Rohan had had a son, called Matthew, and Matthew had married and had a son called Jonah, who would be a young man now . . . Zachary's wife dead and gone, Malachai dead and gone, Mary's husband dead and gone. They were all dead and gone except for Matthew and his sister Ruth, for he had had a sister called Ruth.

I put it into my computer brain. . . .

Zachary Myles begat Malachai and Mary. Mary married John Rohan and begat Matthew and Ruth. Matthew begat Jonah Rohan. . . .

"I doubt we'll ever see hide or hair of any one of the family again," Mr. Barleydrop was finishing.

Up in the Female Orphan House, we were ungrateful enough or perhaps frustrated enough to call Mr. Barleydrop "Old Jelly Baby." I felt ashamed that I had indulged in the practice, as he leaned down to where I crouched in the grass at the bottom of Zachary Myles's grave and pressed a warm bag of jelly babies into my hand.

Here indeed was richness. I thanked him in my politest manner though I could not get to my feet to do it properly for the book might cascade into the long grass and betray me. I edged it round towards my pocket and presently I got it more securely grasped and transferred it into the pocket and out of sight. Then I chose a jelly baby and bit its head off, chewed it to put it out of its pain and lingered luxuriously over the sucking of the body, as any cannibal might have done. Later on, we would have a feast in the bedroom at the home, but just for now, I knew such luxury as long grass and a warm sun to cheer the day and Mr. Barleydrop for good company.

"I don't know why I tell you all this about the doctor's family. Perhaps they're right to say you don't take in a word they tell you, for all the brightness in your eyes."

I looked up at him without guile . . . and cast back on my computer brain.

"Zachary begat Malachai and Mary," I said. "Malachai died without issue. Mary married John Rohan and begat Matthew and Ruth, and Matthew begat Jonah . . . and he's to be a doctor soon."

I paused and looked over what I had said. Zachary deceased and also his wife . . . also his only son, Malachai.

"Never heard you say but 'Yes' or maybe 'No' till today. Not a word out of you, though they did say you mastered the alphabet! You talk with your hands and with your black eyes, better than the rest of us talk with our tongues. There's no doubt that the young doctor was right about you. Still waters run deep and you'd have had no chance in a 'daffy asylum' . . . no chance at all."

I got to my feet and bobbed him a curtsey of politeness for his graciousness to me in words and in sweetmeats and he was kind enough to say I was a well-mannered lassie. He stooped his head down level with mine.

"Does them females up the hill belt the good manners into you?" he shot out at me and I shook my head vigorously and felt my plaits strike my cheeks, as if they condemned me liar.

"Do the ones in charge of the walks give you the sweets I pass on to them? It struck me a time or two that a bunch of girls might have been happier at the sight of a bag of sweets."

The only armour was silence.

"Do they keep the sweeties for theirselves, maybe?"

I shook my head and again the plaits flew wide in denial that I was telling the truth. I offered him a jelly baby, which he refused, then chose another from the bag and munched its head and then settled its body between cheek and tongue.

"Thank you, sir, for all your kindness to us."

Yet still he went on.

"If there was anything to be going wrong up at the house, you're to come and tell me. It's struck me now and again that you've got more brain in your little finger than the rest of them's got all put together. Now, if anything unhappy's going on up there, you're to seek me out and whisper it into my ear . . . not just the usual punishments of such blessed places, but anything what wanted sorting. Seek me out and whisper in my ear. I'll see to it directly for I'm on the Board of Governors and that's been on my conscience for a great many years. God pity orphans! They're at the mercy of so many people and circumstances and I daresay that you don't pick up one word in ten that I'm telling you, yet I think you do."

He had a straw boater on his head and a white apron across his fat stomach and he was as jolly a man as ever one could meet in a day's walk. I looked up, searched his face to see if this was the time to confide in him and decided against it, felt guilt that, by my silence, I directed so many sweet delights into the mouths of the mistresses, instead of their charges.

We walked together to the High Street. I read the sign over his shop and noted it down in my brain.

Sam Barleydrop, purveyor of sweetmeats.

Somewhere in the secret part of my mind, I etched it deeply. In case of trouble, send for Sam Barleydrop. He will be the white knight on the charger, who will deliver the orphan from the oppressor. . . .

"It's funny the way you picked up that Myles family as if they were writ out in the Bible. Zachary Myles would have liked you. The son, Malachai would have done better to come to his Pa's help and work alongside of him here—plenty for two, but he took up with a place called a Medical Hall. I don't know if there are such things in the east of England, but they probably have them in Scotland or the north. This was in Ireland. It's where a chemist and doctor kind of work together and one's the doctor and one's the chemist, to make up the medicines the doctor orders, so the money flows in both ways, if you see what I mean. Malachai, put his nephew Matthew Rohan in as a chemist in this town in Ireland and the nephew would make up the uncle's prescriptions. There was a big house and then next door a chemist's shop . . . with coloured glass bottles in the window and that . . . jars of ointment and all sorts of things, that will soon be forgot by the coming generations, with their craze for this new chromium . . . hates chrome myself. It don't polish like brass."

My mind whipped round the situation in the flash it had taken him to tell me and still he looked down at me and the strings on his white apron strained against the thickness of his waist.

"I don't know why I'm telling you all this and you supposed to be half sharp, but there's a light in those black eyes, that makes a man think you understand maybe what he doesn't understand himself."

Zachary begat Malachai and Mary. Mary begat Matthew, who was a chemist, I filed away in my mind. Matthew had a shop beside Malachai's house and he sold chemists' things and made up bottles of medicine. Then Matthew married and begat Jonah and Jonah is to be a doctor and start the dynasty all over again and I did not even know what dynasty meant but that it was a sort of reign of kings.

"There's a pile of old books in the back of the shop," Mr.

Barleydrop went on. Old Mrs. Hills left them in a few weeks ago, asked me to give them to one of the walks passing by. She hadn't the strength to lug them up the hill and give them to you girls personal. I wonder if you'd like to take a few of them with you now. They're what she called light reading, but for all I know, she may have meant that they were good for lighting the stove, mornings."

I went into the room at the back, which was an Aladdin's cave of sweets. Sam Barleydrop armed me with a stick of brown rock and I licked it as I looked at the books, maybe there were twenty of them and they were all school girls' stories . . . epics that might have originated from the Magnet or the Gem, but in the female line of the species. . . . They were as precious to my eyes as the pink and white sticks of candy in the big jars, for here was wealth to last for many a month. They were corded together in fives and I carried them all, as I might have carried a trunk of treasure from Nombre de Dios Bay, full of gold moidores and gems from treasure ships of the Spanish main. Mr. Barleydrop was worried in case I might collapse before I topped the rise of the hill so he lent me his delivery boy's bike and promised that if I left it at the Orphanage gate, the boy would run up and collect it later on. I presented my prize to Mrs. Creek half an hour later and she looked at it without enthusiasm.

"That's a right load of old rubbish, but if Mrs. Hills presented the books, then she did it to stop filling up her own ash pit. Still, she'll hear about it if we throw them away. . . ."

"If we throw them away. . . ." said Miss Frith.

"Shelves in the playroom," I whispered and no more and I kept the joy out of my voice so she nodded her head.

"Stick them up in there for now and do it tidy. In a month or so, we'll put them in the bonfire pile. They'll want junk in the village for November the fifth. The village kids can have the lot."

I had a few weeks' respite and I seized avidly on the books. They were all school stories about schools very different from the Orphan House. I read them with a growing wonder that there should be such super establishments, where a thing called "honour", was held high. There were creeds, of which I possesed no knowledge. One told the truth automatically. One did not tell tales. One upheld the good name of the school and it did not matter if one won a game or lost. The game was the thing.

I became the passer on of these sentiments to the inmates of the Female Orphan House. One of the big girls read a book or two and declared them, as Mrs. Creek had done, just the thing for bonfire night and what a pity it was that we had to give them on to the village kids. It was high time we celebrated Guy Fawkes ourselves, and gunpowder, treason and plot.

For myself, I read the books when I could and I re-told the stories in the darkness of the dormitory or in the long shadows of the evening in the field at the back of the school. I tried to show them that there was a better code of life and Betsey caught flame from my flame. She fished for girls as Christ had fished for men. Some of them came to believe that it might be worth a try. There seemed little to lose. The spirit of school flickered and grew brighter. Then inevitably came martyrdom.

One day, there was a bar of chocolate missing. Each mistress had a bar of chocolate at the side of her plate at supper-time, a confection that made our mouths moist throughout the meal. About a month after the induction of my mission to the heathens honour, a bar was missing from beside Miss Frith's plate.

The Matron's head bent as Miss Frith stooped to mutter in her ear and the white of the cloth was no whiter than Betsey's face.

"There is a thief among us . . . stolen a bar of chocolate

43

from beside Miss Frith's plate. . . ."

The voice of the God of the Old Testament can sound no different at the great day of judgement, when all mankind is gathered together. There was a smell of chocolate on Betsey's breath. She sat by my side at table, surrounded by an aura of chocolate, with tell-tale chocolate smears on her lips and she was shaking with fear. Worse than that, she had wet her knickers with fright. I could smell the ammonia-chocolate aura to her and feel her trembling against my side. I was on my feet in half a second, my legs full of feathers, my heart thumping my ribs to bid me return to my senses. Betsey had got herself into an upright position too, but she clutched at the edge of the table and dragged herself to stand, her skin was like wax. Together, our voices quavered.

"I took it, Ma'am."

Then in surprise we turned our faces to look one at the other and Betsey shifted uncomfortably inside her wet knickers, while I looked down with dismay at the pool about her shoes.

"Lesley didn't take it. I took it, Ma'am," she said quietly, and I shook my head in denial at her sin and took it on my own soul as all the girls in the school books would have done and been acclaimed heroine. This was how "to play the game", but it was not the idea of the staff of the Female Orphan House. One of us was a thief, and the other a liar, and too brazen to escape just punishment.

In the boot room, we leaned over the bench and took the cane on our bottoms, skirts held up, calico knickers far too thin to absorb the sharp cuts of the cane. Worse than anything was the knowledge that the whole school knew what was happening to us. They knew our ignominy, every last dreg of it. This was what happened to the disciples of honour in schools. Honour was not for any one of them. The cause was well and truly lost. No more, could we expect anybody to own

44

to their transgressions or play up and play the game. In the future, one lied one's way out of things and kept lips tight shut on any confessions one might feel called upon to make. It was the same old cold, hard place and "Missis" was the law within the four walls. There was no court of appeal and no escape ever from harshness and cruelty, no bright banner of honour, under which one might find nobility. It was the end of the dream for a crusade. There was no crusade in the Female Orphan House. Mrs. Creek decided the way life would run and that way it ran. There was no diverting the stream into golden buttercup pastures. Unless I was taken out into service in some house, I was destined to be "incarcerated" within the grey walls for all I knew, for the rest of my life. That evening, I think I knew total overthrow of spirit. There was just nothing to be done, except to put on silence, the best armour of all. There was the curtsey to authority and the meek bob of the head, the scrubbed floor and the blackleaded grate, the dust gathered up and not swept under mats, the "Yes, Ma'am," "No Ma'am" and submission and submission and submission. The years crept slowly past till I was fourteen, fifteen, sixteen . . . and then Betsey married the assistant in Mr. Barleydrop's sweet shop and left me alone without her brightness.

Without Betsey, the Female Orphan House was a lonely place. Before she went, I may have felt lonely, but after her wedding I knew what isolation really was. I had never mixed much with the others. I had few friends, only for the younger children, who valued me for my stories and for being somebody to whom they could turn for help. There was no chance of anybody wanting to adopt me. I was ineducable. I was not bright. Mrs. Creek still called me "the Dummy" on occasions, when she was incensed with me and plenty of the girls followed her example. Still I bent my head and answered "yes" and "no" and still in the twilight in the field behind the house,

45

I spun fairy tales, but there was no Betsey to share my innermost thoughts.

After her wedding, she came to visit me, but Mrs. Creek did not think it fitting that I go as a guest to Betsey's cottage, even to tea.

"No knowing what vulgar habits you might pick up and I'm in charge of your welfare. If anything were to happen to you, I'd be held responsible. . . ."

So a time or two, Betsey called on me or met me in the street, told me that marriage was not all that it was cracked up to be. "Don't wed just to escape from yon place, Lesley. It's much the same outside the gates and there's things in marriage . . . I don't think you'd get on well with any man except maybe a prince in white armour and there's precious few of them about the place, if there's any at all . . . and I'm to have a baby and God knows how we'll make out."

"But a baby, Betsey, a baby of your own. That's good."

"It's nothin' but another mouth to feed my fella says, and not enough for the two of us as it is. I admit it's better grub than we had in the Home and Mrs. Barleydrop's kind, but there's no flowers along the path of this life and there never were and if anybody ever tells you there are, it's a lie."

She put her arms about my neck and hugged me tightly to her and I felt her tears on my face.

"Do you recall the way we tried to find honour for the school and all we got was two sore bums? That's the way of it, my girl, and that's how it will always be. Your best plan would be to go out as a kitchen maid in one of the big houses. You was always best at polishing and shining. In a place like that, you'd have somebody to tell you how to go on, what to do and what not to do. You'd not want reading nor yet writing nor yet sums. Any road, you can do anything you set your mind to. We all know that, except the powers that be, but don't go running into wedlock, just to escape from that hell

46

at the top of the hill. There are plenty of other hells, find 'em in our own selves."

Her arms tightened about my neck till they came near strangling me.

"And you, Lesley, don't tell me there ain't a mystery about you. You're no gyppo's child, nor yet a fairy foundling. I've known plenty of kids, in the House and elsewhere, but never a one like you. By the way you stand, you might be a royal princess. There's a shine to you. You've just to smile and the sun comes out. It's my belief that you got lost some way and never got found again and one day, some great lord will come and claim you and you'll live happy ever after."

Chapter Three

JONAH ROHAN

There was a rumour wisping round the Home. It spread like smoke from a starting fire . . . a little wraith at first and then a more definite fluff-puffing fume, a twirl of white feathers in the chimney throat, to a great grey mist invading every last corner of every last room.

There was trouble on the way. Even Mrs. Creek and Miss Frith looked worried and it was whispered they might lose their jobs. The establishment was not paying. The money was running short. For all the frugality of our daily bread, it seemed that we had overspent the money left for us by Zachary Myles. His relative's solicitors were at our gates. Inflation was upon the nation and everybody was familiar with hard times and we not least. There were just not enough funds left in the endowment and that was bad news. It went from mouth to mouth and spread in the telling. The Orphan House would be closed and we might be put on the street. More likely, we would be scattered to other homes throughout the length and breadth of the country. All these years, the money left by Dr. Myles had been enough and to spare helped out by rates and taxes. He had been a shrewd man and he must be unhappy, even in heaven, to know that the Orphan House was in financial trouble. His heir was Jonah. Did I not know his whole family tree? It remained for Jonah to meet with the family solicitor and arrange what must be done, but the guess was that the Orphan House had known its last weeks . . .

and that Mrs. Creek and Miss Frith would soon be without employment and that explained their grim faces, but then their faces were often grim.

"There is a thing called a depression on," one of the eldest girls explained to us in dormitory. "Capital, that's money, isn't bringing in what it did in the way of interest. They say there's not enough cash left to run us in the style to which we're accustomed, which, God knows, ain't much."

It was all in the wind and then it became more real. There was to be a Board Meeting and Jonah Rohan would be present with his lawyer. The solicitor from the town at the bottom of the hill would be there too, but Jonah would represent "the Family". Maybe it was true and maybe then it was false, but facts seeped between the floorboards and crept into our ears and filled all the empty space in the Orphan House and fear crept into our hearts. What would become of us? There could not be enough domestic jobs to employ us all. We were paupers, if ever there were paupers, but now we would be official paupers. As for me, I wanted to see Jonah Rohan. I had identified myself with his family to a great extent. I visited Dr. Zachary's grave regularly and thought of the Medical Hall and Matthew and Ruth, the brother and sister, who still lived there and were Jonah's people. Most of anything, even if the Orphan House had to be closed, I wanted to see Jonah Rohan.

Mrs. Creek sent for me the day before the Board Meeting.

"I want my room spring-cleaned and mind you see that it's done out properly. They'll be looking for signs that this place hasn't been run right and they're not to find the place covered with dust. You have a bad habit of not shaking out cushions and dusting beneath them. I'll make it hot for you if you don't do your job right today."

I straightened my grey dress and looked about the room as soon as I had the tools of my trade all ready . . . the broom

49

and the wet tea leaves, the mop with mob cap on its head and the tin of Ronuk . . . the fresh-washed duster.

Jonah Rohan was soon to be a doctor, and now he had all the worries of his ancestor's legacy on his young shoulders. Surely his father Matthew might have come, but Jonah was already in England and maybe they had counted it the convenient thing. It would have been a long journey for Matthew all the way from Ireland and he could not leave the Medical Hall, which had to have a qualified person in charge, or so I heard Mrs. Creek tell Miss Frith.

I picked up the carpet with both arms and lugged it out on the grass, beat it soundly till there was no speck of dust left in it and put it back in position again. Then I hung one rag rug after another on the fence and beat them till the sweat ran off the end of my nose. Miss Frith hovered in the vicinity to see that I shirked none of my chores, but today she was not as sharp as steel, but rather blunted and dispirted.

"That's enough for now. See to the dusting and the polishing last, else the dust will settle over everything."

I left the desk till the end for I admired it. It was my one link with Dr. Zachary Myles, who had loved little children and who must surely be sad that the money had run out and he was not on earth any more to put things right. There had been this slump and as good men as he had lost fortunes.

The desk was worth a good polish. I knew of old that repaid all the energy one put into it. The drawers gleamed like old satin, ran on their runners as if they were oiled. I turned out all their contents, for I had got into trouble for not doing this once before, I put everything straight and then set about the pigeon holes and martialled the writing paper into envelopes and paper, size matching size. I checked the stamp drawer, the ink well. I waxed and polished and cleaned and tidied and knew that maybe somewhere old Dr. Myles was watching me. I put a finger up to the keyhole of the small central cupboard, the "Alice in Wonderland" secret place and was surprised when the door of it opened. There was an empty space behind, and I slid my hand in, dusted round . . . then my fingers. There was a slot at the far end. I put an index finger in at the back and the pillar on the right, that looked fixed for ever, slid out. I pulled out a hollow compartment like a book, and it was full of papers, and letters. I turned the hollow book sideways and as if the doctor himself had guided them, the contents fell out on my lap . . . letters, a parchment, a red sealed document. This was a secret drawer. I knew it beyond doubt, knew too, that this was something I must keep to my own heart. I slid the papers into my apron pocket and put the desk back as it had been and as soon as I could, when Mrs. Creek had inspected the room and found it to her satisfaction, I went upstairs to the dormitory and looked at the papers from my apron pocket.

There were too many of them to read them all. I scanned them quickly and hid them away again . . . letters from Mrs. Creek to the butcher, to the baker, to the candlestick maker . . . a legal document, under the hand and seal of Zachary Myles and dated long ago. My heart beat fast for there was something I had not seen till now.

There had been a second compartment on the other side, that matched the one on the right. There were bundles wrapped in soft tissue paper and I rolled them open on my grey gingham lap, the bundles from the second secret drawer. There was my head band, that Mrs. Creek had taken for safe keeping. With it, was a longish parcel, also wrapped in tissue, a child's knife, fork and spoon. I turned the little items of silver and cutlery over in my hand and was surprised that they were in what I knew to be "King's Pattern." They were the same as I had seen in my dream of the cottage, on the table of the gingerbread house, but such things as a child might use. I picked them up and bent my head over them

51

and they were tarnished with age and with lack of polishing.

These things are mine, I thought and imagined that Zachary Myles was beside me, nodding his grey head and echoing.

"These things are yours, Honey."

My face flamed with guilt for I had no business in the world to pry into Mrs. Creek's secrets. I rolled the papers up and pushed them into one pocket and thrust the parcel into the other. Then, I went down the stone stairs and wished I had Betsey, to confide in, as never I had wished for her before.

Into my head, from somewhere, came the voice of Mr. Barleydrop, the sweetmaker.

"If there was anything to be going wrong up at the house . . . you're to come and tell me . . . if anything unhappy's going on up there, seek me out and whisper in my ear, anything that wanted sorting . . . I'll see to it directly. . . ."

Had I not just read out letters from the butcher about payment to Mrs. Creek for meat never delivered . . . from the baker for cakes and pastry we never saw? Where was I to go? I had no person in whom to confide. I slipped through the Orphan House gates and down the hill, found the limestone wall of the churchyard and the tall grass, that covered Zachary Myles in his last sleep. It was high summer and the bees were buzzing in the foxgloves and in the wild roses, that grew near by. There was a heavy scent from the cypresses and the pines. By Zachary's grave without a wind to riffle the papers, I spread them out, the letters and the parchments. I read them carefully, one after the other, and the tradespeople of the town hanged themselves, one after the other. There were receipted accounts for rich mixed biscuits and best dried fruit and candy sugar and centre back rashers of bacon, eggs by the score, sausages of the highest quality, sides of lamb and quarters of beef, lamp chops and sauces and gravies and things, that we had never heard tell of. Each account was receipted and there were many letters, thanking Mrs. Creek for her custom and hoping they gave satisfaction and they enclosed pound notes value to her proportion of the profits. I turned from the letters in disgust to the purity of Zachary's parchment, instructions to his solicitor and he made them clear enough. It was his birthday. It had come into his head that a birthday was not enjoyed much in old age. It must be seized upon in youth and each girl in the Orphan House must have a cake on her "Natal day", made by the baker with her name on it in icing and candles befitting her age. It would not require a large sum to supply each girl with a cake and his will was to be altered. A copy had been sent to his solicitor, Jones, Jones and Son, but did not the matron think that "Mr. Solemn Binding" would fit him better, the young Mr. Jones? It was all so long ago and for many years, there must have been great happiness from one man's generosity.

"It has come to me that the children may lack a personal interest . . . somebody who cares for them and is concerned about them. Could not 'pseudo' foster parents be sought out in the town to ask them into their houses to tea" It was spelt "houffes", so long ago it was. "These children are unwanted and they must feel it keenly. Let us give them gentleness and involve them deeply in the affairs of the town. After all, are they not our future citizens and we do unto them. . . ."

Things were different now, so many years on. Orphans were simple ones for confidence tricks and who was there to complain, of rich mixed biscuits which never appeared on the table, or if there never was even one birthday cake with candles to blow out and the delicious smell of the smoke in one's nostrils?

There were so many small kindnesses. Zachary should have been a father of twelve children and not just two. He should have been surrounded by his children and grandchildren, but he was alone. His practice had been his family and that was the way he wanted it. His best loved patients were the orphans and he had made it sure, or thought it sure, that he made their future one of comparative family happiness. He had not counted on the Mrs. Creeks of this world. I piled the documents up carefully and put them back in my overall pocket and then I took out the silver, wrapped in its tissue paper and the gilt head band, wrapped with it. Well I remembered the red rosettes, that somebody had sewed at each end of the band. I had thought it in bad taste, for the band was beauty by itself, and now, the two rosettes, one for each ear, were faded and tattered and they quite spoilt the dignity of the band. Then they were all in my pockets again for somebody in black came walking down between the graves and startled me and I had the evidence concealed and was walking demurely to the gate.

It creaked on its hinges as if the day was too hot for it and I heard Mr. Barleydrop's voice again.

"If there was to be anything wrong up at the House. . . ."

There had been no letter from Mr. Barleydrop to Mrs. Creek, acknowledging consignments of sweets, that she had never received in our name. Besides, Mr. Barleydrop was an honest man. In my innocence, I was quite sure of it. I went along to his shop and at last found myself in the back room, that he called "his counting house."

"Is there anything amiss, lass?"

I said nothing, just spread the papers in front of him and he put on his glasses, but first of all he went and shut the door. Then he set the letters and the papers out on an old-fashioned desk he had, and looked at me for a long time, then back to the papers.

"How did you come by these?"

"Secret drawer in Mrs. Creek's desk. . . ."

He took out his watch and looked at the time and then put it away again with a slowness that made me impatient.

"They'll miss you up at the House, lass."

54

The thought had already entered my head, but I had thrust it away. Now I pushed the papers toward him.

"You said to come to you."

He went into the shop and fetched a long stick of striped peppermint, and gave it to me, then leisurely he set about the reading of the papers, one after another, and it took him far longer than it had taken me. When he had finished the letters, he moved on to Zachary's parchments and he hummed and hawed about these and I had to decipher some of the words for him.

"He was a good man. I told you he was a good man," he said.

Then I presented him with the cutlery and the head band, but he made nothing of them.

"That's something she took off one of those poor girls for safe keeping, but the child will never see 'em again. They're no value, gilt and ribbon and a set of knife, fork and spoons . . . nothing to that, it's the papers. . . ."

He walked up and down, then he sat and thought for a while, walked up and down again.

"It's time I put up my shutters," he said at last and sent for his apprentice, who did it for him and the back room was darker than ever.

"It's best we visit the solicitor . . . Jones, Jones and I don't know how many Joneses and Son."

We went out of the door into the street and my hand in his, then all at once he stopped up short and turned in his tracks back to the safety of his honest shop. I shall never know how I picked him as being one of the honest tradesmen of the town, but picked him I had. He sat me on a high stool and he walked up and down again and demanded of me how I knew Mr. Jones and the other Joneses to be incorruptible.

"Incorruptible?" I asked him and he told me. "Straight."

I shook my head at him.

"If the others were in on it, so was he. He would have had the copy of them papers of Zachary Myles's. The doctor were careful and he would have tried to make certain that what he wanted done, were done . . . and now what's to do? Here are you, out of the House and far past locking-up time . . . and here am I with no idea in the world who to go to or where to turn."

"Jonah Rohan," I said and no more than that and he might have heard me utter the finest pearls of wisdom in the world, by the way it solved his problem for him.

"He's at the Boot Inn this very day for the board meeting tomorrow, and his own solicitor with him. It's common knowledge. Of course, he's the one to turn to. If Jonah Rohan don't know what to do, his law man will put us right."

He looked at me in consternation all of a sudden, and asked me if I were likely to get into trouble for absconding.

"I can slip in again without being noticed," I told him.

He took my shoulders between his hands, as I sat on the stool and he looked into my eyes.

"Go you back then and don't let on what's happened. Hold yourself ready to be called to the meeting tomorrow. You know there's a meeting of the Board of Governors. Don't say a word to a soul, but hold yourself ready and when the time comes, tell the truth."

I nodded my head.

"You do trust *me*?" he demanded and again I nodded my head.

"How did you not think I'd be one with the others among the thieves? How did you know I wasn't taking money out of the till too and charging for sweeties you never had?"

"You fed the crocodiles," I said and at that he laughed, told me that he would see me on the morrow, opened the shut door and pushed me through, watched me till I reached the corner of the street. I went up the hill and climbed the oak tree and it dropped me over the wall into the long grass of the field behind the Orphan House. I had the misfortune to run into Mrs. Creek, as I went in by the back door and she demanded where I had been.

"Field," I said and hung my head and she lifted it for me with a slap across the cheek.

"Dummy, daftie, fool," she said. "You should ha' been at your home work, though what you learn from it, I'll never know. Still you're not supposed to be asleep in the long grass in the field, when they're at the learning."

She regarded me with distaste and asked me if I had done out her room properly and I told her I had, by nodding my head at her, the humble, bobbing, little nod, that she must have been well used to by now.

"Go to bed then, straight away and no supper. You'll have to learn you can't go asleep in the summer sun, every time you feel tired. You'll have to be up early tomorrow and get the stairs done down. There's a meeting of the Board, and we'll want the place clean for them. . . ."

I lay in bed and wondered where Mr. Barleydrop was and what he was saying to Jonah Rohan and Jonah Rohan's lawyer. I hoped that they would not lose the gilt band, for it was all I was sure was mine. True, the King's Pattern knife and fork and spoon had been wrapped up with it, but I only knew that from my nightmares of the Gingerbread House. I could remember the gilt band and somebody who had sewn the red rosettes on the ends of it . . . could not remember who had done it, only that I had not liked the rosettes, had not wanted them sewn on, but she had liked them and said they were pretty against my black hair.

I woke up, when the others came to bed and they laughed at me, because I had been punished for sleeping out in the field.

"Gyppos like to sleep rough," one of the big girls said, but

I only told her that the bees had been in the foxgloves.

"Who cares about bees?" she demanded in the brassy way she had and another girl told her that presumably she did, for they made honey.

"A lot of honey we get in this here establishment."

I lay there and remembered the account for a dozen jars of best honey and how Mr. Barleydrop had it now, or Jonah Rohan's solicitor. I closed my eyes and went to sleep and presently I was dreaming it again, the old nightmare of the gingerbread house.

"There's treacle in the well," somebody told me. "Like in Alice in Wonderland. It's nice down there, with the others. I read it to you the other day about the three girls, who lived in the well of treacle. The Dormouse told the story. You can't have forgotten it. Their names were Elsie and Lacie and Tillie and they lived at the bottom of a well. . . .

"What did they live on?" I asked her and she told me treacle and I knew she was telling me a lie.

"They couldn't have done that," I said. "They couldn't have done that, you know. They'd have been ill."

"So they were," the woman agreed. "Very ill. . . ."

There was a barrel organ playing somewhere, but I could not know where or why, only that it was familiar. When I stopped turning the handle, the music stopped too. "There's a long, long trail a-winding . . . into the land of my dreams, where the nightingales are singing and a white moon beams. There's a long, long night of waiting till my dreams all come true, till the day when I'll be going down that long, long trail with you. . . ."

There was a fault in the music some way . . . a space where the song stuttered for two seconds between the "long" and the "long night of waiting" and every time it came round, it was the same. The music skidded the words and I waited for the fault and my arms ached with the turning of the handle.

58

There was a man's cap on the ground and sometimes, but not often, the chink of a coin. It was all a dream. I recognised it as such and with luck, I would wake up soon and be back in bed in the Female Orphan House. There was a scream then, but often I heard it in nightmares . . . the same sort of sound, choked off short, the thud, the hollow splash, the knowledge that something awful had happened. The scream woke me up and there I was in bed, my pillow, damp with sweat and the day breaking. There was to be a meeting of the Board in a few hours. What if Mr. Barleydrop had been playing me false? What if he were dishonest too? What if he arrived and told the whole tale to Mrs. Creek and together they made a plot to shut my mouth up for ever? This thought was just the last shred of the nightmare and it was time for me to get up. I was glad to get out of bed and out of the dream.

It was my day for the stairs. I scrubbed them from top to bottom and sweat ran down my nose and ended in the zinc bucket. Every now and again, I went to the kitchen for fresh water. The dirty water ran away down the sluice, with the grey dirt spinning amongst the suds and there was a fresh bucket of hot water hazed with soda to carry up to the place I had left off scrubbing the stone stairs. Each step was hollowed out by time . . . hollowed out by generations of youthful feet, hollowed out by scrubbing with hot water and soda. . . .

It was a bright summer morning and the sun was well up, when I glanced into Mrs. Creek's room to see that the chairs were set out for the meeting. A ray of the new sun caught Zachary's parchment, made ebony of the frame and honey of the wood of his desk. I caught my lip in my teeth and concentrated on counting the chairs set out and the fact that one of the younger girls had been in and polished them to a high gloss. There was a long table and the chairs round it and at each chair today was a blotter pad, a note pad, and a glass for water. At the last moment, a carafe of cold water from the tap must be carried in and the sherry tray. I checked the pens and the ink wells. It was all ready and I asked myself if it was ready for Mrs. Creek to come to her judgement. She would sit at the table. There was a special chair she had, with arms on it. Now according to her instructions, there was another chair, the same as hers, for the solicitor, an important man, who would be present, she had told us. I was tired by the time my housecraft was over. I sponged myself with cold water and put on a clean dress. At breakfast, I could not eat. My throat had closed. I might take a spoon of porage into my mouth, but it refused to be swallowed. I waited till the girl beside me had finished her porage, waited till there was no eye of authority upon me. I pushed my full bowl in front of the girl and she fell on it as if she had been starved for years . . . and perhaps she had. Then my duty was in the kitchens to help wash up and after that, to monitor a class of young ones in the school room. The hands of the clock had stopped moving and yet there was no holding back time. Mrs. Creek sought me out at fifteen minutes to eleven.

"Lesley Summer, you've got a clean frock on. See to answering the front door to the Governors."

They arrived one by one, just as they always did, calmly and with importance, dressed very correctly in navy serge and bowler hats. I knew them well, only Jonah and his solicitor. There was a drive out in front and a gate a hundred yards from the door. Then they walked to their fate, the butcher and the baker and the candlestick maker and all of the others. The town solicitor, Mr. Jones of so many Joneses came in a black square respectable car, but there was no sign of Jonah Rohan. Mr. Barleydrop handed me his hat, as he was admitted and winked at me.

"They've all been called to attend before the Board—the purveyors of food and other goods to the Female Orphan

House. When we're all within, sit yourself down there and wait. I'll call out when I want you to give evidence."

He was full of importance, for it was an honour to be on the Board of Governors. Today, Mr. Barleydrop was far more important than ever I had seen him. He had his best Sunday suit on and a white shirt with a stiff collar. He had a good inch of cuff at each wrist, as he took out his watch from his waistcoat pocket.

"We're on time as usual, my dear. Trust shop-keepers to know the value of time."

He had told me to wait at the foot of the staircase. He disappeared through the door to Mrs. Creek's room and I caught a glimpse of them sitting round the table. One of the girls came tip-toeing along the flags of the hall with the carafe of water on a brass tray. Another behind her had the silver tray with sherry glasses and decanter. I should have opened the way for them, but I was totally unable to quit my post at the front door. I might have been an old tree which had rooted there a hundred years before. The door had a square Judas window and it was possible to see who stood on the front step outside and asked for admission. I kept vigil now and waited and knew that it was all a dream and that Jonah Rohan would never come. I had dreamt it between night and morning and nothing had happened, as I had thought. I had not found letters or parchments, nor yet a gilt head band and a set of child's silver cutlery. The girls were finished with their task and they looked at me in anger as they went back past me, muttering that I might have helped them.

"Just you wait till you want helping with something. That's all!"

There was a shot from outside the door, that made me jump and they disappeared like partridges in a field. One moment, they stood in front of me, their faces unfriendly and the next the hall was empty. Through the Judas window, I saw a car, such as I had rarely seen before. It was green and there was a rakish angle to it and an impossible length. The hood was down. The bonnet was fastened with a leather strap. There were bright pipes at the side. The engine had the roar of a lion, but it coughed itself into silence after the single back fire and a cloud of black smoke. A young man got out by lifting his leg over the side door. I had expected the navy blue of ceremony and maybe a bowler hat. He was dressed in an old pair of grey flannel trousers and a grey tweed jacket, that had leather patches on the elbows and another on the right shoulder. There was no doubt that he must be Jonah Rohan, for there were six feet of college scarf round his neck to prove that he was a student. His solicitor had traditional clothes, not that I looked very much at him, for my whole attention was on Jonah. The sun shone on the fairness of his hair and almost put a halo round his head. His shoes were fresh hulled chestnuts. He was amused at the solicitor's attempts to open the door.

"Just step out over it. If you do manage to get it open, the door's as like as not come off in your hand."

I must wait till he knocked. We were taught that it was not good manners to be waiting outside when a visitor called. Yet I found myself on the front step and did not remember how I got there. Jonah Rohan stopped before me and took me in from head to toe in one glance, the grey high-waisted dress, the white Puritan collar, the flat black shoes.

"Hello there, young lady, and what's your name?"

I thought how dark blue his eyes were and I answered him before I knew what I said.

"My name is Honey."

It was years since I had said that. I had learned the hard way not to say it. Mrs. Creek had appeared behind me and her nails in my shoulder reminded me that I should not have opened the door before the visitors knocked . . . that I should have given my correct name.

"Her name is Lesley Summer," she said and put out her hand to take his. "I presume you'll be Mr. Rohan and this is Mr. Barr."

He did not notice her outheld hand, only stood there and smiled at me, touched my shoulder lightly and told me that I was far older than he had realised. Mrs. Creek was put out with him and pushed me to one side, told me roughly that I was to go to the garden to pick a bunch of flowers for the hall. Then she cut me out of her attention and turned back to gush over Mr. Rohan and the solicitor, about how honoured she was to meet a descendant of the late Dr. Zachary Myles.

"Everybody has arrived. The tradespeople are here too, but we're all of us at a loss to know what they're wanted for. I expect it's to do with cutting down expenses. . . ."

They disappeared through the door and it shut behind them but I lingered by the wall and thought what a pleasant young man Jonah Rohan was. I wished myself grown up . . . wished that I had the beauty of a princess, that I might impress him with my grace and loveliness, so that he would come back through the door and talk to me again. I took stock of my dress with its round orphanage neck, was glad at least that this was one of the days when we wore the white Puritan collar. The collars were traditional garb for the Female Orphan House but only for church attendance and for the days when inspectors came, or important people. I had a black plait of hair down each shoulder and I looked out at the front garden from under a black fringe, with as much self-possession as a Kerry calf. I had never met anybody who remotely resembled Jonah Rohan. He was my idea of Hamlet and maybe Romeo. I leaned against the outside wall of the Orphan House and dreamed a little and then remembered that inside was Mr. Barleydrop and presumably by now Mr. Rohan or his solicitor would have the documents in hand

63

and also the small parcel tied in soft paper. Presently I might be called in to give evidence, for, after all, I had found the things. At any moment, somebody would come and call my name and I would be in the room in front of them all, to show how I had found the secret drawers . . . and there was a bunch of flowers to pick. . . .

The garden was convenient to the casement window of Mrs. Creek's office. She had forgotten that, when she told me to pick flowers. The window was wide open to the summer's day and if I wanted to hear what was going on inside, I had only to move a little closer. It was high over my head. There was no chance of anybody seeing me. From where I stood, I could hear a humming, that was exactly the sound the bees were making in the tall yellow verbascum. I stooped to examine the marigolds, for they were pretty, but they did not smell sweetly enough. There was the lemon verbena that I loved better than anything in the garden. I pinched a leaf now and held it to my nose, tucked it into my pocket . . . took a step towards the window and another and another. They were reading the minutes of the last meeting and it was of no interest to me. The poppies were sleepy with the heat of the sun and soon they would droop and lose their petals. I concentrated on the bank of delphiniums in the bed below the window, deep, deep blue spikes like palace spires. I tried to remember the shade of Jonah Rohan's eyes. I had never seen any person with such darkness in such blue and for all his fair hair, his eyelashes were dark. There was the look of what I imagined a French aristocrat would have been, but it was probably myself, who would go to the guillotine. I was right under the window and had only to stretch out my hands to touch the wall of the building and inside Jonah Rohan was speaking. He had come to represent the family. His father would have liked to be present, but it was a long journey and he himself had been on the spot. . . .

64

The first thing for discussion was the Zachary Myles Bequest and cruelly, times were hard and money had lost value. However, there had been a meeting between the solicitor for the Home and his own solicitor and the County Council representative had been there too, of course. Between them, they had tailored how best the money would be spread in the present day. . . .

Mr. Jones of Jones, Jones and Son had not been dishonest. Mr. Barleydrop and I had done him a disservice in suspecting him. They were all very much in agreement and there was no hint to come of the dreadful issue that must soon be joined. The tradespeople were waiting in the hall, I supposed, and eventually they would be challenged.

Mr. Jones was speaking.

"We will still be very grateful for Zachary Myles and his generosity. I think you can take it, Mr. Rohan, that the memory of a kind man will live on here, down the years to come."

I could imagine him nodding at the parchment on the wall. . . .

"To provide each of the inmates with three pence every week to spend on some frivolous item which might delight her sad heart," he said. "I never come into this room without thinking of the wide humanity of the man and his great understanding of a child's mind. So many kind small fancies, all gone with the winds of change long ago."

Then the summer was gone and the autumn too and the cold blast of winter was in his words and I could imagine the way his moustache would go up over his white teeth and the way there would be no friendliness in his smile.

"Now, however, we come to a very serious and unpleasant matter. One of the members of the Board has very correctly brought to my notice and to the notice of Mr. Rohan and my colleague, some documents and letters, that have been brought to light. . . ."

I wonder if Mrs. Creek's eyes had gone to the desk and felt my legs go as feathery, as if they refused to hold me up.

"I think we should ask Mrs. Creek and Miss Frith to withdraw for a few minutes. . . ."

I was up and away in a second. No partridge in a field could ever have disappeared so quickly. I tore in by the kitchen door, my hand empty of flowers and dashed on into the hall and there were the tradespeople grouped together and Mrs. Creek too and Miss Frith and whispering filling the hall from floor to ceiling. The door of Mrs. Creek's room had shut her out and the butcher had moved over towards it and had his beefy cheek on one of the panels, though I could not blame him for eavesdropping, for had I not been doing just that three minutes ago?

"They've got the letters," he said, "we're done for." Then his eye caught my arrival and the whole assembled company seemed to spin on their heels to face me. Mrs. Creek's face was like lard and there was a pinched look about her nose.

"Who said you could come in here, Summer?" she asked me. "In this house, you come when you're sent for and not before."

"She was to get flowers," Miss Frith said vaguely, but her mind was far away from flowers.

"Well where are they then? Do what you're told for once, but get out. . . ."

Her voice whipped into a rage.

"Clear out of here at once. Clear out! Do you hear me?"

I melted through the kitchen and the scullery and crouched down beside the blue delphiniums again. I crept among the military blue spiked ranks, till I hid from view and I heard the recall of Mrs. Creek and Miss Frith and the appearance on stage of the tradespeople. I wondered after a while, if the whole little town had been involved in stealing from the

66

Orphanage, for that was suggested at one time by Jonah Rohan.

"You sat down there in your comfortable houses and you lived off the miserable children in this place . . . with the connivance of the Matron and her assistant."

There was a storm of denials and assurances and one after another, the letters were produced and last of all poor Betsey. I had not seen her arrive, but I knew her voice with its hoarse kindness and earnest quality. I had not recognised her for Mr. Jones introduced her as "Mrs. Betsey Judd, a respectable married woman of the town."

They asked her to describe the food and she did it very well. She had passed out of the reach of Mrs. Creek's hands and she knew it. It all came out in its lean meanness, the breakfast of thin porage, the Poor-House stew, the starvation diet.

"Missis would have kidneys and bacon often, but we never did!" The poignant hunger was clear past thick brick walls, via the open casement.

"The staff had eggs and rashers and chocolate and that. One day I was so famished, I stole a bar of chocolate."

They called girls one by one . . . read out items of food to them, explained what a leg of lamb looked like and a side of beef.

"I never seen the like of that come into the 'ouse and I work in the kitchen . . . have done for the past two years."

It went on for what seemed a very long time and then Mrs. Creek was making a total denial. The whole thing was a trumped up charge. The bills and receipts were forged to give her a bad name. Where had they come from and who had made up such a pack of lies against the town shops and the staff of the Orphanage?

I buried my face in my hands and knew that she would triumph over the whole of us. She would wriggle out of the morass and everybody would go away and leave us at her mercy. I shivered and huddled myself more deeply down among the delphiniums and heard my voice called and made no answer.

Then there were steps along the flagged path.

"I can see where you are because the flowers are shaking more than you are, Honey. Come out of there and give us your account of what happened. There's nothing to be afraid of."

Jonah Rohan took me through to the room with his arm round my shoulders and explained in his pleasant voice, that I would show the Board how the letters had come to light.

He stood by my side at the desk and gave me his handkerchief in lieu of duster.

"The desk had to be tidied and dusted. Lesley here had full permission to do it and to do it thoroughly. Indeed, so she did."

He nodded at me to repeat my work of the day before and I went through the miming like a marionette and wished I had strings to hold me up. I might have wandered into one of my own nightmares, but this was no dream but reality. I dusted the pigeon holes, pretended to tidy drawers, that were tidy already. I found the tiny key and opened the central door, slid my finger into the back of the space and moved the pillars out, first one and then the other.

There was a silence in the room more terrible than any words could be.

I pointed to the letters and to the parchments and back to where they had been. Then I showed them where the white wrapped parcel had been kept.

I unwrapped the parcel there before them all and put the head band down on the table, set out the cutlery as if I laid a place for a child. I do not think they had discussed the parcel, for there was a murmur of astonishment.

When I spoke at last, my voice was a thin whisper of sound, but I think it reached into every corner of the room.

"The head band is mine. Mrs. Creek took it from me when I came, I think the silver is mine too, but I can't be sure . . . only that I remember something like it."

Mrs. Creek was still standing at the foot of the table and the tradespeople were all about her, as if they would support her against me.

"Of course, they're yours, Summer. I never said they weren't. As far as I'm concerned you can have them this minute. You came here from jail and before that, you'd been bought from the tinkers for five bob. There's a history of honesty for you! A gypsy woman bought you on Midsummer Common and she got herself into jail for stealing and I daresay she taught you to steal too. I never believed that she hadn't stolen them things, or that you hadn't pinched 'em yourself. . . ."

She came down the table at me like a spider, but slower than a spider, more like a toad might crawl.

"You found them things and you gave them to the lawyer. You made mischief for us all and if it's the last thing I do, I'll pay you even. You've turned the whole town upside down. You've ruined us all. I'll lay for you and one day, I'll get you."

Mr. Jones was begging her to be more restrained, but she had lost all restraint.

"There's nothing anybody can do to save you. You can think you'll get away with it, but you'll never. They can't stay here for ever and the time will come when you and I are alone, Miss Summer. They called you 'Summer', because you was took on the fair on Midsummer Common. That's where your name came from, like I said. My God! I'll give you winter instead of Summer. I'll not leave an inch of skin whole on your backside."

She sprung across three feet at me and her nails clawed

69

the side of my face. She grabbed me by the shoulders and shook me like a terrier with a rat. Jonah Rohan took me away from her, but she dodged back and forth behind him like a shadow boxer, trying to come at me, screaming all the time.

"You can lay in your bed and think yourself safe and snug, but I'll creep up on you and I'll find you, do you hide ever so near or far. . . ."

There was a story of a boy, who encountered a convict in a graveyard. I thought of it with half my mind, thought of Pip and Great Expectations and Charles Dickens and knew that fiction was no stranger than fact. I knew the terror that had possessed the heart of Phillip, otherwise known as "Pip".

"It's no good your begging me with them big dark eyes of yours. I'll not see you go unpunished for this day's work. You'll not get away with it."

"I don't imagine there's much chance that you'll get away with it yourself, Mrs. Creek . . . nor that any of you will," Mr. Jones pointed out in his dry legal way and she took a step back at that. Jonah Rohan had had enough of the scene. He took me by the hand and led me to the door.

"I'm going to take this child out of here now," he said. "She's being put in fear of her life. She's been starved and bullied and beaten, I daresay. I'll leave the rest of the Home in your care as a Board, but for this one child, I'll take the responsibility."

There was argument that went on and on over my head. Mr. Rohan's solicitor was very averse to his client's plan. I was turned fifteen years of age. I was no child. The law was strict on the taking of a child into care. It would be quite out of order . . . a breaking of regulations.

"There's been a deal of disregard for regulations one way and another," Mr. Rohan said. "I'll see the girl comes to no harm."

"I hope you know what you've got then," Mrs. Creek

shrilled out at him. "If you take her out of here by force, you'll find yourself in a bigger fix than if you landed up in the whale's belly like your namesake. She's half sharp and she's a wrong 'un. She can't read or yet write. She don't talk much come to that. Daffy, thief, tinker! We call her 'the Dummy' here. Only for my care and kindness to her, she'd have ended up in lunatic asylum. Ask any member of the Board, that's here now. I said she was a good worker and they kept her on."

My gilt band and the cutlery wrapped again in the soft white paper was gripped tightly in my hand, yet I had no recollection of picking them up, wrapping them again, only remembered Jonah Rohan's eyes looking down at me.

"Do you trust me?" he had asked and I nodded my head.

He was arranging for Mr. Barr to go home with the other solicitor in the square respectable car. I looked at the tableau in the room, with the villains bunched together, dressed in commerce and broadcloth at the foot of the table, all respect stripped away from them, as if they stood naked. The desk was there, but its secrets had escaped. The chairs were higgledy-piggledy, this way and that. The casement windows were open to the summer and soon I would be outside away from fear.

"I was on my way home. I'll take her with me. You can contact me at my father's house in Ireland and we'll go on from there."

I was not to fetch my coat, nor any of my belongings. I was to walk out of the front door in the clothes I stood up in. I got into the passenger seat of the green car and pulled my skirt down over my knees. The car purred like a tiger and took the drive at a bound. At the bottom of the hill, we thrummed through the siesta of the little town and I imagined the anxious faces, that might be hidden by pulled aside lace curtains. Then we were out into the country and the wind

71

whipped the fringe from my forehead, while Jonah Rohan debated to himself if he had acted too impulsively. I sat silently, listening to him.

"It was odd, you know. For a while back there, I thought Zachary Myles stood beside me and projected his thoughts in my mind. There's imagination and Tom-foolery for you."

At that, I put a hand on his arm and did interrupt him.

"We never said goodbye to him."

He glanced at me and asked me what I meant and I explained that we should have visited the grave.

"I never thanked Mr. Barleydrop either . . . never said goodbye to Betsey."

"Betsey?" he said.

"Mrs. Betsey Judd, a respectable woman of the town," I explained.

"I see," he said, but he did not see one bit. He was beginning to wonder what sort of a difficult position he had landed himself in.

"They said you didn't read or write, or talk much. You talk with your eyes, of course . . . but maybe I should have waited. Zachary *was* in that ugly room. The only item of furniture with any beauty was his desk and if ever a ghost haunted a place, he haunted that room today. I knew what he'd have done, thought myself man enough to do it too, but now, he's left me."

He was worried. There was no doubt about it. The car chundered the miles away and he said no more. Then he stopped in an aisle of trees, great beeches, that turned the road to a cathedral. The switch off of the engine brought a church silence too.

"Will they be all right in the Home?" I asked, and he promised me that the girls would be happy from now on.

"Yet nobody bothered about the parchments from the desk. There were things that Dr. Myles wanted done and they

72

hadn't been done."

"Those bequests were from years ago. They've no importance now, only as history, been discontinued for a long time."

He understood what I was getting at then.

"You were thinking that Mrs. Creek hid up the parchments on purpose. You're blaming her in the wrong there. Those little fancies of Zachary's had all withered away, as money got less purchasing power. The parchment on the wall was one of them, put up there as a memorial. The parchments in the desk had sentimental value only but you found treasure trove in the letters and receipted bills for things that had never been delivered to the Home. They were fiddling the accounts, Mrs. Creek and her first echoing lieutenant, half the townspeople too, splitting the proceeds between them."

"Will you take me back there, when she's gone?"

He looked at me again and said nothing. He did not know the answer himself and I knew he was wishing he had left me where he found me. I would have been safe enough, for Mrs. Creek must presumably go to prison and surely she could never carry out her threats? He was wishing that the ghost of Zachary Myles might never have walked across his mind.

"I was on my way home to Ireland. We'll go there and see how things turn out."

I did not ask him any more questions, but he thought he owed me some more explanation. He swung his leg over the door of the car and picked up a dried beech stick.

"My father has a chemist's shop. He's the son of Zachary Myles' daughter. Look here. I'll draw it for you.

In the beechmast of last year, he drew out his family tree.

Zachary Myles
↓
Malachai . . . Mary

73

"Now Mary married a man called John Rohan, a doctor."

Mary married John Rohan
↓
Matthew . . . Ruth

"Matthew's my father and Ruth's my aunt. Aunt Ruth looks after the house, for my mother died when I was born. We'll take you home and see what they think of you."

He drew a circle round the name of Ruth scratched out in last year's husks.

"Aunt Ruth's a Betsey Trotwood. I suppose you don't know what I'm talking about, but I think you might be a second David Copperfield. I could do with a Mr. Dick myself this minute, but you won't understand that either."

"Mr. Dick always knew what to do," I said. "He said 'I should wash him and another day have the boy measured for a suit of clothes and I should put him to bed. . . .' "

He climbed back into the car and started the engine and shook his head at me.

"Couldn't read or write !" he said. "But for now, I'm going to take you to the only person I can think of as a substitute for Mr. Dick."

After a while, we reached Cambridge and I thought I had never seen such a beautiful town with its narrow streets and lovely buildings. He parked outside a cake shop and went in, came back and put a bag of buns in my lap.

"Eat some of those, while I go and take advice from Mr. Dick."

We were off again, along streets that barely could make room for the car. Then we stopped half way along a line of dignified houses, with two stories and a basement.

The paint was fresh, the curtains fresh, the windows shining.

"University lodgings," he explained. "I live in this one.

Eat those buns and I'll be back directly."

He went up the steps and let himself in through the front door with a key, and I caught a glimpse of a plump comfortable woman. He unwound his scarf from his neck and she took it from him and hung it on the hall stand.

"If ever I wanted your help and advice, I want it now, Mrs. G."

The door shut and I sat there and waited. After a bit, I opened the bag and the smell of the sticky buns filled me with desire. I thought it might not be good manners to eat one openly in the street, but I broke off a small piece and put it in my mouth and chewed it, knew that I had never tasted anything so delicious. Little by little, with great discretion, the bun disappeared and still the door stayed shut. Once, the lady came to the window and looked out at me. Then after what seemed a very long time, she came out by herself and put up her arms to help me over the car door.

"Well there, my little darling. Mr. Jonah's gone to phone his pa and his aunt. You're to come into the house with me and be made very welcome."

In the hall, she took the bag from my hand and looked inside, exclaimed in delight that Mr. Jonah had been a wise one to get some of Fitzbillie's buns.

"No buns in the world like them! My young gentlemen come back to see me sometimes, years after they've gone down. I've always to get out my bike and go over to Fitzbillie's. Sticky buns! It's the first thing they ask for. I daresay you don't understand a word of what I'm saying, but this is a University Lodging House. That means that I'm registered by the University to take in the young gentlemen from the Colleges. I've had them in all shapes and sizes and from most parts of the world, for the past thirty years and if they're in this direction, they always come to mine to see me."

"And Mr. Jonah is one of your young gentleman?"

It seemed that he was and he had asked her to get some tea and soon, he would be finished with the telephone, though the line to Ireland was bad that day, he said. If I would come down to the kitchen, she'd put the kettle on. The kitchen was gloomy in the basement, and you could see the legs of the passers-by on the pavement outside the railings, but there was a cheerful stove and a scrubbed white table. I helped her put the sticky buns out on a plate, while she cut very thin bread and butter and filled a jam dish from a pot of home-cooked strawberry jam.

"I made this here jam myself last year, two weeks after Midsummer Fair was on the Common."

"Midsummer Common," I echoed as Miss Frith might have done.

"It's down the road to the corner and turn left. It's near enough that you can hear the music from the gallopers, if the wind's laying right."

"And are there gypsies there?" I asked her and she said there were more gyppos than you could shake a stick at . . . a line of caravans with a lady in each doorway waiting to tell your fortune.

She passed me a packet of doilys and asked me to set out the cakes on the plates and I did it very carefully, wondering if there had been truth in what Mrs. Creek had said. It might be possible that in the clouded forgotten past, I had visited Cambridge before.

"Has the Fair been held on Midsummer Common for a long time?"

She laughed at that and said that it had gone on for hundreds of years.

"I think it were called 'Stourbridge Fair' once and folks used to come to hire maidservants and that, but I don't rightly know. Now, it's all china stalls and sweet stalls and coconut shies and roller coasters and walls of death and the like. The

76

children go mad when the Fair comes on the Common. Usually there's only a few horses graze there, but the Fair's as big as a town in itself . . . right down 'most to the river bank."

We carried the trays upstairs to "Mr. Jonah's sitting room" and it was a very special kind of homely place. There was a table set out with a white cloth and shining china . . . a silver jug for the milk and a table napkin in a ring, a little bunch of roses. The chintz covered armchairs were deep and comfortable and there were rows of books on shelves . . . a desk at the window.

"That's where Mr. Jonah does his studying. He's reading medicine at Downing and soon he'll be off to London to walk the hospitals. I'll miss him when he goes down. He's one of the nicest young gentlemen I've ever had, but then he's Irish or half-Irish. I expect he kissed the Blarney stone. Anybody who's done that could talk the birds out of the trees."

We had tea together, he and I, while Mrs. G. insisted on waiting on us. I had discovered that her name was Mrs. Greenall and felt awkward that she would not sit down and take tea with us, but she said it would not be proper. She had "her own tea" in her little room below stairs. Really I think she insisted on the waiting because she wanted to hear what happened on the phone and of course, I was full of curiosity too.

"It's all right, Mrs. G. They quite understood and they're looking forward to us arriving tomorrow evening. The line was so bad we could hardly understand what we were saying."

He insisted on treating me as an adult with all my brains intact, for he explained that he had spoken to his father and to his aunt in Ireland and told them as best he could what had happened. They understood most of what he said and agreed with what he had done. Then he had telephoned the undergrad, who shared the car with him and it would be O.K. if we took her to Liverpool and parked her near Prince's Dock. His friend would get a lift up with somebody going that way on Sunday and fetch the car home again. It was his friend's turn to have it for the Long Vac.

When tea was finished it was quite late, for me at any rate. He smiled across the table and between us hung the memory of Mrs. Greenall being like Mr. Dick in David Copperfield.

"And now, Mrs. G. I think it's time for Lesley Summer to be getting to bed. I'd be obliged if you could see to it . . . wash her and maybe tomorrow have her measured for a suit of clothes . . . but put her to bed for now."

I had a bath and put on one of Mrs. Greenall's night-dresses, which was so soft and white and lace bound and filmy that I thought it might have done very well for a ball gown, if I took it in a good bit and wrapped it round myself and banded it with a ribbon for a belt. I was admiring myself in the glass when she came in to say goodnight and she stood at the window and beckoned me to come and look out.

"You can see Midsummer Common from here."

I stood by her side and looked out at the lovely soft light of a Cambridge summer evening and saw the expanse of grass, that stretched to infinity, with the houses throwing long shadows in the street below us. Somewhere in a secret recess of my mind, I remembered the grass common and the smell of the fish and chip stalls and the trampled grass, the ozone quality of the power units that ran the gallopers and the dodgems and the cake walk and the Jollity Farm, the raucous cries of the show men. There were stalls of china, set one beside the other. There were rows of gypsy caravans, gay with gilt china and "gaudy" was the keynote and "spotlessness", for travellers must be as battleship-spick-and-span as the British Navy. I did not know how I knew it. I did not know from where the picture came. It was from the past and it had happened and been lost.

"That's where they put the Fair every year. It's a great place for china. We all use china from the Fair and every June we replace the pieces we smash before Midsummer comes round again, replace them from the china stalls."

"The gypsy caravans, the fortune tellers," I whispered. "Did they stand just there near that entrance and run in a line along by the trees?"

"Oh, no, ducks, they were all at the front way in. You haven't to go far, do you want your fortune told, just inside that front gate where the bar is now and along a bit on the left."

"I thought it farther along . . . up near where the paths meet, just where that white horse is grazing."

She looked at me in surprise and then laughed.

"They were there just the one year. Have you got second sight or something? The Council wanted them to pay more money and they reckoned they paid enough already without extra dues. The Council wouldn't give them the old site, but that were some years ago."

She smiled at me and asked me how I could know anything about Midsummer Fair and there was no answer to that. I did not know myself and soon I was tucked up in bed and on the edge of sleep. It was the first time somebody had kissed me goodnight and tucked the clothes tight about me and I lingered before I slept and could not sleep and I was out at the window again by myself and it was dusk. The green common was darkling and yet I knew how it would be with the Fair at full height. I knew the lit bulbs and the crack of rifles on the firing ranges. I knew the hawkers' cries and the screams from the roller coaster. I knew what it was like to ride the great wheel and look down on the dwarfed houses. I recalled the sick lurch of the swing boats. I knew the intimacy of a caravan and the shine of a crystal ball and it was time for me to go back to bed and stop asking myself how I could possibly

79

know these things. The bed was soft as only a feather bed can be and my sleep was deep as death. I did not open my eyes till Mrs. Greenall appeared at my side in the morning and told me that it was a fine day.

Then it was time for her to carry out her version of measuring me for a new suit of clothes.

My dress had been washed and ironed overnight and the white collar was fresh starched. My shoes were polished like guardsman's boots. All my underthings were freshly laundered, ironed and aired. . . .

"He didn't actually mean that about being measured for a suit of clothes, Miss Summers. The young gentlemen haven't much money by them especially after May week, but not to worry!"

She produced a nurse's cloak of blue lined with red, with a cowl that hung from the shoulders. It belonged to some relation of hers, who had quit the nursing for wedlock and would never want the cloak again. It fitted me to perfection and went very well with the grey dress. As a crowning glory, she gave me a straw boater, with a school ribbon. It had belonged to one of her foreign young gentlemen and all it wanted was a strip of paper, inside the leather band, and it would fit me a treat.

She tilted it over my eyes and I looked in the mirror and scarcely recognised the orphanage child. Mrs. G. certainly had a flare for the unusual. Mr. Rohan was waiting for me over breakfast and his eyebrows went up at the sight of me. Mrs. Greenall was all smiles as she waited for his opinion.

"An undergraduate of Jesus College, Mrs. G. and a member of the nursing profession!" he said. "Lesley Summer! Mr. Dick has 'measured you for a suit' and had it made up, all gratis and for nothing too . . . and it's perfect. Come and have breakfast and then we'll set out for Ireland. I've got an idea we'll take the Medical Hall by storm."

Chapter Four

THE MEDICAL HALL

We set out after breakfast "to take the Medical Hall by storm" and the old Bentley gave what Jonah Rohan called a noble performance between Cambridge and Liverpool. Only once, did she come to a stuttering halt and then it was a hundred yards from a garage. That showed great consideration on any car's part, even though in this case, it was not necessary.

"Don't worry. It's nothing lethal. . . ."

He had the bonnet up and was bending his head over the engine so that his voice was muffled.

"And don't call me Mr. Rohan all the time. Call me Jonah. Everybody else does. Mr. Rohan is my father and you'll meet him tomorrow."

He had taken some parts out of the car and was wiping them on his handkerchief, putting them back again. The engine purred at the first touch of the starter, but Jonah pointed out that the car had still had the decency to stop near the garage just in case.

He settled himself into his seat and sighed.

"Mr. Rohan, my father, Mr. Matthew Rohan. You talk very little for a woman. I don't rightly know how much you understand or don't understand. I'd better tell you a bit about the Medical Hall, for it's an old-fashioned place, part of history, I suppose, or soon will be."

"Mr. Barleydrop told me what a Medical Hall was," I said. "I think I understand it."

81

"Barleydrop?" he exclaimed and looked at me sideways in surprise, till I reminded him that Mr. Barleydrop was the sweet seller, who used to give sweets to crocodiles, and at that, he said it was all perfectly clear to him.

"Not that the crocodiles ever got any of them to eat," I continued, "But I didn't think it fair to let him know that."

"I see," he said, but like the blind man, he did not see at all, so I explained it to him and he laughed, though I did not think it funny in the slightest, but then neither would he, if he had gone walking, two by two, with his companions past the sweet shop for the last five years and had the same thing happen to him.

"Mr. Barleydrop must be a splendid old chap," he said and then he went on to tell me about his own family, for he thought it best if I knew something before I actually arrived at the Pharmacy.

It was in a small town called Ballyboy and Zachary Myles's son, Malachai, had practised there. Malachai's house was next the chemist's shop and had been run by Malachai's sister, Mary. There was another doctor in Ballyboy called Rohan, John Rohan, and he had married Mary. There was another chemist in the pharmacy part of the Medical Hall at this time, no relation or anything like. Then the doctor's house had fallen on evil times. There had been an epidemic of typhoid and Malachai had died. John Rohan had moved into Malachai's house and had carried on both practices, and two children had been born . . . "Matthew Rohan and his sister, Ruth, that is, my father and my aunt. Mary Rohan, as she was now, my grandmother, died before my father Matthew was quite grown up. I suppose she seemed the last link with Zachary. It left John Rohan my grandfather, with two growing-up children and a fairly hard practice."

"It's all too complicated for you to take in. Maybe it's best if I let you see the set-up with your own eyes. It's just that you may have got the idea in your head that we're rich, when we're as poor as church mice."

We had stopped the car to eat some sandwiches Mrs. Greenall had packed for us, and I looked at him. He read the surprise in my eyes.

"Just because I'm up at Cambridge, it doesn't mean that I'm a wealthy chap. I don't know how I expect you to pick up all the threads of this, but John Rohan died too and that left Matthew, my father, with a sister Ruth to look after and a living to make in the world. Matthew worked at nights as he read for his degrees as a pharmacist. Then he took the pharmacy over from the old man, who had been the chemist there. He was to have been a doctor, my father, but there was no money left. My grandfather had a long illness. I'm at Cambridge because of Zachary Myles. He left one of these strange old bequests, he was so fond of, a kind of tontine. It was to be shared out between his great grandchildren for their education and I was the sole surviving one and there was money to put me through University and I got a scholarship choice for Cambridge and jumped at it. . . . We make ends meet or almost meet. You'll see what I'm talking about. I suppose it's not the done thing to say how proud one is of one's father, but I've no shame about it . . . my aunt too. They've gone without to see me get on. My father's motto is 'Aim High.' He's never done saying it."

It explained the neat darns in Jonah's shirts and the patches on his elbows. It explained why he had not very much cash in his pockets and why he had to travel with care. We did not stop for meals but were both very glad of Mrs. Greenall's packed sandwiches and that good lady had obviously known what she was about too. Yet I wondered where I would fit in into the family. Almost surely they would keep me for a little while before they got rid of me. They could not want another mouth to feed with Jonah on his way to "Walk the hospitals" next term. I could only guess at what an expensive procedure that would be.

I sat back in my corner of the passenger seat when we started again and tried to work it out. I had the family tree etched in my mind and I went over it again. If only John Rohan had not died early and left his son and his daughter "without much means!" This son and this daughter, would become my host and hostess and according to Jonah, Zachary's ghost had practically made him take me out of the Orphanage. Why should Zachary's ghost want such a thing, if there were such things as ghosts? There was no solution to it. If I had thought to go along to Dr. Zachary's grave, he might have made it clear to me, but I had not even gone to say goodbye.

I pushed the thought of the Myles-Rohan families out of my mind and remembered my own heritage. I had had no time to think of what had been revealed to me over the past day or two. I sorted out what Mrs. Creek had said to me in anger, or said to the Governors or to Jonah. I had been "a tinker" and bought for five shillings and the gypsy who had bought me had been put in jail for theft. I was called Summer, just because I had come to the Home with the policeman and had been taken, presumably with the gypsy on Midsummer Common and Cambridge was not too far away from the Female Orphan House, not miles and miles away. Then in the University Lodgings, I had remembered in a kind of fugue, what Midsummer Common was like at the height of its season. As far as I knew, I had never been there before, but I had remembered the line of caravans and the gaudy china and the shouts and the music and probably it was all imagination. Then there was the recurrent dream, the Gingerbread House with the hollyhocks climbing up the front of it, the garden with the well. Always there was a deep shaft into the ground and surely I could not dream the same horror over and over again, without something very real implanting it into my mind? Yet I was "daffy and dummy and a thief and a tinker." That's what Mrs. Creek had said. I went asleep against the side of the seat and the Bentley hummed me to deeper slumber, into a happy dream, I, who scarcely ever had a happy dream. He was an old gentleman in a black frock coat and he had white hair, white side whiskers and a white beard. There was gentleness all about him and he picked me up and carried me in his arms.

"I had to come back to see to you," he said and laughed. "I couldn't leave everything as it was, but you're not to worry any more. I'll see to it that things are better in the future and after all the time I've been up there, I know how to get things done."

He had exactly the look that Mr. Barleydrop had had, when he said much the same thing.

"If there was anything to be going on . . . anything wrong, you're just to call out for me. Zachary Myles's the name."

Then I woke up and found that we were well into Liverpool and it was time to park the car at the garage near the Prince's Dock and board the B. and I. boat for Ireland.

There was a great bustle of getting the car safely parked with instructions of who was to collect it and when. The garage man made quite foolish difficulty about not giving Jonah the ticket to collect it. I may have been called "daffy" many times, but the garage attendant could not understand that one man might leave a car and another collect it. Only the sight of a Cambridge University Student's card convinced him that we were honest folk and not villains and then all the apology he made was that you could expect anything from University folk, especially in the south of England. Then unexpectedly, he became all friendly and Jonah and he discussed the points of the Bentley, till I thought we might miss the boat.

"We can go aboard at eight o'clock . . . have dinner if you like. She doesn't sail till ten."

I felt that it might be more tactful to refuse dinner and did so, but he read my face and laughed . . . told me that funds would rise to it. I never hope to have anything more splendid than that dinner aboard the boat, with "the steam up" all ready to set sail for Ireland. I kept my cape on and the waiter took me for a nurse. That would have explained the chapped work-quality of my hands, though I kept them tucked as far out of sight, as I could.

It was a feast, such as I had never had before, the sort of thing we might have imagined the staff of the Female Orphan House to be eating, while we supped our gruel.

There was grapefruit or soup, but I had had enough of soup. The grapefruit squirted juice into my eye for thanks and Jonah said it was no matter and did I like steak rare or well done, I, who had never tasted steak in my life, as far as I knew.

He chose for me at last with the wisdom he seemed to possess. We had "medium steak" and fried potatoes, after the rebellious grapefruit. His soup was unlike any I had seen in the Orphanage and in a way I was sorry not to have chosen it. It was clear brown, clear as a trout stream, or what I thought a trout stream might be like, pieces of vegetable suspended in it. You could see the richness without tasting it. The potatoes were "deep and crisp and even" Jonah said, to make me laugh.

"You've got dimples when you smile," he said and he began to take more notice of the look of me. Before that, I think I had no real identity to him, except that of a shade that Zachary had conjured up for him to take earthly care of.

The puddings were wheeled in on a trolley and I sat and gazed at them and wondered if the orphans would be able to keep their seats in hall, at the sight of such delights and not come scrambling all over the table with excitement.

"Meringue glacé," Jonah suggested, "or profiteroles, if you would like them. That's a posh name for cream buns with chocolate icing on the outside and cream inside. There's nothing to choose between them or the meringues. I'll have cheese myself, but I'll not inflict cheese on you."

The waiter thought that nothing was too good for the nursing profession. He had a soft Irish accent and he came from County Cork. His voice lilted and his eyes were the eyes of a friend. It seemed that the nurses in the Convent had saved his sister from certain death with their skill. There was nothing he could do to repay me but to give me both the meringue glacé and the profiteroles as well, and I made short work of them too and wondered if Zachary Myles had such food in heaven or if it was all plain ambrosia.

Then we did without coffee, which I did not want anyhow. Jonah said it would keep us awake and I imagined that expense had reared its head again, yet he left a tip. I had never seen anybody leave a tip before and thought it a lordly gesture, but it was not the tip that made the waiter see us to the door. He thanked me for my care of his sister in the Cork Hospital and it did not matter if I was not in that hospital. Weren't nurses all over the world doing the same blessed work every day of their lives? I felt all the shame of false pretences, and hoped my blushes might pass for modesty.

We stood on the top deck and watched the boat edge out through the docks and then Jonah left me at the door of my cabin and I lay down and was asleep between one breath and the next. It could not have been a whole night later, when there was early morning tea at the door and a biscuit in the saucer with Jacob written on it. It seemed that biblical names followed me even to biscuits.

I had planned where to meet him and I met him and we disembarked and got his big trunk out of the hold and collected up the hand luggage. A taxi was necessary, because of the trunk and we travelled along the edge of the Liffey in style.

I had never seen such a lovely river for all that it ran through the centre of a big city. It bore swans on its bosom and there were tug boats butting their way up and down the tide and sirens calling against the querulous overlord notes from the big ships. There was a smell of malt and coffee. As we drove along the quays, the sun glittered on the water and cars flashed past, taxis, buses, lorries, vans, and trams. The trams were like land ships, even to the ting ting of the bell that might have marked the watches. There was a magic about the flash of electric sparks from the cables.

The railway station was a long platform and there was a smell about it too, not quite the same as other stations had, I thought. Then I remembered that I had seen no station before. The voices of the people were soft and as sweet as poetry. . . . They were slower than the voices I had known up till now and the folk had time to stop and smile at us. There was more smiling than I had seen for a long time. In the carriage, and we had one to ourselves, I sighed, as the train slipped out along the length of the platform. There had been a green flag that waved and a whistle that shrilled and we were on our way and there were so many engines and spare railway carriages and the smell of railways. I could not know what railways smelt like, but Jonah told me this was Inchicore, the birth-place of rolling stock and then laughed at my earnest "wanting to learn" expression.

In half an hour, we were in mid-country. In far less we were in beauty, but within an hour, I was back in my familiar "have been here before" mood. I knew it all so well, the small green fields, the cows and the horses, the sheep, the cocks of hay, the mountains blue in the distance . . . but the green of the fields, there was never grass so green, not yet fields so small. I had been here before. I had turned a corner somehow and got lost and maybe now I was found. There were small cabins, washed white and thatched roofs to them and clamps of turf against the winter. There were donkeys that walked the lanes by themselves, hens that scattered from cottage doors . . . and this was no foreign land. I knew the smell of it . . . the smell of the turf smoke that rose, as straight as Nelson's column in Dublin, from the cottage chimney stack. There were small rivers that we flashed over, and I knew they were full of fish for the taking, yet I could not know these things. From somewhere, I remembered a river, where salmon lay side by side like sardines in a tin, on their way against the current to spawn.

If I was right in imagining that I had been on Midsummer Common in Cambridge, than one hundred fold, I was right in knowing that I had been in Ireland before. I had never felt so moved by any emotion. I had come home, I, who had never known what home was. I had come back to my mother and I had never known any mother. This was where I belonged. I knew it to the depths of my soul. God help me ! Maybe, I was a tinker child, but if I was, we had wandered Irish roads. Up to that train journey to Ballyboy, I had wondered who I was. I had wanted very much to find who my parents had been. I had been jealous of Jonah for his fine certain family tree. Now, very much indeed, I wanted to know my origins. We changed once and then again. Each time, the train got smaller and less important and more lovable, more full of character. As we made the last change, I decided that when I had settled what must happen in the Medical Hall, then I would begin to seek out my own beginnings. First of all, I must see what happened in Ballyboy. When I left there, I must set out on a long journey and it would be a trek into the past. I decided not to give up till I reached back to the day of my birth, even if I had to spend the rest of my life doing so.

If I did nothing else, I would find out who I was . . . I

swore to myself, on, on, on Zachary's grave and then the train was running into a short platform and we had arrived at Ballyboy.

I saw the name written in English and then in Gaelic characters and the train pulled up and Jonah jumped out. There was a man there to meet him and a lady. They had eyes only for him and he for them and I felt an intruder, turned back into the carriage and gathered the hand luggage together, got out on the platform and set it in a neat pile. Jonah was Matthew's only child and they had not seen each other for a whole term. Aunt Ruth Rohan, the second Betsey Trotwood, was expecting her nephew and not a stray David Copperfield. It was quite natural that they should be engrossed with each other and forget the outcast, that Zachary might have thrust upon them. At least, I had plenty of time to study them. Matthew was a tall scholarly man with a lined face and dark hair. I thought that he looked delicate. He had neat darns, where the points of his collar had fretted his shirt and the shirt cuffs could have done with turning. There was no prosperity about the little family, but who was I to look for prosperity? Aunt Ruth Rohan had an old tweed skirt on, and a cardigan, a white blouse. I was glad that she wore no hat, for a hat would have been a shame on such shining white hair. There was an almost visible love between the three of them and a great excitement. I felt the sharpness of being odd man out. All the same, I knew that I had no cause to expect them to come running to me with outstretched arms. I was a stranger . . . another mouth to feed, even for a little while.

"You've lost weight, Jonah. We'll have to get you fattened up before we let you go back."

"You've been too hard at the studying. 'All work and no play.' That's what it is, my boy."

I waited beside the luggage and presently the Station Master appeared and said he had the trunk out of the van. We might leave all the traps and Tommy would run them down later. He looked at me if he expected an answer, but there were no words on my lips.

"We'll take the bus today, but thanks all the same," said Aunt Ruth Rohan.

I studied the platform and noted the stone kerb it had. The main part was asphalt like the school play yard, very clean and tidy with a flower bed at the back. I watched the feet that scurried past, feet that paused, people that embraced. There were greetings and conversations, where everybody talked at one time and I was jealous that no joy overflowed a face for me. Presently I told myself, I would find myself back on the asphalt of the Orphanage. How could it be otherwise? I closed my eyes for a moment and prayed that I might never have to go back there any more and when I opened them, a pair of flat brogue shoes with fringed tongues had come walking towards me and a stick with a bright brass ferrule, tip tipping along. I followed the stick up to her hand and from there to her face and the white hair without a hat. Jonah had not told me she was beautiful, but if ever beauty sat in a face, it was here, in the wide brow, the straight nose, the square jaw, the cleft in the chin. She walked slowly, Miss Ruth Rohan, and she leaned on the stick. She limped, but there was grace about her that seemed to overcome the halting gait, and her hands awry, as if the fingers shied away from the thumb.

"God forgive us that we neglected you with the sight of this boy of ours! We've been watching the rail track for half an hour with our eyes worn out for the sight of you both."

She made no attempt to take me in her arms or kiss me, just held my shoulders between her hands, searching my face.

"Jonah told us about you on the phone, but the line was bad. I don't think we understood anything much he tried to say, only that you were from the Orphanage and it was time you left it."

She put up a hand to my face and smiled at me.

"Heaven save us! He's brought home stray kittens and puppies all his life and one time he found a few hundred tadpoles in a ditch and thought they were lost . . . put them in the pool in our garden, where they all turned into frogs . . . not been short of a frog or two since. We've had a thrush with a broken leg that we had to feed every two hours, night and all, and a hedgehog that covered us with fleas, but I don't think he's ever found anything quite like you before."

Again I seemed to have forgotten how to talk. I just raised my eyes to hers and tried to make them say what my lips would not say, that I was sorry that I had been foisted upon them, when they could ill afford a guest. I would stay a while and help as much as I could, then I must be on my way.

Matthew Rohan had my hand in his and he was laughing and scolding his sister, that he had never heard a guest get such an odd welcome.

"Welcome to Ireland, Lesley! Is this your first visit?"

I nodded my head and then shook it and still found no voice.

"Let's get on," he said. "There's a bus that takes us into the town and I daresay you haven't been in such a grand conveyance before."

It was like a miniature tram on four wheels with an old horse under the shafts. The driver sat on a seat on the roof and we rattled down the hill into the town, with the luggage behind the driver on the roof. The town was small and neat, mostly in limestone houses, but nearer the station, there were some white-washed cottages with half doors and hens that clustered about. The centre of the town was the most important place, for it had a Bank and a Post Office, and on the corner of the Main Street was the Pharmacy. I got out of the bus and stood looking at it in wonder for I had never seen such a place before. It was black-painted, marked out with gold lines. There were windows with contents that might have belonged to a genii's cave, great bottles of coloured liquid, green and blue and red, that caught the light and held it and turned it to magician's stuff. There were big china containers, three feet high with gold lids to them and foreign writing on the sides in flowing script. The shop was open and in charge of an old man, who shook my hand and bade me welcome, but I was caught up with the strange floor, that was jig-sawed in tiny pieces of marble, all to make us a splendid coat of arms with a serpent coiled on a staff. There was an essence to the whole place, a smell that I will never forget as long as I live. Along shelves behind the counter, were regimented oint-ment jars in pink with the gold line again and the foreign script. There were gleaming bottles with rounded shoulders and ornate labels and glass stoppers. There were treasures beyond price to my reckoning. The windows of the shop were bow fronted with small square panes and some of the glass looked bottle-bottom-flawed. I daresay you might find such a place in Bond Street, today, or even in a hundred years hence. I had seen an illustration in an old book of just a shop window, but these places have moved down the stairs of history.

Ruth Rohan went up to the first floor one step at a time and even that day, I recognised that she dragged her body along, by the strength of her will. There was a square room on the right, very much like the room in the University Lodg-ing House, a table set with a white cloth and polished glasses and bright silver. Of course, it was celebration. There was chicken for dinner, but perhaps I would like to wash my hands and tidy up after the journey? As I came back to the room, I overheard something not intended for my ears.

"But she doesn't talk at all? She hasn't said one word."

"Of course, she talks. She's intelligent, highly intelligent too. She's got a sense of humour and if you can imagine any-body having a sense of humour after five years in that place, you'll know her qualities. She's shy as a fawn, and she's a stranger in a strange place. Give her time."

I had taken off my nurse's cloak and my "Jesus boater" and now I appeared in the plain grey of the orphanage.

Aunt Ruth Rohan was more interested in dishing the dinner than she was in my wardrobe and I helped her, as naturally as if I were in my own home. There was a flight of stairs down to the kitchen and I sped down and up and had the potatoes in their dish, mashed to a cream in no time and the chicken spitting on its serving plate. I had been truly imbued with the household arts and the knowledge came in handy.

Yet obviously when I had been upstairs tidying, Jonah had filled in some blanks in their knowledge of me and there was a new awkwardness in the room. They were worried about the extra mouth to feed, or I thought they were, although nobody even intimated that they might calculate how to make do and mend and even maybe go without. The food was delicious and cooked to a turn, but my appetite had disappeared, as such things do. I helped myself sparingly and ate slowly and when we were all done, I asked if I might clear away. There was an apple pie next and there was no necessity for anybody to move. I had seen it in the oven. Jonah himself came down the stairs and helped me dish the second course.

"Maybe they don't like me," I whispered to him and he laughed at that and said that everybody liked me.

I had lost the power of speech with everybody but Jonah, and I wondered if I could ever find myself talking to his father or to his aunt. Mr. Rohan had to go back to the shop soon after dinner, and he took Jonah with him. In the kitchen, Aunt Ruth Rohan and I did the washing up, and she chatted away about Jonah, but I only nodded my head and smiled and

washed the dishes and put them away when she had dried
. . . took the tea cloth from her hands at last and finished the
drying and set her in the chair. She scolded herself for "letting
me do all the housework, but Mary wasn't well!" She sighed.
"It's no way to treat a guest, especially on her first visit to
Ireland, Honey."

Maybe she just called me "Honey" as a pet name, maybe
Jonah had told her. It was a key that unlocked my words.

The colour flushed my face and I tried to right what I had
said. I knelt by her chair and took one of her hands in mine.

"I'm sorry. My name is Lesley Summer and you'll know
that. I sometimes think that my name is Honey or was Honey
and sometimes I forget it's Lesley. I thank you very much for
letting me come here . . . having me in your house . . . and
as for the shop, it's like something out of the Arabian Nights.
It should be put in a glass dome and kept as it is, for ever and
ever and not allowed to change in any way. I had a friend
called Mr. Barleydrop once and he was a very good man and
he liked the old things too . . . never took to chromium plat-
ing. He liked brass, for the shine you could get out of it."

That was the start of my conversation with Aunt Ruth
Rohan and it went on for an hour or two before the kitchen
stove and neither of us with enough energy to move up to
the sitting room, where there was a turf fire wasting itself
away and deep armchairs too as I found out later. She sat
on the wheel-backed chair with her feet in the rag rug before
the bars of the kitchen grate and I knelt at her side. Now and
again her hand would come out to stroke my hair.

"I'll call you Honey, if you'll let me. It's a name that suits
you and I think somebody you loved a long time ago called
you that, and you never forgot it. There's a mystery about
you, for you're no tinker child, like that woman said you were.
Jonah told us about that, but he said that the Matron had a
tongue that would clip a hedge and a spite against you like a

spitting snake."

She looked down at me and shook her head.

"First of all, you must settle in here and after you're at home with us, we'll all put on our considering caps. There's nothing that Matt and Jonah and yourself and myself can't solve, if we put our minds to it. Just now, rest tranquil, like a salmon in the quiet reach of a river, after he's lepped the weir, with the rush of the water tearing the life out of him and the stones battering his poor sides. Stay with us a bit, Honey. Stay just as long as you like. It's a funny thing the way an old house stirs back to life, with the coming of the young ones to it. It creaks its old bones and smiles again and there's laughter and happiness in the dark corners and it's not all empty and dead, the way it was before the coming."

She talked to me very confidentially about Jonah, for she was worried about him. He worked too hard and she was of the opinion that he did not eat enough. She was very gratified when I told her about Mrs. Greenall and she thanked me for putting her mind at rest.

"Still, it's a good thing you're here for you can get him to take you walking the hills, get the country air into your lungs and colour in your faces."

She had a wish for me to let my hair free of its plaits, for she said it was not right to keep such hair in prison. I was to run up to my room and bring down a brush and maybe a fresh bit of ribbon. I found the old gilt band and brought it down to the kitchen and I told her about it.

"And this is yours?"

She asked me to get the scissors from the drawer and then she snipped off the two rosettes. After that, she examined the band very closely and got up from her chair, filled a bowl with warm water at the sink, came back to the table. She cleaned the dullness of the years from the band, as if is were some precious piece of old china, washing it gently between her

96

fingers with soap and water. After a while, she found a brush with a long handle and soft bristles and for a long time, she rubbed the band with suds, back and forth and back and forth . . . then took a tea cloth to dry it, and an old bit of silk to shine it again.

"You're quite sure this is really yours?"

"I had it on the day the policeman took me to the Orphanage and there was a wardress with him. Mrs. Creek took it from me for safe keeping. I found it in the secret drawer in the desk and that last day she said it was mine and they let me take it away. I don't think it's any value except for remembrance. I had nothing of value."

"So we can be reasonably sure that this is your own?"

I nodded my head and she said that the mystery deepened and she hoped that the band might still fit me.

"Let's hope your head hasn't grown out of it. There's a mirror on the wall there. Brush out your plaits and mind you do it properly. No, come over here and sit down by my feet on the floor. I'll do it for you. Maybe it's a long time, since you had anybody. . . ."

She broke off suddenly and started in on my hair with great vigour and there was a Betsey Trotwood side to her, in the way she did not like to show too much emotion. She counted up to a hundred strokes in a military way and said that was how hair had to be done in her day. Then she turned me about, fitted the band over the crown of my head, her hands awkward for the task.

"It still fits you fine. Go and look at yourself in the glass."

It was not the same gaudy thing it had been, ornate with red rosettes. It had a gleam that had not been there before and I could see a faint pattern worked on it.

"Take it off. Look at it very carefully and put it on again."

I did as she bade me and found two marks on the under side of it I had not noticed till now.

"Do you know what those marks are?" she asked me sharply and I said I did not.

"And neither did Mrs. Creek, I'll be bound," she said. "Put it on."

She picked up the poker and speared the grate of the range as if it had wronged her. I took the poker from her and made up the fire, fixed the dampers, straightened the rag rug, while she sat in her chair and watched me.

"I have a girl called Mary, who comes in every day and all day, to help me with the work, for it's past me to do it myself. She couldn't come today, for she had a terrible old tooth. I packed her off to the dentist and told her to go home afterwards to rest, not that that mother of hers will let her get much rest, but that's beside the point. I admit to you that if there's one thing I hate, it's stairs. I gave in to the temptation of the fire there and the warmth of the rug on my old feet, but there are perfectly comfortable chairs above in the sitting room, with fresh-washed covers for Jonah's benefit. The turf fire should be glowing grand by now. There's a fine view of all that goes on in the world outside the windows. Maybe we should stir our stumps and climb the stairs and sit in grandeur."

The sitting room was beautiful, opposite the dining room across a landing and the windows looked over the Square, so that you could see the Post Office and the Bank and the few passers-by on the pavements. The time was high summer but there was a chill outside and the warmth of the fire was a luxury. It was coming on to late afternoon and there had been a shower of rain, but it had gone over, leaving the streets wet, the air fresh-washed. There was a softness to the sky and a tranquillity to the room. It was just as peaceful as the reach of the river might have been to the salmon, who had conquered the weir. If I had not been there, I thought Aunt Ruth Rohan would have dropped off to sleep, but she obviously did

98

not want to appear rude to her visitor. Yet her voice grew sleepier and sleepier as she told me about Jonah. It was a good thing he was home, for his father would be like a dog with two tails. Jonah would be down in the Pharmacy now and the two of them talking over all that had gone on since the last vacation. Jonah helped out in the shop too and "Matt would be glad of it." I was not to allow him to work too hard all the same. He studied too hard and I was to get him out in the fresh air, as she had said already.

"There's so much to see out there and young legs to carry you. There's the river and the mountains and the town. There's nothing half as peaceful as a white-washed cottage with a clamp of turf and a flock of fowl and an ass and cart, and maybe a few geese . . . and a turf fire in the hearth. Turf smoke is the essense of Ireland and once you get it in your soul, it's there for life, so that the smell of it will call you back from half across the world."

She was almost asleep and I tucked my feet under me and leaned back and listened and was as quiet as a mouse.

"I wish Jonah hadn't gone over to Cambridge. After all, Malachai went to Trinity in Dublin, and my own father, Dr. John Rohan, was a Trinity College man too. It was Zachary pushed Jonah over to the grandeur of Cambridge University with his strange legacy and Zachary, long dead and gone, and Jonah's brains to back the bequest. I suppose it was meant some way, but he would have been nearer home in Dublin. I don't like the sea to be rolling between us. Yet Zachary was a Cambridge man and he'd have been glad Jonah went back. It was funny the way Jonah said Zachary put it into his head to bring you here. I often wonder if the dead can influence what a person does or doesn't do, but then why should Zachary want you here and Jonah in Cambridge University? Och, Honey! Take Jonah walking and let him show you the quicken trees and the nut groves and the wood-quests. I miss

99

the way I'd be able to tramp the hills with a dog at my heels. . . ."

She was asleep and I stood up and crept to the window to look down on the Square. There was a donkey wandering along the street opposite and yet wandering is not the right word to describe his walk, for there was a purpose to it, although he was completely alone. He had a look about him as if he had some important message to do. Then I saw he was bringing in a herd of cows for the milking or maybe taking them out to pasture again. He walked a hundred yards in front of them and they came behind him, a dozen or maybe more, treading in a most leisurely manner, as if time was of no consequence whatever. One of them stopped and put back her horn to stratch her side and then went on again, till presently they had crossed the Square and disappeared along a street at right angles. There was no traffic to confuse them and nobody took the slightest interest in them except me. I felt I had wandered into an enchanted land. I felt again that I had come home.

The people on the streets were as leisurely as the herd. There was no bustle of shopping and always there was time to stop and talk the minutes away.

After a while, I returned to my chair and leaned back against the bright chintz. My eyes were heavy with the weariness of travel and the lids weighed down and I slept and immediately I was in the dream world again and it was the Gingerbread House. I recognised it as the house, but it was different, for all that it had thatch on the roof, that overhung the walls with deep shading eaves. It was white-washed and it had a half door and never had I seen it so. It was alive instead of dead, yet still I knew it for my dream. There was a half door and bright flowers at the windows and a rose that climbed the front wall. There were hens, that waited with hopeful expectancy outside the door and presently somebody would come out and throw down crumbs to them out of an apron. I slipped the catch of the lower part of the door and went in, shut the hens out, for they would have followed me. There was a table for supper . . . oval and shining, all polished silver and glass. At every place, there was a knife and fork and spoon and they were the same as the one I had found in Mrs. Creek's desk, of King's Pattern, made in the right size for a child. There was a birthday cake lit with candles and they were all alight and I knew there were seven of them and soon I must try to blow them out with one breath and it was a lovely happy dream, a dream such as I never had, a dream where the Gingerbread House was alive and full of happiness and the cloth on the table was like snow and the tea cups small, perfect, and dolls that sat along the chairs . . . I was filled with excitement and happiness, that bubbled up in me like champagne spilling from a shaken bottle. Then, the click of the door latch wakened me and for a while, I did not know who I was, or where or why. Then the world spun a circle about me and I was in the sitting room with Jonah at the door smiling and me with some fragments of great joy and happiness clinging about me. Aunt Ruth Rohan slept at the other side of the fire and Jonah signalled to me not to wake her.

"Come and help me get the tea. We don't have much now . . . have something more substantial, when the shop's shut."

In the kitchen, we were conspirators, who made a plate of small cucumber sandwiches from thinly cut bread and set a cake we found, out very grandly on a silver basket. Then we took a tray up to the sitting room and Aunt Ruth Rohan woke up with a start and declared she had never been asleep at all. She had just closed her eyes. She poured out some tea for Matthew, who was still on duty in the shop and arranged some cake and sandwiches for him.

101

"We have no assistant. They're not to be come by and the shop is a terrible tie. Oh, I know you saw a man minding the place when you arrived, Honey, but he is a very old gentleman . . . a retired chemist and he helps out occasionally, but of course, we can't afford to employ a regular assistant. Let's be frank about it. It's a small town and there's not the business. Besides, we like it like that, Matt and I. Who would want to live in Piccadilly Circus and earn a fortune, when you can pass your days in peace?"

I smiled at her and we understood each other very well.

"And watch the donkey take the cows to and from the field to the milking shed," I finished for her and laughed and my laugh seemed a strange sound, that echoed from the cellars to the roof of the old house and the sun came out and the fire glowed warmly and I could still feel the happiness of the dream about me.

"I'd better take Mr. Rohan's tea down to him before it gets cold," I said and went down the stairs with it to a room at the back of the shop.

He thanked me as if I were a human being and not just a foundling orphan and told me to run away and have my own tea upstairs. Presently, we would all have a proper tea, when the slavery of the day was over and the till counted and the blinds pulled down and the gate closed against the night.

It was over the same proper tea that Aunt Ruth Rohan burst her secret like any anarchist.

"I've been wondering whether to tell you now or whether to bide my time a bit, but I've decided it's Honey's business and she ought to be told about it. Yet after all, there's no sense to it. There's no telling where the thing came from or if it was stolen, though it's my opinion that it was not stolen. Nobody recognised it for what it was. No word spoken in this room between us now, will go out the door. I'll tell you what I know and we'll say no more about it. Let the child get her feet down and herself settled in here and make her home with us as long as she wishes. There's so much for her to do and so much to see, and such time to catch up on."

She was serving rashers and eggs from a china dish out on to plates and she looked very fiercely at me, making sure she showed no emotion whatever.

"Do you see the band she's wearing across the top of her head?"

Their faces turned towards me as I passed a plate along the table to Jonah and he grinned at me and shook his head as if to signal me to take no notice of his aunt's nonsense.

"Now, listen to me and listen to me well, Matt and Jonah. I'm going to tell you this and we'll turn it this way and that in our minds. Then we'll leave the subject alone to mature like good wine and presently we'll penetrate all this mystery, that hangs round the child, like the mists round a mountain peak, and don't dare tell me I'm mixing metaphors, Jonah Rohan!"

There was silence in the room except for the ticking of a marble clock over the mantlepiece, that I thought was very fine indeed. It had black marble pillars and four gold balls that spun round and round and it chimed the hours with a golden voice.

"Honey! Listen to me. There's no explanation I can give you of how you came to an Orphanage poor-house with that band in your hair, or how you ever escaped out of it with that band still in your possession. It's a very splendid piece of jewellery and it's solid gold and there's no doubt about that whatever . . . not nine carat gold, which would be grand enough for any lady, but eighteen carat gold, hall-marked to prove it. If you thought you went to that place with nothing, you thought wrong. One of these days, we'll find out the truth about you, but just for now, will you all start off on the rashers and eggs before they go cold on you? One of these days, we'll sit down and work it all out, but we'll not do it now. We'll eat up our tea like the good sensible people we are and not go chasing rainbows. Haven't you got your whole life stretching out before you, Honey, and time for the spending and the world for the seeking and the finding . . . and love in all our hearts warm for you . . . and what's the importance of the gold in a fillet on your head against the love you'll find in this house?"

Chapter Five

THE TOWNSHIP OF BALLYBOY

Looking back now, I can see that Ballyboy had a certain quality about it, that Brigadoon might have had . . . a dream town in a musical comedy, a town that was spot-lighted by the sun, as it lay peacefully in the Vale of the Shannon. You might come upon it in the setting of the evening and think it a place of enchantment and come back another day and find nothing, but the wind whistling through the quicken trees and the cowslips a harvest on the hills and the town quite gone . . . no Bank, no Post Office, no Medical Hall with bow-fronted windows, no thin stooped, rather delicate pharma-ceutical chemist, who looked at you over the high counter and made up your prescription in a bottle in white paper, which must be just the right size, and sealed it with red wax and tied it up securely with pink string. Nowadays, there are tablets in a plastic case, handed straight in their container into your hand, with the label stuck on and your name scrawled along the bottom of it and the name of the tablet too, written above the instructions and no mystery about it in the world, for the old days are dead and gone when medicine was an art. So now, you breathe the metered aerosol and swill down the factory-made pill, turned out in its millions, by girls in nylon overalls, to keep the nerves of the nation sedated, and you never realise that there was once an art, where the Apothecary rolled pills and coated them with gold, made his own syrups and processed his own tinctures and had moulds for making his own suppositories, with wax melted down and poured into a shape, set like plaster of paris might be set and it was all so personal and private and there was time for one person to feel concern for another.

Yet, I wander from my theme. Ballyboy was a dream town, or at least, so I found it. I was afraid to venture too far afield, lest I might never find it again. I remember the first walk I had with Jonah, when we went to see the weir by the Chapel Bridge, where the salmon jumped. It was the town river and it was beautiful and the drama of the leaping of the salmon was a thing that happened when the fish were coming home to spawn. There was a bell in the Chapel, that pealed out twice a day, noon and six, and the people in the streets stopped whatever they were doing to pray. It was a moment in the day, but it was God's moment and perhaps his ear was down-turned to Ballyboy. Even on a Fair Day, the farmer would stand in the streets bareheaded and prayers went up like turf smoke to heaven.

That day, I stood at the Chapel Bridge with Jonah and looked down into the pool below the weir. From somewhere in my past, I knew a place where salmon queued up to leap a weir. It was round a bend in my brain, but I had seen it and remembered it . . . salmon like sardines. Who could ever forget such a sight?

Yet that day, there were no salmon waiting to jump the weir in Ballyboy. It was a high graceful bridge with a good deep drop into the water and the stones of the bridge were polished by the sitting there-upon of "cornerboys" and cornerboys, according to Jonah were unemployed men.

"When the salmon are leaping, you see a few fish here, 'screwing their courage to the sticking point'."

There was the old maziness in the thoughts of my head. I had seen salmon somewhere, lying like sardines in a tin, but all alive. You looked down from a high bridge and saw them, side by side, faced against the run of the water, with the struggle for survival still high on their priorities.

I had seen them, but I did not remember where or when or why or who was with me, or anything else. It was a thing you went to see and apparently never forgot.

"Jonah, is there any place in Ireland, where there are salmon to be seen, swimming close together with their noses pointed upstream, a tall bridge maybe, but it's an impossible thing. There might be people there fishing, with the salmon about their feet."

I had see it and not in a dream, just in one of the old rememberings.

"They're like that in the River Corrib, where it flows through Galway city. It's one of the tourist sights. I only saw it the one time myself and you couldn't believe it, even as you watched."

Jonah rarely went walking with me. It was hard to detach him from the Pharmacy, where he liked to help his father.

"It's the least I can do to stop him killing himself."

Yet again I have wandered from the theme of Ballyboy, which was a town of no importance, set on the edge of the Bog of Allen, near enough to the Vale of the Shannon. It was not on any main road, not on the road from Dublin to Cork or Dublin to Galway. The great road from the city by-passed it as a thing of no account, and there were no famous ruins to see there and nobody of great international importance had been born there, or had died there. There was only peace and beauty and quiet and trippers do not come seeking for those qualities any more, or perhaps they seek them, and never find them. It was a small town and it was the centre of a farming community and once a month there was a Fair Day, when the farmers brought their cattle into town for sale. Then there was total confusion, with beasts penned up against house walls and horses trotted back and forth by young boys, bargains to be struck and the farmers' wives in to do the shopping and maybe to bring eggs and butter to sell . . . and all the news of the community to be exchanged and a hot dinner to be had at either of the two hotels or at the one restaurant. There was a personal quality about it, which seems to have departed forever. If a client wished for steak, there was a minion to run up to the butcher's and it could be rare or medium or well done . . . and there was an eternity about rashers and eggs, for surely nobody but an Irish woman can cook rashers and eggs to such perfection? There was Irish soda bread, brown or white, and these days you buy it pre-made in tinfoil packs and make it up yourself with the addition of something, milk maybe, or only water and it is sold in the supermarkets of the world, but it is not the soda bread we ate in Ballyboy, where I learned how to make it, "like an angel", according to Aunt Ruth Rohan. Now I stood with Jonah and leaned on the polished stones of the Chapel Bridge and saw the clear crystal water far below and the boulders, edged with white foam, that stood against the current. Maybe that day, there was an old tin or the frame of a bicycle, for there were spoilers in those days too, but offset against them, was the solitude and the sparcity of the population.

"Look down there just at the edge of the rock. See him."

After a while, my eyes picked him out, a fine trout, flecked against sight, his side fins holding his trim straight to the flow of the water. It was a fine place to cast your line if you wished to fish for trout, was the Chapel Bridge, but it was equally good, anywhere along the riverside walk. There were places, where you might sit, just to watch the water curl over the stones and listen to its music and let life pass by in peace.

"The house next door to ours was the place Malachai Myles came to when he set up practice here," Jonah told me. "The two houses have always been closely connected, for my grandfather, John Rohan lived there and my father and Aunt

108

Ruth were born there. It's a fine house and the local doctor —man called Cane—lives there now, but he's no relation to Zachary Myles nor to the Rohans either. Have you seen the door in the room at the back of the shop, the place my father calls 'the dispensary'? It's locked up, but it leads through to the house next door. There's another communicating door between the houses, not used, but still there."

I had seen the mahogany door on the top landing, had turned the knob and found it locked, had wondered where it led. Now Jonah told me it was locked by mutual friendly consent and it would take me through to the top landing of what used to be the house of Dr. John Rohan.

"You haven't met Dr. Cane yet, but you will. He's an old man and he says he has hopes that I'll practice here one day, if ever I have the luck to pass my exams, but let's go home now. The evening is coming down and Aunt Ruth will be wondering where we've got to."

It was dark enough for the shop windows to be lit by the time we came to the Square and I was drawn again by the beauty of the square-paned bow-fronted windows, the glow of colour from the giant bottles, the glint from gold lettering on tall jars. There was writing that proclaimed itself from the shop blinds that here "all prescriptions were carefully and accurately compounded," as if anybody would ever doubt it, after one look at Matthew Rohan. He smiled at us from behind the counter and beckoned us to join him in the small space where he did his dispensing. There was a shelf that pulled up for a work space and here he had three bottles and he was finishing compounding his accurate prescriptions for the day. The bottles were full, corked, labelled. The paper to wrap them was to hand. The spirit lamp was a genii's bottle of methylated spirit that burned from a wick in the top with a blue flame. I leaned against a row of dark old drawers with writing on them that I in no way understood, Magnesium Levis, Magnesium Ponderosa, Bismuth Subnitras. I watched him, as he went about his work and talked to Jonah meanwhile. There was a square of white paper, that must receive the bottle at just the right angle and there were folds to be made, along the sides as firm as tongued and grooved boards, pleats about the neck of the bottle, two at each side, and a blob of red wax, from the stick heated in the genii's lamp and dabbled against the paper . . . and then pink string and the wonder of the neatness of the pleats and the white of the paper. I waited till he wrote the patient's name in copper-plate hand and then I watched him wrap the second bottle. When it was finished, I asked him with my eyes, if I might try to wrap the last bottle. My brow was frowned in concen-tration and my hands followed every move his hands had made and it had looked so easy, but there was skill that my hands had not. I thought I did the same operation, he had just done and I ruined a perfectly good sheet of white paper, but he smiled and let me try again, as if he humoured a child. I bit my nether lip in concentration and this time I got it near enough right. I held the red wax against the heat of the flame and touched it against the top of the paper and again against the bottom and then I reached for the pink string. I set the pleats in place between my fingers and offered him the wrapped bottle like a retriever dog might lay a shot bird at his master's feet. He ran his fingers over it and in his hand was perfection. It stood beside its two brethren, eight ounce bottles of medicine and although he had finished my work off to his perfection, he was too kind to say so. He poured praise down on my head. Never had he seen an apprentice make such a good attempt, first try.

"I'd like to help you, if you think I could," I said hesitantly.

Again, he was kind to me. There was nothing to stop me taking up the profession, if I had a mind to. When Jonah went back to Cambridge at the beginning of term, maybe I might help in the shop. I might even take my Preliminary examination and in time, get my degree. There was nothing to do in life, but to "aim high" at the beginning and then it was no disgrace to you, if you missed the target and ended up in a heap at the bottom of endeavour.

"Aim high, Lesley. Never accept the second best thing, even if the first's not in your range."

"But I can't stay on here, when Jonah's gone back to England," I said and he raised his brows at me and asked me why ever not.

"I know that my sister had Mary to help her, but you've made yourself a very useful person to have about the house upstairs and it seems you might fit in here too. We've no hold on you, if you want to go or if you have other plans for the future."

I thought that he must be sarcastic, for I did not consider myself of much value anywhere, but then I saw he was in earnest. There was a welcome in the Medical Hall, if I wanted to stay on there. If I wanted to stay on in Ballyboy! Even with Jonah back in Cambridge, I wanted more than anything to stay on in "the reach of the river where a salmon might rest after its struggle up the weir."

So I stayed on in Ballyboy and Jonah went back to Cambridge, but we all knew he would be home again for the Christmas vacation and meanwhile, there were his letters to read, one every week, written in Mrs. Greenall's and addressed to Mr. Matthew Rohan, but meant to be read by us all, even by myself.

"Dear Aunt and Father and dear Honey too,

Cambridge may remind some people of the days of Sherlock Holmes and his hansom cabs, but as usual, I miss the quietude of home and the soft brogue and the way that over there, everybody knows everybody else's business and maybe cares about it too. There's a detachment to one's fellow man

111

here that I can't take to. The University is a very special social club, where we all sit like gods and take the world to bits and put it together again, as if we really live on Olympus. I have been to London and fixed up to share a flat with three others, all of them medical students too and each of us with a brand new stethescope, through which we can hear nothing but the blood bumping in our own ears. At least, the other three are friends of mine in Cambridge. One of them shared the Bentley, God help her, for her big end is gone and we must wait till we get her botched up. We can do it between us and we won't 'let poor Nelly starve.' She will travel past Drury Lane one of these days and surprise the natives, if she backfires. They will imagine that Chicago has come to London, which we must all regard the centre of the civilised world, or so they tell us, but we have reservations. Father, I am studying hard but not to exhaustion, Aunt Ruth, I have as yet no holes in my socks and if they come, I am well capable of cobbling them myself. Honey, my hospital nurse from Jesus, complete with boater and Jesus College ribbon, are you settling down in the township of Ballyboy? You know the donkey you so admire, Breen's old ass, who leads the cows to and from the fields, I imagine by now, he knows how to take a carrot from your hand or maybe an apple or a potato. You're that sort of person, though you don't know it yet. Everybody likes you, even Breen's ass. Look after yourself and be happy and rest a while."

God help me! I was in love with Jonah Rohan. He was the white knight in shining armour, who had delivered me from that unhappy place and at inconvenience to himself too. There had been no obligation for him to do anything, except to settle legal affairs and go off with a carefree backfire from the Bentley, but he had got caught up with his conscience, or perhaps, as he said, old Zachary in his black frock coat and white bearded face had leaned down over the golden bar of

112

heaven and ordered him to see to "the orphans in their afflic-
tion".

I did not know what love was. I had never experienced it.
Now I knew there was a state where one person got involved
with another or the thought of another to the exclusion of
everything else. One left father and mother and sister and
brother, it said somewhere, but I had none of these. All I
knew that when I was with him, the sun shone brightly and
warmly and there was happiness all about, even down to the
trout in the river, who was happy because Jonah watched
him with me. The Medical Hall was empty without him, but
there was so much to think of, that his going was bearable.
My world was expanding about me at a tremendous rate and
there was so many things to assimilate, so many friends to
make, so much to be seen, so much to learn.

It was a wonderful life after the Orphanage for it was all
kindness and laughter. There was no trouble for anybody as
far as I could see. People might not be rich in worldly goods
but they were rich in happiness and friendship. There was a
peace that hung over the hills and stretched to the distant blue
mountains and up to the bright island sky.

So I was content to stay on in Ballyboy and dream of
Jonah and the day when he would come riding in on his
white charger and take over the practice from Dr. Cane in
the house next door. Dr. Cane and I were already good
friends, for he met me in the shop one day and was interested
in my case. It was obvious that he had talked about me with
Matthew and that Matthew or maybe Aunt Ruth Rohan had
asked for a professional opinion.

I found myself in his consulting room one day for a medical
examination and was glad that he was one of the people I
could talk to. Besides, he seemed to have heard it all before.

"I hope you'll bear with me if I take a look at you, for you
don't add up. You just don't add up. . . ."

113

He shook his head and sat down at his desk.

"Tell me about your childhood."

There was nothing to answer to that and he saw he had made a false start and began again.

"I'll run the rule over you, for we can't have Matt and Ruth worrying over your health."

The stethoscope searched and found nothing, but how could it seek out what was in the innermost part of a person's head?

"You're as intelligent as a bag of monkeys and you can read and write and count. You just told me that two and two make four, unless you put them down side by side and then they make twenty-two. Your I.Q., as the learned professors call it, is as high as the sky. You're not daft or dumb or deficient in any way, yet you got away with such a picture of yourself for five years and I'd like you to tell me how."

I said nothing, just looked at him out from under my knotted brows and he told me I would frighten the crows if I didn't take that face off myself.

Slowly and with great hesitations, I told him about the Gingerbread House and about the dreams I had of it. I told him and he made me go back over it and again and again, made me tell him every little detail of the house and of the Witch who lived there and about the three girls, who lived in the well of treacle . . . and about the thoughts that came up through the mists and vanished again.

He wormed it all out of me and he cared very much about my welfare. He wanted to put my feet on the stairs to happiness. He radiated his involvement with me and his assurance that he would help me all he could.

"The brain is a strange kingdom, girlie. It holds complete dominion over the body in every way. It's my considered opinion that you had tremendous mental trauma one time, early enough on in your life too. It seized everything up,

114

locked up your mind like a fly caught in amber. We've just got to find a way to get to that poor fly and let it go free again, but I daresay I'm talking, like a real doctor, and not the old quack I'm becoming as the years drag me down. I shouldn't have used the word 'trauma', for 'tis for the medical books. It means hurt or injury. They say that a person could be frightened to death and that would be a kind of mental trauma, I suppose. At any rate, I think we're going the right way about your cure, if there's any cure needed, for you're a very nice girl just as you are. Still, if there's a fly in prison, we'll let it out."

He turned away from me and went to the fireplace, kicked at a lump of coal with the toe of his shoe and the sparks flew up the throat of the chimney and glowed like little bright will o' the wisps in the soot on the back.

"I can't abide the thought of all the creatures that get into a car and then somebody closes the windows on them, a fly perhaps or a bee or even a ladybird. Then the car drives away and for all anyone knows, somebody puts it on the boat for England. There's nobody to open that window, for what customs man would worry his head about a fly or a bee or a ladybird? You or I might think that perhaps the lady's home was on fire and all her children gone, but not a revenue officer. Then at last the window's wound down, but say the car's in London, when it should be on the Curragh, with sheep grazing and horses running. What does our poor ladybird do in a big city with no air to breathe and no green in the grass and her friends and relations all gone for ever, not to mention her home?"

He looked at my reflection in the mirror over the mantleshelf and smiled at the concern in my face. Then he was all professional again.

"Matt and Ruth next door want my opinion, but now I must give it to you, for you're my patient and my first duty is

115

to you. Then, if you'll give me your permission, I'll discuss your case with the Rohans."

I nodded my head and he turned back to sit at the desk his elbows on the pink blotter and his chin in his hands.

"As I said before, I think you had a great shock, a shock that shut a car window on a ladybird. Maybe, and not knowing that she was doing it, she closed her thoughts of who she was or where she lived, refused to weep about the fact that her house was a-fire and her children all gone. She put down a mental barrier and it will take a long time to dynamite it. Now and again, when she's asleep, her mind takes over again, because she herself is asleep and doesn't know how things escape in the dark of the night, doesn't know that ghosts haunt and ghosts not from the dead, but just up from the past. We've got to turn back the calendar, but there's no hurry about it in the least. Besides, it's easier said than done. The first thing I'd ask you to do is to let Ned Oakapple take a look at the gold fillet you wear in your hair some days. Miss Rohan knows about such things. She says it's old and probably very valuable. We just want one loose thread to start unravelling. God knows, child, I'm talking far above your head and you know every word I say and what I mean by it, but Ned Oakapple might be able to tell us something about the gold band. There's nothing he likes better than bygones and he's an individualist. I like individualists and you're one, if ever I met one."

He stood up and went to open the door for me and stopped up short as he turned the handle, for I tried to thank him.

"Don't thank me, but just to oblige me, go on helping Ruth in the house and Matt in the shop. I see what goes on and I'll tell you a thing that's true. If the Angel Gabriel instead of yourself, had walked through the door that day in Jonah's care, the Angel or Archangel or whatever rank he has, could never have carried more happiness for the Rohan family in

116

his two fists, than you did. . . ."

Before I had time to visit Ned Oakapple, there was a Fair Day and we were very busy in the shop . . . not that I did much but wrap bottles and tidy up and dust and polish and help unpack the great crates of drugs. By ill luck, one had come by carrier that day from the station. There was some shopping to be done for midday dinner, not that Mr. Rohan ever ate much on Fair Days. Aunt Ruth Rohan gave me a list of things she wanted me to buy and she knew I could read by this, although nobody in the Orphanage ever suspected the fact. We had decided that Uncle Matt, as I called him now by his request, would do far better on busy days with a rich nourishing soup, so I had to get some lamb bones and a little barley. We had the vegetables by us in the garden. A bowl of hot broth was soon gone without the trouble of eating it, as Mary said. I was also to find the woman who brought in eggs and butter for us every week and see that I got the butter home in time, for we were nearly run out.

I did all the messages faithfully and then I saw a tinker woman going along the Main Street from one shop to the next. She had a black shawl over her head and a baby wrapped in it close to her breast. She was a handsome woman, or could have been, if she had tidied herself up and washed. Her hair hung in wisps on her damp forehead and she smelt of dirt and wood smoke and sleeping out of doors.

She slunk into each shop apologetically with her hand stretched out to one customer and then another. The country women rummaged in their handbags for coppers, but she hinted for more than they wanted to give.

"Spare another copper for the poor starving child. Don't turn me away without the wherewithal to buy milk for the poor little creature and nothing in my breast left for him. God bless you, Ma'am, and send you good luck for your kindness to a poor tinker girl!"

The shop-keepers knew her sort and were short and sharp with her.

"Go on out of that. You've been in here before and you've got my customers fleeced. If they knew the way you pinched that child to make it bawl! Hungry! Take it out and let's have a look at it and it as fat as a pig."

She spat against the door post as she sidled out of some shops, her face a storm cloud.

"God curse you for the mean old divil you are and you taking in the coin, fist over fist, and no thought in your head for the ones that live rough."

There was a black and tan terrier, that crouched at her heels and she kicked its skeleton ribs and all my pity for her was gone in a flash.

'Go to hell out of that, you mangey cur!"

If it were possible for him to crouch lower against the cold pavement, in apology, he did it, but she strode on to the next shop, all thought of him forgotten.

He crouched where she had left him, shivering with the fright he had of her, and I went over and stroked his smooth coat. He broke my heart with the wag of the tail he gave me and I could do nothing but open the bag of bones that I had for the broth, for Uncle Matt's lunch and offer one to him. Uncle Matt would never object to such charity by proxy. The terrier had the bone out of my fingers, but gently, and was gone, running at full tilt, still crouched low, round the corner out of sight. I got through the messages quickly after that and I did not see the dog till I reached the Market Square, which was at the other end of the Main Street from our Square. There was a monument to Daniel O'Connell and it had a plinth to it and on the wide kerb at the foot, the small terrier sat "couchant" in a spot-light from the sun. There was no sign of the bone, but no mistaking his content. He was satin black except for his muzzle and his paws and his chest and

118

now, his head was up as if he was sun-tanning his already rich gold chest. I had never seen an animal with such proud air. His right fore paw was daintily crossed over the left and his eye half closed. There was a small tan mark above each eye, as if our Lord had blessed him and left the marks of His fingers, when he created him and saw that he was good. My heart missed a beat. I went closer, to make sure there was no mistaking it. He was the dog on the crest of my King's Pattern silver . . . in mien, in pride, in cross paws, one over the other.

I put out a hand to stroke him and he smiled at me, as a human being would smile, his teeth bared and his face happy. Then he was crouched down again, but all a beggar-man again, his tail between his legs, the voice above my head as brass as a gong.

"Where the hell have you been, you idle baste of a dog? Don't you know that your job is to drag at my heels behind myself and the child as if we was all dying of hunger?"

She aimed a blow at him and he ran away down the street and stood looking back at her.

"One of these days, I'll tie a rope round your neck and ornament it with a stone and swim you in the river for the good-for-nothing cur you are."

"Why does he sit with his paws like that?" I asked her and she was conscious of my presence for the first time.

"Paws like what, me lady?"

"One over the other and the look of a prince about him."

I could talk when I wanted to. There was no doubt about that and now I had hold of one end of an unravelled thread. He had crept back to my side and I felt again the pink lick of gratitude against my wrist. Had he not done the same thing, as I handed him the bone? He had not snatched it, although he must have wanted it very badly. He had paused to lick my wrist and had taken the bone gently. Then and only then, had he rushed away, as if the whole world was in

119

pursuit to do him down.

"Crost-wise you mean," said the whine above my head. "Maybe he has it in his head that he's one of the Corby Hounds."

She aimed a second kick at him and this time her boot connected with his skeletal ribs and he was gone with a whimper of pain.

I leaped to my feet and grabbed her by the arm, got the musky, dirty, smoky smell of her at close quarters.

"Corby Hounds?" I demanded like any great lady. "What do you mean by Corby Hounds? You're an Irish gypsy and you might know. . . ."

My mind was back with the crest on the silver knife and forks and spoons of the King's Pattern, that lay in tissue paper in the bottom drawer of my dressing table and had been seen by very few people. Here indeed I held the end of a thread to unravel the mystery.

She pulled herself out of my grasp and her face was mottled white with fear under the dirt that besmirched it, yet there was my duty to the poor creature.

"You kicked him. You kicked him for nothing and I could tell the police about what you did. I could get you punished for it, for he'd done nothing. . . ."

"Maybe you'd like to buy him, my lady?"

"Tell me what the Corby Hounds are. I'll buy him from you, but tell me that first."

"And how much would you pay for him? He's well bred, from one of the Hounds as I said. That's why he had his paws crost-wise."

"What are the Corby Hounds?"

I was no match for her and well she knew it. Mentally I counted out how much money I had in my change.

"I'll give you half a crown."

I had no right to spend money that was not my own, but

I could not release the thread of evidence I held and as well as that, he had come back to cower against my feet.

"Hand it over then."

I gave her Matthew's half crown with guilt in my heart and she snatched it from me and hid it away in some secret place under her noisome shawl and the baby began to cry again.

"You're welcome to him if he'll go with you and he knows how to beg the shops. Maybe you saw me kick him, but he needs a kick now and again to keep him in his place. Take him, my lady, and welcome, but maybe he'll not lave me. He knows who's good to him. He knows what side his bread is buttered."

She turned away from me and I grabbed her by the arm again, but she twisted from me and I might as well have tried to hold a wet wriggling eel. She ran off across the Market Square and dodged under the neck of a young horse, that was being trotted, darted under its hooves with no thought for the squealing baby in her arms. I went after her as best I could, but at every stage I was blocked. There were pigs penned against a wall and they broke the hurdles and escaped between her and me and she was farther and farther away. Then a woman with geese across my path, asked me if I was after a young goose for the oven that would be as tender as a new born child might be from the cooking, if I basted it well. For a while, I roamed the town, even stopped some tinker men to ask them if they knew the woman with the black and tan dog . . . a dog with tan marks above his eyes and a black coat.

"We call a dog like that a four-eyed dog, missis. Tinkers don't like a four-eyed dog. He sees more than's good for him to see."

"But the tinker woman?"

"We've no such woman in the town this day. We'd know any tinker woman that'd be in it. We'd not deny our own

121

kind."

"But I spoke to her. She told me about the Corby Hounds. . . ."

They turned their backs on me and I stood there, quite alone, boycotted by them. Then a black jowled man turned round on me as if he owned the earth.

"Give us some silver for a pint of porter."

"I have no money left, for I gave it to the woman and it wasn't even mine. If you know what the Corby Hounds are, for pity's sake tell me."

"Get to hell out of here then. There's no such thing as Corby Hounds, never was."

There were men at the street corners and in desperation, I stopped to talk to them, men who had driven the cattle in from the farm in the dark of early dawning.

"Did you see a tinker woman in a shawl with a black and tan dog? I'm trying to find her."

"Did she rob you then, for if she did, it's the police you should be after. The guards don't like them tinkers with the trouble they cause on a Fair Day."

"I gave her money. She didn't rob me. I bought a dog from her, but I daresay, it followed her when she ran away."

"Well then, you're wrong there, miss, for the same dog is crouching at your heels."

I turned and saw him there, just as they had said, his tail stirring up the dirt of the road in an apology for a wag.

I sank down on my knees beside him and cradled him in my arms and got the feeling of the brightness of life in him, the vitality, with the hope he had, that the mean times were at an end.

"The mean times are over," I whispered in his ear and scratched him at the base of his tail and a flea jumped out and lit on my wrist.

"He knows when he's well off," laughed one of the drovers.

122

"I wish a pretty young lady would buy me from the wife, for she's dared me to go into the Fighting Cocks today and my throat cut for a drink."

I cared nothing for the flea, only just a little that I had just done what Jonah had done, to Matt and Ruth. I had landed an orphan of the storms at their door or would do so presently.

"That fella has more brains in his head than to follow a tinker streal, when a lady like yourself takes a fancy to him. They likely stole him from some big house and took him tied under a caravan, bate him, and starved him to put pity into the hearts of honest people. Don't worry yourself about him, Miss. He knows when he's well off. Look the way he's took to you."

They were kind men now. Later on, they would be the worse for drink and might split each other's skulls with the ash plants they used on the cattle. Now they were tired with the earliness of their rising and soon, they would find the porter that made a Fair Day fairer still. I looked round the ring that had gathered about myself and the dog.

"The tinker woman spoke about the Corby Hounds. Do you know what they are or where they're to be found?"

They shook their heads and their eyes were empty of any knowledge that might help me.

"That chap's a black and tan . . . and he'll stick to you through hell fire. If he takes to you and he's taken to you, he's your man and you're his. He'd ate anybody that would try to harm you. I've seen a dog like that go for a big dog, with no fear in his chest to stop him and it was the little fella won in the finish and the skin in tatters off him for his trouble . . . and you'll be the chemist's young lady, Miss. You'd better take your man here home and ask Matt Rohan for a tin of flea powder, for there was a great animal lept on your arm a while back and if I'm any judge, it was what we call a 'flay' hereabouts. You're beyond from England and maybe they don't have 'flays' there, but over here we still have the human frailties."

They were very amused with the whole situation. They even found me what they called "a young rope" and by that, they meant a piece of stout string. They fashioned a loop for his neck and fixed it so that it wouldn't choke him.

"I don't know his name," I said as I thanked them. They even christened him for me.

"Sure, what can you call him but 'Tinker'?" they asked me and so "Tinker" he became and "Tinker" he remained. Meanwhile, I had to present myself at the Medical Hall on a super-busy day, with a dog on a rope . . . a dog that maybe had never lived in a house before, a dog, who, for all I knew would take to his heels and vanish up the street after the tinkers, as soon as they quit the town.

"I'm sorry, Uncle Mat, I bought a dog with the change I had from the messages."

"For God's sake, Ruth, would you come down here and look at what herself has brought home?"

It was a busy day and we were all worked off our feet, but Tinker did not get in the way. He stayed beside me and behaved very well, considering the fact that I fitted in space to give him a bath and a dusting of powder. He took it all in good part, as he did the last half of Uncle Matt's Irish-stew-soup, for he helped out with that, when Uncle Matt had had enough. He went round the house and examined every inch of it and Aunt Ruth said that maybe he was looking for snakes. Then he came and curled himself up in a ball at my side, wherever I happened to be. I would look up and see him there, but his eyes watched me, even though for the look of him, he might have been asleep.

Maybe he was something they called a Corby Hound. Always he Trafalgar-Lion-crouched in that aristocratic way, with the right paw held over the left. In the sun light, always he lifted his noble head to let the light strike full on his chest . . . and little did I know that day what I had bought in Ballyboy from a tinker woman for the sum of half a crown, old money, for I had bought me a faithful heart.

As for Matt and Ruth Rohan, they took him in as they took in all homeless unhappy things, be they lost kittens or nestling thrushes or tadpoles or orphan girls or tinker dogs. It seemed that the old house opened the concertina wrought iron gate and then the shop door and let the stranger pass through and once inside the bastion, there was peace and love and tranquillity.

"That dog's no more a tinker's cur than Honey is a tinker's child," I heard Aunt Ruth say to Uncle Matt one day, when they had no idea that I was in earshot. "He's got the manners of a prince of the blood and somewhere, somehow, he's been trained how to behave himself . . . and so has she and not in that tread-mill of an Orphanage, though adversity may have tempered her steel through the fire."

It was true that Tinker was well-mannered. If he wanted to go out, he went to the door and looked back at me and whined a little. He never expected to be fed from our plates at mealtimes, just waited with dignity, till we had finished and then accepted his scraps with the gratitude of pink tongue on wrist. He liked a bone, better than anything, but first he brought it to me and laid at my feet and looked up into my face, as if he offered it to me. He went like an expert on the leash. There was nothing of the pull of a hard-mouthed horse about him. If you said "Sit," he sat and if you said "Down" he crouched and if you said "Stay," he waited till it was your pleasure to release him. If you said "Walks," he fetched his lead and put it by your side. He was appreciative and polite to other members of the household, but he was my man, never happy unless he was with me. He sat with complete patience while I helped in the shop or with the household chores. With all the understanding of a gentleman, he knew that it was fitting that Aunt Ruth and I should toil away the hours with scissors and sewing machine, for I had to be equipped with clothes. Aunt Ruth declared that I could not spend the rest of my days in a nurse's cloak, a workhouse dress and a Jesus boater. She set her wits to the task of clothing me. God knows her purse must have been almost as empty as mine had been, when the gypsy men asked me for money for a pint of porter!

Our book of patterns was given away free with some paper or another. We just had to send a stamped addressed envelope and we had patterns of every object a young lady of fashion might need. There was good hand-made Irish Tweed in suits long laid by since the days when Aunt Ruth went walking the hills with a dog at her heels. Together we worked, unpicking seams and fitting cloth to pattern. The old Singer sewing machine was capable of running for another hundred years and I could use it. I had learnt the household arts and hand-sewing and machine-sewing were child's play to me. Yet I had never realised what enjoyment one could have, with setting out cloth, and cutting and tacking and trying on.

"The house is full of cardigans and jumpers and them not worn at all."

So we searched cupboards and drawers and unravelled and cast on stitches and Aunt Ruth was still able to knit and proud of the fact. I tried to thank her for all she did for me, but she shook her head and asked me what repayment she could ever hope to give me, for the way I had switched on the light for her again and we left it at that.

I have no excuse that I did not seek out Ned Oakapple, as Dr. Cane had advised. I even quite forgot the silver with the hound dog crest. It lay in the bottom of my dressing table and there were times, when my mind was misty again. I wonder if a normal girl with her full intelligence would not have gone

126

fast about solving the mystery that surrounded her, but as it was, I went from day to day and slid into the habit of putting things on the long finger. No more, I wore the orphanage dress. I had two good skirts of tweed, that would wear for ever and I had three sweaters, warm against the winter, with high necks to them and long sleeves that turned up over at the wrists. I had warm wool mitts and a winter coat with a fur collar to it, such a garment, that I had never hoped to possess.

Then, with the thought of Christmas approaching, there was the plum pudding to make and the mince for the pies. The pantry shelves were beginning to look ready for the winter. Mary Brady and I were great friends by now and we had gone out one day and stripped the hedges of blackberries, had boiled them and strained them through the flannel sleeve and now they were pots of bramble jelly, dated on the labels and ranged with pride.

Mary was the domestic help, who had had the bad tooth the day I arrived and she reminded me of Betsey in the Orphanage, for she lived in a miserable hovel with a mother and many sisters and brothers. Her family gave her no joy. When I told her about the Orphanage one day, she amazed me by the sentiment that maybe Betsey and myself hadn't missed much.

"God forgive me for saying it! Ma has no thought but to grab the bit of money I earn out of my hand and hide it from my old fellow, for he drinks every ha'penny he can get. I'd change places with your Orphanage pals, but it's a sin for me even to think that. Haven't I a grand house to work in and since you come here, I'm that content. I wouldn't call the King my uncle."

So Mary Brady and I gathered tomatoes from the tumbled down greenhouse in the garden and tried our hands at setting seeds and made chutney and pickles and jellies and jams, and soda bread, white and brown, and I knew a great new contentment.

Then the Christmas vacation started in Cambridge University and Jonah was on his way home, and every time I thought of it, my heart beat faster.

There was so much to be done. There was the airing of his bed and his blankets and a fire to be set in the grate in his room and a tin of biscuits by the bed. The Christmas cake was ready for icing and the mince ready for the pies. We knew the time his train would leave London and that he had not to change and what time he arrived in Liverpool. Any one of us could pass an examination on the times of every stop on his journey home. Only at the last moment, I knew I was to meet him at Ballyboy station. The shop was very busy, for there was an epidemic of flu in the town and Dr. Cane had come in. He wanted some aspirin tablets and I told him that Aunt Ruth was far from well.

"I came to tell you the same thing about the old chap, who's supposed to mind the shop today, when you go to meet Jonah. I've just packed him off to bed and I'm going upstairs now to Miss Rohan. That lady would not send for a doctor till she was in her grave. I've no doubt I'll pack her off to bed too, for the whole town is down with this damned thing."

I helped Aunt Ruth to bed and gave her two aspirins and a hot drink of milk . . . put a hot water bottle against her feet, while she grumbled at me that Dr. Cane didn't know what he was talking about. If a man was to fall down and break a leg and the bone was to be sticking out in two halves, he'd not get the right diagnosis.

She scowled at me and knew well that she was speaking from disappointment and exasperation and that she trusted Dr. Cane in much the same manner as she trusted God.

"And Matt will not be able to meet the train either. You'll have to go, Honey. He'll be past Ballybrophy now and not

128

an hour left. Thank the Lord, Mary Brady is below and the fowl in the oven. You'll have to go and meet the train yourself and tell him what's happened and that our hearts are broken with the thought of not catching the first sight of him."

She looked at me and sighed. Then she lost patience with her body which had let her down at such an important time.

"I suppose you'd tell on me, if I were to put a foot out of the bed?"

I said nothing, just nodded my head and she told me to take myself off. Then she called me back again and bade me make sure I wore something warm.

"Put on the coat with the fur collar and wear the orange sweater with it . . . and put your hair up on top of your head, like you did the other night. If you don't, it will look a holy show with the height of the fur collar."

I was a very different girl from the one Jonah had last seen on Ballyboy station. I had just glimpsed myself in the mirror at the entrance that advertised Pears soap. It said "Use Pears soap and you'll be a beautiful lady one day. . . ." I was still short of sixteen, but only just, but I had lost the childhood look . . . lost the hunger and the unhappiness. The high bright colour of the sweater brought vivacity to my face and highlighted the dark coils of hair on top of my head. For good measure and with vanity, I had wound the gold fillet round the base of the bee-hive of hair and I thought it gave me sophistication, but perhaps I was wrong. At any rate, when the smoke of the train came in sight, my heart started to pound my ribs and my face went white, or I felt it went white, for there was no time now to go back and look in the Pears mirror. Then the little train puffed in with importance and the doors slapped back open and Jonah jumped down to the platform and looked about him. He was excited too, but the excitement drained away from him, like water through a leaky sieve and that's the leakiest thing I can think of.

I could hear the man who drove the bus horse talking to him, but Jonah had already looked at me and away again.

"The whole town is down with flu and your poor uncle is run off his feet with the medicines he has to make up. I daresay herself is bad with it too, but it looks like as if they sent your young lady to meet you."

I walked over to where he stood, putting one foot carefully down in front of the other. There was no way I could get my tongue to utter words and no thought of what I could say if I could talk. I just stood there and looked up at him and he looked down at me and he was taller than I remembered him. Then he had me by the shoulders and was looking at me, running his hands down to my knitted mitts, holding my arms out from my body, looking at me, just looking at me.

"It can't be. It just cannot be . . . but it is."

Of course, Tinker had come with me to meet him. He had followed me along the platform and now sat at my heel, as any well drilled guardsman, yet he could not control his curiosity. His paw came up gently on to my shoe and I took myself out of Jonah's grasp and there was an awkwardness between Jonah Rohan and myself, that Tinker bridged for us with his great sagacity.

"And if you're Honey, then this is the famous 'Tinker'."

Tinker was such a wise dog that he probably knew that my shoulders tingled, my arms tingled. I might have got a severe electric shock at the touch of my knight in white armour.

"Let me introduce you," I said formally. "Tinker, this is Mr. Jonah Rohan, soon to be Dr. Jonah Rohan . . . and Jonah, this is Tinker, a dog, of great talent. He will shake hands with you and he'll fetch your slippers for you."

I did not say that I would be very happy to fetch them for him myself, given the chance.

Tinker had extended a paw and was shaking hands with

gravity and I noticed that he gave Jonah the lick on the wrist that meant gratitude and for a second, I wondered why he should think he owed gratitude to Jonah. It was impossible that he was aware of the fact that Jonah had been responsible for bringing me to Ballyboy from my bondage and that I, in my turn, had freed him from his slavery.

"We'll walk home, Tinker . . . not take the bus," Jonah told him as if he was talking to another person, but Tinker trotted off and stood at the step of the bus.

"You see, Jonah, he knows it all. He knows that they're waiting for you in the Square and Aunt Ruth is ill with flu' and Uncle Matt worked off his feet and they're both waiting to see you."

So we travelled down the hill by the horse-drawn bus and Tinker very sedate on my lap, looking out through the window at everything that went on.

I told him about Aunt Ruth and said she would be better in a day or two and we would both help Uncle Matt in the shop and that there was really very little to worry about.

"It will do them good to have you home, do us all good."

"But the Corby Hounds? What have you managed to find out about them? You told me in your letter that you meant to try. You were to see Ned Oakapple and show him that gold band that you have in your hair this minute. What did he say about it?"

I stroked the satin of Tinker's coat and scratched behind his ears, but still he kept his unblinking gaze on the streets, that were framing past the bus windows. I sensed that he might be as disapproving as Jonah of "laissez faire."

"I didn't get the time to go to Ned Oakapple's yet, Jonah. I know I ought to have gone the day after Dr. Cane said, but you have no idea of how much there was to see to. There were the blackberries to pick, for they'd have dropped in another day or two and we had to get them in, and the nuts were just right for picking and somehow I put it off and put it off."

"And that's Ireland all over with its 'time was made for slaves.' The bus will drop us off now at the Medical Hall and then there will be all my things to be unpacked and I'm quite capable of unpacking them for myself. There are no socks to be darned and the laundry's been done. There's a girl in the flat above does all our laundry for us."

How could he know he drove a dagger through the space between my ribs and found my heart and that the blood ran redly?

"We'll eat our feast of roast fowl and and raspberry trifle to follow and then Uncle Matt will be worked to exhaustion in the shop downstairs and I will sit and talk to Aunt Ruth, but I'll not tell her anything about the four girls in the flat above ours. She'd have a fit if she knew what they do for a living, but at least they can iron shirts and that's all the capacity I'm interested in."

There was silence between us and Tinker turned his head to lick my cheek, for he knew I needed it badly, the comfort he gave me.

"They're good hearted girls, that sort always are," he laughed. "And don't for God's sake breathe a word of it in the Medical Hall, or they would all drop down dead with the shock, but that's Lunnon for you."

He laughed at his own humour and I bared my teeth in a smile.

"Tomorrow, yourself and myself and this sagacious animal here are going to make a trip to Ned Oakapple's . . . and we're going to bring along that golden band that you wear in your hair. We're going to take along the silver with the crest and we're going to ask Ned if he knows anything about it."

He laughed again and stretched his arms up to the roof of the bus and went on.

132

"But this is Ballyboy, so if we don't do it tomorrow, we'll do it the day after, or the day after that."

The windows of the bus laughed at his joke, but there was no laughter in my heart. There were so many people he must know, patients, other students, nurses, and all of them free to fall in love with him and what chance did I have that he even knew I existed?

Then his next words sent me like a rocket to heaven.

"It's a funny thing you know. Three months ago, or thereabouts, I rescued a maiden in distress, a child, maybe a little scrubby boy, for all the notice I took of her! and she's grown up. She's become a graceful and beautiful lady, with silence, no not silence now, with wisdom on her lips and serenity in her smile. It makes a fellow think. My God! It makes a fellow think."

He gave me a sidelong look and his eyes were champagne sparkling with laughter.

"But the day after tomorrow or the day after that, we go to see Ned Oakapple and we take along the silver . . . the crested silver and the gold band. I can't bear not to know the answer to a question or the solution of a mystery. If it's the last thing I ever do, I'll find out how you landed up in that Orphanage with all the wrong values fixed on you, you, who might hold the gorgeous East in fee . . . or the West for that matter, if you'd a mind to. God! God! God! It's great to be home again. There's no place like it in the whole universe and it reaches out its hands to me and begs me to make haste and come home and take up the art of healing the sick, in the house next the Medical Hall."

Chapter Six

NED OAKAPPLE

It was not the next day, nor the day after that, for Aunt Ruth was more ill than even she had supposed, when she had suggested that she should put a foot out of bed after I had put her firmly in there. She got congestion on her lungs, which made her cheeks purple and we were all so frightened that we dare not even discuss her future with one another. Then just before Christmas, Uncle Matt came down with flu as well, refused all talk about bed and crawled round the shop till Christmas Eve, when he was so ill, that he could hardly close shut the door, after Jonah and I had put the concertina wrought iron gate in position.

"Don't look so worried about me, children," he said hoarsely to us. "There's a holiday tomorrow and it's only morning duty on St. Stephen's Day. I'll throw the damn thing off in twenty-four hours."

He sat in his armchair in the sitting room and asked me to make him a hot toddy.

"I forgot to bring up a few aspirins from below. There's nothing like aspirin for the flu and never will be, and thank God, Ruth is better. She's got the pudding on to boil tonight and she has been fussing me about it all day and I don't feel as if I could eat anything, even to please herself."

Aunt Ruth was still in bed and there was no doubt that his mind was wandering. Jonah took him off upstairs and sent me next door to fetch Dr. Cane.

Dr. Cane painted a grave picture of him. He knew that Uncle Matt had been coming down with the flu, but there was no talking to him.

"As it was, Matt's determined that the shop must open after Christmas and if we don't open it, he'll be down there behind the counter himself. If he is, he'll be in his coffin in twenty-four hours."

Dr. Cane was well over sixty and he had a shock of white hair and bushy white eyebrows.

"He won't be much better than he is tonight, not for a week, but Miss Rohan can get up tomorrow if she stays quiet. I've promised that the three of us, Jonah and Lesley and myself will run the Pharmacy without his honourable presence and I think it can be done, for there's need for medicine in the town, even if some of us are a bit short of qualifications."

I will never forget that Christmas. The pudding did not get eaten till New Years' Day and I doubt if the cake was ever iced. We had mince pies at Easter and pulled crackers on somebody's birthday.

Aunt Ruth Rohan and Mary Breen managed to run the top floors of the house and keep the food coming down to us. Jonah and I took turns at the counter and at the dispensing and at the unpacking of the crates and the cleaning and polishing and dusting . . . at the packing of aspirin tablets into boxes of twenty or fifty or a hundred, at the making up of the eight ounce bottles from stock mixtures, diluted down by taking one part of the concentrated mixture and adding seven parts of distilled water. Jonah left the wrapping to me and addressed the bottles himself, but he lacked the copperplate hand of his father. Still the customers were well content. Hadn't they got a doctor over from London to see to their ills and I was still the nurse, that had arrived in Ballyboy in my cloak with the red lining.

We never went very far into the question of whether Dr.

Cane's supervision made it all legal, but anyway the Pharmaceutical Society seemed content to turn a blind eye. There were too many patients lying in bed and too few doctors and chemists to see to their needs. Dr. Cane looked in on us between his sick visits and said he hoped that we were not killing off too many of his clients, and if in doubt, give aspirin, but never forget that "aspirin was dangerous on an empty stomach."

"It's the salicylic acid that does the harm. Jonah will explain it to you, Lesley. It must be taken after meals or milk.... 'Ter in die, post cibum,' three times a day after meals. Jonah will tell you the jargon and if you don't know Latin, write it down in English. 'Ex aqua,' in water, 'Ante cibum,' before food. 'Mane,' in the morning. 'Misce bene' . . . mix well. 'Si opus sit,' if necessary. 'Tussi dolente,' if the cough is painful. My 'scripts' will be coming in like the flakes in a snow storm. I'll try to forget the Latin tags and only write plain English and I'll write in block letters, if you prefer that, for nobody but Matt can read my writing. I'll only bowl you easy ones and no bumpers, but if you're in doubt, don't run any risks. I'll come in every now and again. Legally, I think I'm in charge . . . and don't go 'sine cibo', either of you and that means without food. You'll end up in bed with the flu yourselves and if you do and I want some strength in your bodies to work on."

He stopped at the door and held the handle with a hand that was skilled and kind, and he lifted one of the white bushy brows at Jonah.

"I suppose you've done your Materia Medica course or is it Pharmacology, Captain?"

"We start it next term, sir."

"Well you're starting yours now, or maybe you started it when you went to the trouble to help your father with the work here. 'Nil desperandum,' either of you. We'll get by and

136

may God direct our hands and protect the poor patients!"

We opened at eight-thirty every morning and we shut the concertina grill at eight every evening and after that came the out-of-hours callers, who had been taken ill, too late for civilised timing. We took turns to wolf down sandwiches or hunks of cake or a bowl of thick pea soup with squares of fried bread floating on the top and we both discovered job satisfaction.

As Dr. Cane had told us we would, we got by. We earned ourselves quite a reputation in the town. I even got credit for saving a lamb that was on the point of death, for there was a veterinary side to the Medical Hall too. The lamb had gone light and had stopped eating. It was shivering and it had slaver running out of its mouth and Dr. Cane was out of Ballyboy seven miles away in another town and there was no Vet in Ballyboy. In the privacy of the dispensary at the back, Jonah argued that the lamb was "a goner", but I wondered if a lamb might have flu too . . . or an ewe no milk.

I wonder what I looked like that day behind the tall counter, with my orange sweater high about my ears.

"I'd take the lamb into the kitchen and wrap it up warm. Have you got a box it could lie in, well padded with straw, or maybe (remembering Cranford) flannel? Is there a chimney corner. where it could lie near the fire, but not too near? I'll give you a lamb's teat and you'd have a big bottle by you? I've dispensed some tablets."

Only I knew that they were pink aspirins, which many people found far better than the white ones, because the mind has dominion over the body.

"Give her as much cow's milk as she'll take and crush one, no maybe two of the tablets into three of her feeds . . . and be sure you never give her these tablets on an empty stomach."

Behind the screen of the dispensing hatch, I closed my eyes and prayed that the lamb might live. When I came out, I found

137

the farmer still there and I worried because I knew he could ill afford to lose a fine lamb.

"What do I owe you, Miss?"

"You owe me nothing at all unless the patient gets well and believe me now she *will* get well."

Perhaps she would have got well in any case. I prefer to think that God's ear was down-turned to me that day, for my luck went on from good to better to best . . . and they all got better and the shop started its normal sane way of commerce and then it was time for Jonah to return to London. The day before he left us, he turned to me and said we must visit Ned Oakapple.

"I told you that things move slowly, but I couldn't have foreseen the battle against disease and death. My God! It's taught me something."

We walked over to Ned Oakapple's shop together and very companionably, arguing whether the lamb had recovered because of the pink aspirin or whether the ewe had not had enough milk. Neither of us could be said to have any accurate information and we decided that the lamb had lived, because it had had fantastic luck and so had we. Jonah added for good measure that he did not know what the Hospital Board would say if it knew how he had spent his holidays. Then we came to a shop in a side street at a corner, a dim, dusky old shop, that might have been etched in a work by Dickens. The paint on the window sills had not been renewed for many years and the front door was at the side and there was no reading the letters on the sign to say who owned the place or what profession or trade he followed. You just opened the door, which was a double door of a great height, which creaked like the hinges of limbo. Inside was a plain board floor and at your left side ran a high partition, which might or might not have a counter behind it. Jonah led the way along and suddenly the whole vista of the shop opened out into a huge spacious room, packed with furniture from floor to ceiling in front of us. There was no first floor, the shop reached to the roof and behind the partition was a counter and the counter was cluttered up with objects of every sort. There was a musical alarm clock all taken to pieces and a glue pot boiling on a spirit lamp and a picture waiting its frame—a half-hunter watch with the face open, a small miniature of a girl with curly hair, a box of dominoes and a silver cigarette case, with the hinge wrenched, an ornate ink well, a gold chain for a watch, with links as thick as they could possibly be. It was all higgledy-piggledy.

The walls were twenty-five to thirty feet tall and they were covered in paintings. Some were hung so high and were so cob-webbed, that the subject could not be made out, but there were portraits of ladies and gentlemen from ages long gone, whose descendants had lost them in the dust of the years. There were cases of medals, hundreds of war medals in maybe a dozen cases, all pinned in ranks, side by side. The furniture was a solid phalanx at the far end of the great room but it was stacked with care, for all that it looked thrown down by a giant's hand. I saw tables with claw feet and wardrobes and desks and chests of drawers and tall-boys and whatnots . . . and on the floor there was china stacked, some of it very fine look-ing, hand-painted, worth a fortune, to my way of thinking.

There was nobody at all about. If Jonah and I had pleased, we might have drawn up a pantechnicon in the street outside and stolen a fortune in antiques, but Jonah knew the place of old and called out, for the bell, that was supposed to ring when a customer entered through the rasping, squeaking door was out of order.

"Ned's a fool. If he took the time to get this stuff sorted and catalogued, he'd make a mint, but he's like them all. 'Put it off till tomorrow and it may go away'."

I did not remind him that sometimes circumstances can

force a person to the doctrine of "Manãna", as it had just done to both of us. Yet here I was at last, with the gold band on my hair and the silver knife and fork and spoon still wrapped in its tissue paper in my hand and with Tinker, following at my heels, on his best behaviour, in case he might be told to go outside the shop and wait for us. He lay with his nose on my foot and there was an anxiety about him.

"Ned makes what money he uses for living out of the dead," Jonah told me in a whisper. "He's the one undertaker in the town and he's making a coffin in the room inside now."

I heard the tap-tap of the hammer that Dickens describes so well and smelt the planed wood. The glue was obviously wanted soon, for it was hot and the water bubbling under it.

We went across the room and through another door and Ned Oakapple was at work with a plane in his hand and a coffin on trestles.

He put everything aside, when he saw us and his eyes took in every last item of me, in my tweed skirt and the white sweater and the long wool scarf, the black beret, that Jonah had given me for Christmas and which I knew had been made in France.

"Good morning, Jonah. It's taken you a long time to bring your lady to see me, but her fame has gone before her."

He was a round faced man and yet there was a Christ-look about him. He had black hair going grey and a black beard that made a circle of his face and gave him the round look. There was humour and kindness and a great understanding in him and his back was bent a little from stooping over his tasks.

"I'm Lesley Summer," I said, and he smiled at that and said that he had heard my name was "Honey".

"Everybody in this place knows everybody else's business, but it's no harm. It's because no man is an island, as John Donne had it, and each one cares for the next, and I bid you

140

welcome."

He laughed and put up his arms, stretched his hands towards the ceiling, that was so high and so festooned with dusty cobwebs that it was a land of mystery and imagination, that might have interested Edgar Allan Poe.

"Come out into the outer shop and show me the silver and that band you have on. You see, I know it all before you tell me and also that you're a grand nurse, for the way you snatched Mr. and Miss Rohan out of my clutches, the way you even have a way of lifting lambs out of the jaws of death."

Tinker had advanced himself to the fore and stood on his back legs and begged, a thing I had never seen him do and Ned searched in his pocket and found nothing, went over to a cabinet and came on a biscuit tin . . . put Tinker through "on trust" and "paid for" and Tinker tossed the tit-bit into the air, caught it, crunched it, running his tongue round his upper lip and then squatting below my feet, when Ned had sat me on a high stool in the outer room.

I laid the wrapped silver on the counter again, he looked at me, did Ned Oakapple and knew all about me, or I thought he did, down to the last mist-veiling of my soul.

"There's no need to tell me where you came by these things. Matt's my best friend, so I have it from the horse's mouth."

We talked for a long time about this and that, mostly about the great deal of sickness there had been and how glad he was that it was past and done with.

"It kept me busy too and I don't like that side of my work, for 'tis laying friends under the ground. As you get older, it gets harder on a man to lose friends."

His hands were unwrapping the silver knife and spoon and fork.

"King's Pattern," he said at once, not to us but to himself and he was not in the shop any more, but in some secret part of his brain, where his experience was stored. "It's silver, solid

141

silver and it's Stuart . . . very good that. It's not full-sized, maybe made for a child . . . a loved child, to fit her small hands. They'd have been a set of these. There's a crest here, of a hound couchant, a man like Tinker there, but this chap knows his breeding. I've seen him before, but I can't think where. There's a coat of arms with couchant hounds and the paws crossed like that and the head held up with the pride in his people."

Tinker was sitting at my feet in just the position he'd described and Ned Oakapple looked down at him and surprise highlighted his whole face.

"Would you look at that now? He might be a sitting model for that engraving, but the tinker woman had him at her heels . . . probably stole him. Now he's fallen on better days. There's breeding in him. The 'Some-thing Hounds' they're called and I should remember. There's a hound called a Talbot, but it's not that. By the Saints, I have it . . . don't know how I came to forget it. This is the crest of the Corby Hounds. It belongs to a family in a big house west near the sea . . . down beyond the Valley of the Shannon. There's two brick gateposts, with bricks as old as the hills, not stone pillars as anybody else would have, but brick of every colour under the sun, mellowed down the years. There's a carved stone hound, on each post. They're supposed to guard the way to the avenue, but they haven't kept tragedy out."

He held his hand out to me and asked to see the band and I took it off the bee-hive of put-up hair, which I still wore, because Jonah said it made me "grown-up".

"Gold band, solid gold. Miss Ruth had that right. It's hall-marked twenty-two carat . . . too soft for hard wear, twenty-two carat, but it's a rich man's present, or a rich woman's adornment and if it wore out, there was coin in plenty to buy another."

He turned it this way and that in his hands and noted the

pattern on it, running a nutmeg finger over the surface.

"It's not all here. I've seen a picture of this same ornamental piece of jewellery in a magazine one time, years ago. There was more to it than that."

He took out a jeweller's eyeglass and screwed it into his eye and he went from one end of the band to the other.

"There was a way this comes into two halves and there's two parts to it here and a third part, that's been lost to you. Was this all there was to it?"

He went to the wall and stared hard at a miniature of a small boy in a blue coat, that played with a pug dog, throwing a ball for him.

"It was like that when I went to the Orphanage, but there were two rosettes in red satin, sewn on, one either side. Aunt Ruth Rohan cut them off and it's far better without them."

He went along the counter to a pile of dusty magazines, picked up the top one and blew the dust off it . . . moved down through them flicking the pages over, seeking for something, not finding it.

" 'Tis looking for a grain of corn in a bag of barley."

There were pictures of furniture and china and jewellery of every sort imaginable on the shiny pages and Ned Oakapple shook his head and mourned that when a man grows old his memory leaks away like a faulty bicycle valve, leaks the air out of a tyre.

"It's best not to wear out your brains with the trying to remember. Just put a thing out of your head and then it comes round a second time. It's like the gallopers at the fair. You go round and the next minute, there's the fact you're after, standing at your side, as if it hadn't come to you but you'd come to it and maybe you had at that."

He picked up the silver knife again and examined it very carefully indeed, especially the blade of it.

"The blade is modern. The handle is Stuart and what do

you make of that? I daresay the original was given to some little Stuart miss, in a set all the same, six I'd think. She'd have it for her dollies' tea parties. Then this century, somebody bought it and took it along to a jeweller's, had new blades put in, for another little miss, but twentieth century now, who would not want to be cleaning the knives on a bath-brick board, every time she had finished her tea-party."

Jonah knew that I was longing to ask about the Corby Hounds, so he did it for me.

"You said that the Corby Hounds, on the crest there, didn't keep ill luck or tragedy out of the house they were guarding."

"Maybe they did, for generations, for they were standing a long time. The family is an old one and it prospered. It's in the last century, that the Hounds haven't managed to hold the devil at bay."

The family name was Corby, like the Hounds. Tinker sighed as if he knew all about it, all about the lovely estate with lands beyond the Vale of the Shannon, and running down to the sea.

"They're monied gentry with coin to throw away for plea-sure, for art, for beauty. Now to give you an idea of what they were, there was an ancestor built a kind of Folly, no use in the world except for the lovely look it had, a mile from the main house, and seen along a vista of oak trees."

Ned Oakapple knew it well, for he had seen it a time or two. Anybody could go through the gates and look at it, but it was ruined now. There had been an ornamental garden to it, that had gone wild.

" 'Tis Regency with all the curves and pillars to it, but 'tis gone to pot and only the jackdaws and the spirits haunt in the rooms now. It's a sin to have let it go the way it is, but you can't blame the present man, for he's had more sorrow on his shoulders than any one man should have to bear."

Ned had gone over to look at the Corby house one half day,

144

but he had not been able to bring himself to get any farther than the Folly, when he saw the neglect all about it.

"It was the Folly I'm talking about—a proper house, built in a curve and there's three stories to it and all ornamented with pillars. They'd have held musical evenings maybe with the ladies in crinolines, maybe gaming parties for the men. The floors are gone in, most of them and oak lying all round the place, oak, that wants kindness and a gentle hand and understanding that it won't get from the jackdaws in the chimneys. If there's anything I like, it's oak. There's a honey colour to it and a flower . . . nothing to touch it, to my way of thinking. It made me unhappy that day to see the way it had been left, and the ceilings down and the floors in and black-berries everywhere, winking their evil little black eyes at you for spite."

He turned his back on us and stared at the glue pot gloomily.

"Maybe we'd take the car and go west there one day, when you're home again, Jonah, and we'll take Tinker along too. Maybe he's descended from the Corby Hounds."

He spun on his heel and looked down at the dog and the fact he had sought down his memory came round on the carousel.

"Give me that head band again. Tell me, does it fit your head the same now as the day you went into the Orphanage? Five years ago or maybe six? A girl would grow a deal in five–six years."

I told him that it used to go down right to the lobes of my ears, but now it was too small really, but still it held my hair in place. He hardly listened to me. He had the band in his hand again and he was looking at the centre of it, probing it care-fully with a needle set in a wood handle, oiling it with a quill feather, moving with as much care as if he were dealing with the crown jewels.

145

"It wasn't in the magazines. I read it in some paper or another. The Master of Corby had it made for his only daughter by some jeweller above in Dublin and there was a third part to it . . . a part that would make it fit a bigger girl. It was a plaque, no, it wasn't a plaque! It was a part that joined together with this band. They say what man has done, man can do, and I don't like it to beat me."

Then there was a snap and the band was in two halves and each half with a catch, so that it could be snapped together again. He cleaned the catches carefully with a respect that seemed impossible in his big hands, which were like lobster-claws.

"This matches up with the Stuart silver, but it's modern. There was a centre piece and how do you think it was fashioned?"

We looked at him in silence and there was triumph in his eyes.

"They fashioned two paws, beautiful work it was and the paws were held one over the other. Look at your man, Tinker there and he might be sitting for the goldsmith. The sides clipped into the central part and it made the band bigger, but it was no Stuart dynasty gold worker that made them. It was done in this century by a real craftsman. It ties in. If you go back far enough, everything ties in, down to Adam and Eve. The Folly, the set of silver with the crest on it, then the gold head band . . . all hall-marked "Master of Corby" as if I was to take a paint brush and mark it on them, but I've no thought of doing any such a thing. I don't know how you came by them, Lesley Summer."

My imagination blew up clouds in my mind, blew up a golden balloon with a solution of all the mystery, but Ned Oakapple popped the balloon almost as soon as it was full.

"They say you were a tinker girl and maybe you were. From the look about you, you might be the Master's daughter,

146

with one of his hounds at her heels, but it's not possible. Don't ever put your hopes on it. Miss Corby . . . beautiful little Miss Corby's dead and gone, with no doubt in the world. Of her bones are corals made. Those are pearls that were her eyes. The hounds didn't keep the devil from stalking down the avenue the day a foreign woman came to call, but a lot had happened before that. The hounds were helpless against death too. They let the enemies in past the front gates and down the avenue, past the Folly and into the big house, like crawling rats."

He told us slowly and dramatically and he got out an old pipe and puffed at it and his face was the mask of tragedy that hangs above a stage in a theatre and I recognised it as such, though I never remember being in a theatre in my life.

The Master of Corby now was "only half a man" for what life had done to him. He had married and had one girl, as pretty as a changeling. The woman he had married was "one of a big family" from Galway . . . a real lady, if ever there was one.

He had set his life on a fair course, but his ship had run aground. First there was the war and then the influenza epidemic, that swept the whole world and the Mistress of Corby was dead. Yet, still there was the small child, and the Master spoilt her more than ever, built a little house down on the sea cove for her to have as a play-house. He had hired women to run the household for him, a housekeeper, parlour-maid, kitchen maids, cook, and governesses, and last of all, following death, past the hounds on the gate posts had come the foreign woman. She was fair and beautiful and she fitted into Corby House as governess to the little girl and she taught her German."

The words flew through my brain and were gone again . . . "Rapunzel, Rapunzel, Lass mire dein Haar hereunter . . ." but my lips were silent. Spieglein, speiglein . . . Mirror, mirror

147

on the wall, who is the fairest of them all? Die Wand, feminine case, a wall. That was "Schneeweisschen" . . . Yet it was all mist and fog and gone in a beam of sunshine.

"Sorrow the day for Corby House when the foreign woman eluded the Corby Hounds for gradually she sneaked herself into the establishment, till she was almost Mistress, but not quite."

"Then the Master took to drink, as many a man has done before him and the foreign woman was always there with a filled glass in her hand. He must have been drunk the night he asked her to wed him, but wed her he did and the little girl's nose was put out of joint. That woman drove her through hell. She had been her governess, but now she owned her, body and soul, and still he liked daughter better than second wife. He saw what he had done. Locally they say she put the evil eye on the house and if that was what she did, wouldn't you think the Corby Hounds would have stopped her?"

The thoughts were running round in my head like trapped rats.

"Would the girl have been my age, Mr. Oakapple?"

He told me that I matched up with the child in every way, but I must wait for the ending.

"It doesn't end with happiness ever after, like a fairy story," he said in a low voice, and I listened to him as he went on and his darker side had taken over now and he was all undertaker and not Ned Oakapple, lover of old wood.

"They weren't happy, the master and the foreign woman. She wasn't a woman content with one man and maybe he was no good to her and his heart in the grave, for I've seen many such."

Jonah frowned at him, as if such conversation was improper in front of me, but he had the bit in his teeth.

"All you have to do is to go to one of the papers . . . even the local paper ran it, look up the back numbers, in the

148

Tribune. They went for a picnic down by the sea, this second wife and her step-daughter. They took a white cloth and dolls and cakes and meat and salad. It was all reported to the last detail. They walked out of that house with a picnic in a hamper packed by the maids and they were never see again, least not alive. They planned to take the picnic by the house the Master had built as a play house. I've never seen it but it was a work of art, just as the Folly had been, that his ancestor built before him. It was furnished and set out like a real house and there was thatch on the roof and turf to burn in the grate. They never knew how they both came to be drowned—supposed that they went in for a swim for the weather was hot . . . got washed out to sea and the little one gone to the green grave."

"They weren't found?" Jonah asked him and Ned Oakapple shook his head.

"The woman's body came ashore the next morning, but not the child's. She'd have been washed out farther towards the headland and then the Atlantic claims them for the green grave. There's an undercurrent there, that whirls them out towards the New World, but there was no doubt she was dead. The coroner brought them both in as accidental drowning. The girl's clothes were found, here and there along the coast, and a teddybear. She'd never have been parted from that teddybear in life. Can you blame the Master of Corby that he gave up all hope of happiness? They say he went strange in the head, wouldn't accept the fact that the child was gone, never has done."

In my mind, I denied it too. I might be that child. It was too good a fit for the piece in my jig-saw. I had the Corby Hound head-band and the setting of Stuart silver. Last of all, I had Tinker, who sat at my dangling feet and was my man.

"Was there no chance the child lived?" I whispered.

"Not a chance in the world, Honey," Ned Oakapple said

149

gently. "She had a new dress that day and it was identified by the women in the house. She had the old teddybear and there was no doubt, she'd not have parted with it. Last of all, there was a dog, that never left her side and his body was washed ashore. He tried to swim out after her. Ah, no, there's no chance at all that Honor Corby is living yet. There's no chance at all."

"Yet I have the silver knife and spoon and fork?" I challenged him and he was gentle with me.

"They had taken such items on the picnic and they're easy to steal. There was plenty of stuff stolen from the cottage by the sea, before the police arrived on the scene. There was poverty about and poverty breeds greed. That coast was searched for miles, north and south, and there was no child's body washed ashore, though the woman came up the next day I told you. If you asked me my considered opinion, I'd say that stuff you have is stolen property. There were tinkers in the neighbourhood and they knew better than to pass a table set out for a picnic . . . and somehow those things came to you, but I'd forget it, if I were you. One of these days, we'll take my car and drive west. I'll show you the Folly and the big house and the cabin by the sea, but you'll be disappointed in the Folly and the Cabin, for they're all rotten and fallen to bits, all because of what a woman can do to a man, two women perhaps, one to enslave him and another to fail to set him free."

There was a creaking of the outside door at that moment and a tall lanky woman came in by the high partition.

"I thought I'd find you talking, Ned Oakapple, with your dinner spoiling in the oven."

We were introduced to each other, Mrs. Oakapple and myself and I forgot all my dreams of being Miss Honor Corby of Corby House, for Ned Oakapple's wife had something important to give me, maybe better than any fortune.

She was full of interest, for my fame, as I knew already, had gone before me. She asked me how I had managed all the years to make them think in the Orphanage that I was daft when I was nothing of the sort.

"Why! You helped run the pharmacy as well as Mr. Matt, when they were all in bed with the flu and you saved O'Brien's lamb for him, you that were supposed not to read or write or talk more than a weeshy bit."

There and then she put me to the test and she was all school ma'am, for that was what she had been when she married Ned. She gave me a quick run through history and geography and then she tried out my arithmetic and I smiled at her.

"Two and two is four, unless you put it out side by side and then it's twenty-two. That was what the young Doctor in the Orphan house said at the board meeting."

She glared at me to see if I was joking with her, but I smiled and seeing that I approved of her, Tinker wagged his tail.

"Maybe I didn't speak, Mrs. Oakapple, but I listened. I heard all the lessons."

"All right then, what in your opinion is the finest English ever written."

Jonah and Ned were quite frightened by her. Ned had blown out the lamp under the glue pot, for he obviously despaired of any more work on the coffin and Jonah had deserted me and was studying the medals in the case.

"And that's the Victoria Cross, Ned! Why has it to be made of metal? Why not diamonds and emeralds, for often it's the price of a man's life, and then he comes to have to sell it, or his widow does, or his son, to make ends meet. . . ."

The finest English ever written, I thought, and there was silence for a long time. I knew so much poetry and prose and had no idea how to answer her. Then I looked down at Tinker

151

and his tail moved against the bare boards as if he said, "You can tell them, Missus." I closed my eyes and thought and then opened them and thought of the unmade coffins and the souls who hoped to get through purgatory to heaven. My voice was as husky as Betsey's as I answered her.

"The Lord is my shepherd; I shall not want.

He maketh me to lie down in green pastures: he leadeth me beside the still waters.

He restoreth my soul: he leadeth me in the paths of righteousness for His name's sake."

The huskiness was gone now and I was triumphant suddenly, yet fearful still, for I had dreamed of places where these words might have been a light to my feet.

"Yea, though I walk through the valley of the shadow of death, I will fear no evil: for thou art with me; thy rod and thy staff comfort me.

Thou preparest a table before me in the presence of mine enemies; thou anointest my head with oil; my cup runneth over.

There was silence in the big crowded room and they looked at me with amazement and Jonah very serious. Mrs. Oakapple had an umbrella in her hand and she gripped it more tightly by the middle and I went on.

"Surely goodness and mercy shall follow me all the days of my life: and I will dwell in the house of the Lord for ever."

Mrs. Oakapple threw down her umbrella on the counter with small thought for Ned's glue pot or anything else.

"They say you've no schooling, but your Aunt Ruth has asked me to school you and school you I will . . . and I'm wondering to myself if you'll be teaching me or if I'll be

152

teaching you."

She paced up and down by the counter and she was obviously moved that I had chosen the psalm. She was not going to let her emotion get the better of her all the same, for she was another like Aunt Ruth Rohan, who counted it a weakness to show too much softness.

She decided that the best thing to do was to discuss the plan for my education there and then.

"They tell me you're planning to work in the Medical Hall. There's an examination you'll have to sit. There's another one after some years, if you're hankering to put letters after your name."

She stopped up short in her pacing and took another look at me.

"I doubt if you need any letters after your name. That lamb of O'Brien's was dead on its feet and you brought it back to life, and it's that sort of thing that counts, not knowing how to quote the Bible. I like you, lassie. They say everybody likes you and I'll join the crowd, but there's something about you that I can't fathom. One of these days, maybe, I'll fathom it, but not just now. Just now, maybe you'd persuade my husband to come home and have his dinner. In a day or two, maybe we'd best start at the Latin for that's important to a chemist or a druggist."

Ned was smiling now and reaching out for the old felt hat with the stained band.

"And one of these days, when Jonah here comes home from that God-forsaken country over the Irish Sea, we'll take the car and go west and have a look at the Corby Hounds. It can't do us any harm and at least, we'll get a breath of fresh sea air."

Chapter Seven

"BY THE PRICKING OF MY THUMBS
SOMETHING WICKED THIS WAY COMES. . . ."

I know of no form of tuition that could ever be half as enjoy-
able as that of Mrs. Ned Oakapple. She lived in a narrow-
fronted three-storied house with steps up to the front door. It
was on the street that led north from the square up a slight incline and it took me, maybe, five minutes to reach it from the
Medical Hall. On my way, I passed the Spanish arch, through
which the donkey led the herd of cows to and from the field
for the milking. There was friendship between myself and the
donkey now and if the time was right, I carried a sugar lump
in my pocket for him or perhaps an apple or a potato. He was
gracious enough to know me on sight after a while and to
take time off from his important work, to lift the gift from
my proffering palm with a softness of grey velvet nostrils, but
he had no time to spare. He would never stop for conversation, only for a scratch between the ears and he was on his
way again, his feet twinkling in the dust perhaps or sticky in
the muddy street, his glance faintly apologising for his hurry,
but he had business in hand.

I would have worked all day in the Square, but it was not
like the toil I had known in the Female Orphan House. I
dusted a room or made the beds or showed Mary Breen how
to run a fork round the rim of an apple pie for decoration, or
cut out pastry petal leaves for the top of it. Then, in the shop
downstairs, perhaps I helped unpack one of the great crates,

that brought the drugs. There was a store-room in the basement and there all the stock was ranged in rank on shelves . . . tins of "mag. sulph.", jars of Virol, great bottles of infusion of gentian or peppermint water . . . boxes of Dolly dyes, boxes of fly papers . . . crates of bottles of every size in the world, two ounce, three ounce, four ounce and eight ounce. It was two shillings and eight-pence for an eight ounce bottle of medicine. That was half a crown for the contents of the bottle and two pence for the bottle itself, so it paid to bring back the bottle for refilling, but that meant that there was a thorough washing of the bottle in the sink in the dispensary and a scraping off of the old label with a razor blade and that was my work too. Perhaps it had some likeness to the work I had done in the Female Orphan House, but I do not think it had. I was washing a bottle and soon, I might learn how to mix up a fresh one. I already knew how to wrap it in the white paper and seal it and tie it with pink string. Perhaps it was from one of Dr. Cane's prescriptions and there was no doubt it would make the patient feel better. I dreamed as I washed bottles and wrapped and sealed and tied. For all I knew, that medicine might be the difference between life and death to somebody. I was enamoured with the art of healing the sick. There was no denying that I was a cog, even the meanest, lowliest, most unimportant cog in one of the noblest professions of mankind. The smell of the pharmacy was the breath of life to me. I was in love with the exotic names of "Dragon's blood" and "Aqua rosa, Aqua camphorae" and "Belladonna" and "Hyoscyamus" and "Ipecacuanha" and all the rest of the magic of the apothecary, for who could refute the magic of the names . . . lost to us now and like not believing in Father Christmas, we are no better off for the loss? Still, I am straying from my late hours of learning, for when I had helped Uncle Matt put up the concertina iron grill, drawn the blinds and seen that Aunt Ruth Rohan was comfortable upstairs, nodding by the fire, I was off like a homing pigeon to the house up the hill. There was a welcome for me there and Ned in carpet slippers and Mrs. Oakapple very comfortable in good tweed skirt and warm jumper and cardigan, if it were winter, or a summer dress if the weather was warm, but winter was the best time, with the grate a mass of glowing turf and logs and Ned growling from his comfortable armchair. "Ash wet or ash dry, for the Queen to warm her slippers by. . . ." I learned so much about wood from him. There was nothing he did not know and ash was for the burning and there was nothing to touch it, but ash made long bows too . . . and bog oak had lain for hundreds of years under the earth, but it was hard stuff to work on . . . and teak was good for wear. A teak front door would last out generations . . . and it made fine ships . . . but now it was time for lessons. . . .

I had mastered "Paradise Lost", first part of it, at any rate and now there was Oliver Goldsmith and the Deserted Village. There was Latin and it was poetry, but I knew English grammar and here it was all over again. Mensa, mensa, mensam. . . .

Violet Oakapple was not one to give praise, whether it was due or not. She had never learnt "the Irish" and we managed to learn a "smidgeon" of it between us . . . enough for me to sit the exam, when the time came.

I went up to Dublin for it and I got it first shot and came back with the Preliminary examination of the Pharmaceutical Society of Ireland behind me. I had done well. I had little documents to prove that I had been found proficient to get on with my work. One day, I might attempt the Finals, but that was well over the horizon. Uncle Matt took it that I could now help more rigorously with the dispensing and that meant that I was allowed to count out a score of pills into a round box and press on the lid and affix a round label on the top and write the instructions thereon, show it to him for appraisal, wrap it in white paper and seal it with the drop of red wax and set it in the queue ready for collection.

Perhaps they took it as a great joke, Uncle Matt and Dr. Cane, but I do not think they did. Dr. Cane would take pains to teach me all he could. He showed me the tubes that had been used when applying leeches to the skin and made me familiar with the outworn practice of using leeches, when a blood transfusion might have been better.

"The medical profession swings this way and that. One decade, it is all the fashion to do one thing and the next, it's all gone the other way. Use the old tried ways, Honey. You can't go wrong. They've started sending out blotting papers, the drug firms, with advertisements for new drugs. If you fly to accept a new thing, you're too hasty. You're a blotting-paper-doctor. Wait a bit and see how the others get on with it. Aspirin has proved itself and Mag. Sulph. paste. . . . Hasten slowly, lassie, Festine lente. It's hare and tortoise all over again."

I was so busy that I had not time to think of my jig-saw puzzle. Maybe in the night, I might find myself in the Gingerbread House and the sweat standing on my face. I might awake and think of the Folly out beyond the Vale of the Shannon, but I never found time to visit it. A great part of my life revolved about Jonah, for all the part that revolved about the acquisition of learning. Between lessons, the Oak-apples and I might talk about going out to see Corby House, but somehow or another, we were always too busy.

Jonah broke my heart with his letters. They came every Tuesday, posted on Sunday night, and he was having high times in the Hospital. He had changed from the unsophisticated young man I had thought him to be. He "walked the wards". He treated the sick. He went into the mortuary without any terror in his heart. He attended dreadful things called

157

"post-mortems". He was proud of his toughness.

"There was a plastic surgery session and one of the chaps passed out."

Here followed awful details, meant to impress us, but I recognised whistling in the dark. Jonah was passing through the fire to temper his steel.

Yet there was worse than that. Did I not know about the ladies that lived over the flat he occupied with three students? I was relieved when he moved into the hospital proper and then a new torment took over. There were hospital kitchens and pretty nurses. At night, if you were on duty there were flirtations and plates of bacon and eggs, stolen kisses for all I knew . . . and "the Sister of St. Mark's was a smasher." This ruined my happiness for a month, till he told me she was long in the tooth and going on thirty years of age, but she knew when the lads wanted a good hot plate of soup with buttered toast thrown in.

There was a Russian princess, who served behind the counter in Woolworth's. He had taken her out to dinner in one of the Lyon's Corner Houses, and the eye of every man present had been upon her. . . . Her hair was silk blonde and it swung as she moved her head.

Aunt Ruth Rohan's lips were a thin line and I wondered how he could be such a fool to write such stuff to her and his father, but Uncle Matt laughed at it and pulled my ear.

"It's but a phase in the stages of the life of homo sapiens, my dear. Jonah's no fool. Don't think it."

I thought of it all the days that followed, and only the lessons at Violet Oakapple's dispelled my jealousy, and jealousy, as I knew well by this, was as bitter as aloes—as the grave.

From Violet Oakapple, in between sessions of chemistry and physics and a dozen other learnings, I picked up pieces for my jig-saw.

"Your Master of Corby, who interests you so much, is a poor creature. He found his love and lost her again. The epidemic after the war took away as many as the war took. He married to try and find his happiness again, to find somebody to take home his jokes to. Do you know, it's very important to marry a person to whom you can talk the same language, and I don't mean English or German or Hindustani, just the common change of little funny things to laugh at? She was a German, the second wife, or Swiss-German or Austrian German, a woman with fair hair, and she was beautiful. I'll give her that, but it wasn't a warm beauty. She was fair and her features were chipped out of ice. There was no laughter in her, only a stiffness and a pride and an "I'm Mistress of Corby now and you'll kneel down to me". She couldn't keep any help in the house, for she spoke to them like dogs. Anybody that stayed on, stayed for *his* sake."

One night she took out an old paper.

"You're always talking about Corby House, though dear knows why you've never made Ned and Jonah take you there! There's an old newspaper I found lining a drawer last week. It has the report of the whole thing."

Maybe I showed how much I cared, or maybe I hid it. I picked up the paper and saw the heading on the front page. . . .

TRAGEDY ON WEST COAST. FATAL ACCIDENT.

Perhaps my face was wax. I know that the blood drained away from it and I felt sick and faint, but I managed to lift the paper and read the first line that came to my eyes.

"In the early hours of the morning, the body of a lady was washed ashore. . . ."

It was horrible . . . horrible . . . and I was having a nightmare yet I was awake.

I picked up the chemistry book and opened it at random.

"I'll take the paper home and read it later on. Just for

159

now, I want you to help me with this next part. I can't understand it."

"I probably won't understand it either, Honey. Don't you know we're feeling our way through strange country with your Uncle Matt rather an indifferent guide? Anyhow, let's see what's bothering you."

We had got electric power in the Medical Hall recently, but Uncle Matt insisted on turning off the main switch at night, for "he didn't trust it." We still had lamps and candles in the bedrooms. That night, I locked my door, did not know why, for my door was never locked. I undressed and got into bed and then opened Mrs. Oakapple's paper and it was brown and creased with the years that had passed, while it did service at the bottom of a drawer.

It was all there, just as they had told me. I learned very little more. The second wife of the Master of Corby had gone down to a small cottage in a cove, on the estate. She had taken her step daughter with her, for a birthday picnic. Honor Corby was seven years old and there had been a cake with candles. The cake was found in the cottage, all the candles burned down and no slice even cut. The body of the Mistress had been washed ashore and also the body of the child's pet dog . . . one of the famous Corby Hounds. It was thought that he had followed the child into the sea in an attempt to rescue her. It was a hot day and they must have gone for a bathe. Objects had been washed ashore all along the coast, the new birthday dress and underthings, a shoe . . . that would have fitted the child's foot. It had been identified. All of it had been identified. The tide must have come in and washed away the shed garments.

Death by misadventure . . . death by misadventure . . . death by misadventure. . . .

I must put the paper away and open the lock. I never slept behind locked doors. It showed mistrust. Then I dreamt

160

it again, the old dream of the Gingerbread House.

Here was the cottage again with its whitewashed walls and thatched roof and the flower bed in front. Inside the house a table had been set out for tea and today there was a cake with candles. The teddybear sat in a high chair and there was a worn look about the fur on top of his head from much kissing. Bruno, his name was. It came floating down to me as if it came on the spume from the running tide. Bruno, I was quite sure of it. One of his arms was loose and soon I must see to stitching it on, or it might be lost. He had already lost his bear's eyes. They had been tawney coloured with black centres, but the Witch had sewn in black boot buttons.

"It is your own fault. You should not have been so careless to lose them and he does not feel pain when I stitch him. It is time you were not a baby any more."

I knew he felt pain at each stab of her needle. I knew that he understood I hated her and that he hated her too.

Then we were up on the cliff and I was still arguing with her.

"Bruno doesn't like honey. Besides you said he had no feelings and was only stuffed with sawdust, so how could he like honey? He doesn't want to go down the well either."

She took him from under my arm and threw him down the hole and I knelt on the edge weeping and Patch was barking at her. He came up and stood at my side to guard me. His nose was wet against my cheek. His tongue licked me and then he was gone. She had enticed him into the well and he had spiralled away into the dark and his bark was cut off short with a splash that might have come from the centre of the earth.

"You've killed them. You've killed them both. The sea comes in there and the tide's full today."

She came at me in a run and I knelt there, cold and wet and almost naked. . . .

161

Then I was awake, terrified and awake and the mist was closing down on my mind again. Had it been a dream this time or had I remembered some awful thing that had happened to me long ago? I shivered with the cold. Yet my pillow was wet with sweat.

I wrapped my nightdress warm round my feet and was surprised that I was not clad in short white pants, all wet with sea water. Yet where had such a thought come from? I lay awake for a long time and decided that the time had come when I must pay a visit to Corby House. I was seventeen years of age now and my hair was permanently up on the top of my head, or flowing down my back in a pony-tail. There had been too much talk of Corby House and the newspaper article had made it all so real. Jonah would be home soon and I would ask Ned Oakapple to take us all on an expedition to see the Folly, even if we went no farther than that. Tinker usually slept on the patchwork quilt, but he had crept between the sheets and was close against my chest, as if he knew I wanted comfort.

"We'll have a picnic to Corby House, Tinker. No, we won't have a picnic, I wouldn't like a picnic there. We'll find the sea and you'll run along the sand and maybe we'll have a picnic. I don't know why I thought I wouldn't like it."

It must have been the end of September or the start of October, when we went to visit the Corby Estate, Ned Oakapple, Jonah, Tinker and I. We went on a Thursday, which was the half-day in Ballyboy and we travelled in the limousine that Ned used for funeral corteges. You might say we rode in style, even if our transport was antique. The car was a black Rolls Royce, polished back to mint condition, as if it had just driven out of the showroom, as it might have done a great many years before. I was impressed by the plaited straps at the side of each passenger's seat, to hold for greater comfort. The roof was so roomy that a lady might have walked in by one

162

back door and out through the other without disturbing a hat crowned with ospreys. The engine was silent. I could not understand how one judged when it was necessary to press the starter. It glided along the road as if wafted by a silver cloud and there was a magnificence about it. People had a tendency to stop and the men removed their caps, in reverence for something, maybe because we might be part of a funeral or maybe because we were the remnants of an ancient aristocracy.

We sat three abreast in the front and Tinker had the back seat all to himself, where he curled into a ball and went asleep. Ned and Jonah discussed the details of the vintage Rolls and I could not understand one quarter of what they were talking about. I cut them out of my mind, for they went on to speak about the Bentley with the straps on the bonnet. I thought again about Corby House with the dogs to guard the entrance, the hounds with one paw crossed over the other, that had failed to keep evil from walking through the gates and down the avenue. I was not Honor Corby. That was quite certain, yet I was connected in some way with the tragedy. Had I dreamt it the other night about the abyss in the cliff that fell straight into the running tide? Could it be that I was beginning to remember things that had happened so long ago? Surely now today, when I saw the hounds at the gate and saw the building they called the Folly, surely when I saw the big house and the cabin by the sea, I must feel something in the depths of my mind? There were so many things that were unanswerable. How had I come by the gold head band? How had I come by the crested silver? Why had I remembered Midsummer Common in Cambridge, as if I stood there with the crowds swirling about me? Most of all, in the "remembering" on that last night, I had felt the dog's nose cold in the "dream". I had felt the warmth of his pink tongue and he had been a Corby hound, if ever there was such a thing.

Jonah's arm was about my shoulders in carelessness and the fact made me feel secure and safe. The country through which we passed was superb. The trees were tunnels of yellow and red and orange and we whispered through them noiselessly. His arm on my shoulder made the colours a glory, gave them a beauty that they could never have possessed before. The leaves danced in the sunshine and spiralled down and carpeted the roads and I wondered if Jonah was beginning to notice that I had grown up. "My hair was quite something," he had told me four days ago. It had been plaited into a long coil and wound round my head like a crown and he had gone on to tell me that I reminded him of Snow White . . . "hair as black as ebony and lips as red as blood and skin as white as snow, Princess."

I had been wearing a white coat, behind the dispensing screen, wrapping boxes and bottles and pouring tinctures and counting tablets.

"The sealing wax matches your lip-stick," he had said casually. "Do you wear it on purpose . . . the lip-stick I mean?"

He touched my shoulder and I got a shock that might have electrocuted a weaker girl.

"Lucky for me that you're not a nurse in the hospital. You'd have a queue a mile long at the ward kitchen every night you were on duty."

It was all a huge joke with him, when he kissed my hand and told me he loved me.

"I'm going to come back here one day and take over the practice next door. Dr. Cane's only holding it for me for he's old-fashioned enough to believe in family doctors and sons and nephews, who follow in foot-steps of some kind or another. You know about the communicating doors."

He imitated Dr. Cane's voice to the life. "We never bricked them up, my boy, I always hoped that you'd take on here and

164

let me rest in peace, out in the cemetery with content in my heart that I had thrown some sort of torch in the right direction."

"Your Russian princess mightn't settle for Ballyboy," I said with some sarcasm and he laughed at that and told me that she was a thing of yesteryear. He laughed about it and he made great fun of me and he never knew how he put my thoughts on a swing and sent them to the skies and let them fall back to earth again, and again and again. . . .

Mostly I kept my silence and that was my weapon against his flippancy. I had plenty of youthful suitors by now, but I fancied none of them. I might turn from Jonah's teasing and try to advise a farmer, who seemed on the point of losing a good milch cow from some dreaded disease with an impossible name. Because of O'Brien's lamb, I had made a reputation for myself with the farmers and they insisted on seeking me out. I did my best to read up books on Veterinary Diseases and I wondered what rules I might be breaking, but at least I had no difficulty in finding partners at the local parties. Yet the young farmers were not for me. I looked for Elizabeth Barret Browning and the silver armoured knight and the white charger . . . not for clumsy fumblings of an arm round my waist and a hot hand that searched for my breast. I had kept myself to myself and Aunt Ruth Rohan was very pleased about this, but she had ended up an old maid and I seemed to be pointed in the same direction.

Yet Jonah's arm on my shoulders was different. It was a gesture of comradeship and a sign of blood-brother-hood, and his fingers found a tendril of hair at my ear and twisted it round and round, and he little knew what he did to my emotions.

We drove in the old Rolls Royce through the furzy bogs, bright with wild flowers and there were mountains ranged along on our left side, as we ran down to the valley of the

Shannon. There were hazel nut groves with the autumn turning them to russet. The berries of the quicken trees were like rubies and the wood-quests clapped their wings out of the beech trees and sent the leaves spiralling down. The bracken was a trail of fire, the shorn sheep white against the hills. The hedges were tall herbaceous borders at first and then as we reached the west, came the dry stone walls and the hungry stony fields. The houses were toy cabins, whitewashed and thatched, and a pile of turf propping the side wall against a hard winter. The windows were polished and the curtains white-clean and always there seemed to be a woman, who leaned over the half-door and smiled at us, thanking us that we had slowed down and not run over the fowl that squawked out from under our wheels to safety. Somewhere along the way we crossed the mighty Shannon, full of fish, and then we began to rise a little, with the skies growing brighter from the sea and the hint of salt in the air.

I must have nodded off to sleep, because I woke up with a start to feel Jonah's lips at my ear.

"Here we are, Honey."

I saw the old brick pillars and the stone hounds, the lichened paws crossed one over the other, and there was Tinker, as if he modelled for them and he fast asleep in the back seat. The brick pillars were as lovely as a patchwork quilt is lovely with the colours melded together and weathered and the cement washed out with the years, but the hounds still proud.

They were the same breed as Tinker, the same breed as the dog that I had maybe seen the woman kick down into the abyss.

Jonah ran a finger round the rope of my hair and told me that Ned had gone to the woman in the gate lodge to get permission to go up to the house. Presently the woman herself came out and smiled into the car at me.

"There's nobody at home, Miss, but go on in and welcome. You'll find nothing there, but maybe old Ben. He wanders about the place and the Master lets him go where he will. He's quite harmless."

The conversation stretched into time, as it had a way of doing in Ireland.

"The Master of Corby was in Scotland for the fishing or maybe it was the shooting. He was restless since the days of the first Mistress, never settled anywhere and the place gone to ruin, for all the care he had for it, not but he minded his tenants and saw they were fed and warm and had good sound roofs over their heads."

"You should stop at the first building along the avenue," she called after us. "They say it's of some interest, history or that, but 'tis gone to pot and that's a true word."

I was properly awake by the time I got out of the car at the Folly, which was round a bend in the avenue and maybe a few hundred yards from the front gate. It bestrode the avenue like a colossus, shutting out the view beyond . . . a pretentious building, three stories in height and ornate . . . curved, with pillars and carved stone spheres. We passed through it under an archway and saw the vista in front of us, but there was an emptiness about it. The hedges were run wild, the walls were gapped, the stock had been driven off. Only the central avenue of oak trees that led the eye to the front door possessed all its old grandeur. There was a garden at the Folly, a pleasure garden, if ever there had been such a thing, but the box hedges were eighteen feet in the air and the roses had run wild and the blackberry thorns were cruel to the legs. You could go inside the building. Ned had taken Jonah to show him the virtues of boxwood, but I slipped past the door at the side . . . no, through the doors, twenty feet high and double. The first length of the staircase was down, but higher up, it was passable, except for the notice

There were rooms along the curve of the building and the damp had stripped the wallpaper off into leaves, that told the taste of people down the years. Surely if I had any part of this place, I might remember the rose-coloured paper, or the Regency striped one, but there was nothing. Here was a kitchen with an oven. As surely as God was in His heaven, bread would have been baked here and sucking pigs taken out with an apple in their mouths. I felt sick at the emptiness in my mind and even Tinker had left me on the track of some small creature, that moved in the weeds outside the windows.

I went back to the staircase and knew there was no excuse for me to try to attempt the climb up to the first floor, yet I found a toehold and then another. Dusty, I stood on the landing and from there it was easy. In no time at all, I was out on the third floor, with the boards giving in dry rot under my feet. Yet at the window, I forgot what rot could do and maybe remembered it again. There was a valley between the land and the sea and it sheltered a big house of matchless beauty, of dark red brick and with ivy, that ornamented the two wings of it. The steps to the front door were grey stone and clean, the windows whole. There was a high turret at the tip and a flag pole with no colour flying, because the Master was away. Presently he would come home and the Corby crest would fly again, two "hounds en sable" on "the vert ground" . . . and where had that sentence come from?

My eye was taken towards the ocean, that guarded the house on the left, a mass of rugged cliffs and coves and the sea sending back the cloud colours.

There was a small cove about two miles off and somebody had built a cabin there, white washed, thatched, with a cliff behind it to shield it from the fiercest gales, a sand like golden carpet at this distance. Yet there was no pricking in my thumbs. I had never seen the place before. I had never seen the house or the grounds or the ornamental lake. I would never have forgotten the ducks sailing along the rippling waters, nor the two black swans. If I had been Honor Corby and if I had had two brothers, then here they were magiced to swans, but I had never been Honor Corby. I had never had two brothers, and black swans were black swans.

Then Jonah appeared at my side, his face white and his tongue angry.

"What sort of a fool were you to climb up here? You might have got yourself killed. Even the dog had more sense than to follow you."

"I don't remember any part of it. I'm just a tinker girl, like they said, who was sold to a fortune teller for a few pieces of silver on Cambridge Common. There's nothing for me here, Jonah. I'm sorry I came, but I had dreams. . . ."

Maybe he took in my emotion after a look at me, for I was not far from tears and I think I had never felt more adrift in the world. He gathered me into his arms and held me for a long time and my face was against the warm skin of his neck.

"For God's sake, my darling, what does it matter? You're safe up here when you might be lying smashed on the brick floor below and my heart broken with your bones. Don't you know I love you? There was a time I thought that I might escape from you, with the fine English ladies and the way their voices would coax the birds out of the trees, but beside you, they're brass and you're gold, for all the ebony of your hair, and it doesn't matter to me who you are or where you came from . . . only that maybe you had unhappiness, and I'll see to it that there's only happiness for the years to come . . . if you'll have me . . . if you'll open the dividing door and maybe do a few prescriptions for me now and again . . . and run the Veterinary side of the business."

Ned interrupted us then and we said no more, only took

the car down the avenue and looked into the windows of the big house, like so many trippers full of curiosity about how the rich lived.

Ned kept us filled in with the picture.

"Never kept up much style, did the Master of Corby after the drownings, closed himself up like a clam and lived inside his own soul and for all his wealth and all the lovely possessions, lands and furniture and beauty of every sort just to stretch out his hand to take or his eye to behold, isn't it all turned to dust and ashes on him?"

There were rooms as big as I had imagined a ballroom might be, though I had no experience of such, and furniture sheeted over, portraits over mantelpieces, walking up the staircase walls and along a gallery.

If one of them had been my mother, I must recognise her, but they were all high-born ladies with no resemblance to me in the least. There was no set of the eye or chin, no tip tilt of nose, no dark widow peak of hair, that I might lay claim to.

"I don't want you to be a rich heiress, Honey."

The words were in my ear and I dropped Tinker, whom I had taken in my arms with the start Jonah gave me. "I have it fixed to practice in Dr. Cane's house as soon as I'm through my exams and get a bit of experience. You know about the connecting doors. We'll leave them unlocked in a few years and maybe we'll turn back the pages of history and set up a working partnership and maybe you don't realise that I might never get my final exams, for the thoughts of you that come walking through my head. I've never found a girl to like, far less to love, for the thought of you in the corridors of my mind. . . ."

"Don't tease me, Jonah. . . ." I opened my mouth to say something else, but I shall never know what, for Tinker was on the trail of some old memory. We had thought he was a stolen Corby Hound and maybe we were right. He had scratched at the front door and now he had gone down across the meadow, that had been a lawn in front of the house, along a path towards the coast. We followed him more slowly and Ned joined us, asking what had got into the animal.

"He's making for the sea, but it's a fair way off."

We came on it eventually after a walk over rough ground, beyond the meadow. There was a path, not used now, though we could make it out, that led over stiles and dry stone walls and down a small narrow sandy way to a small cove. It was rock bound and there was a high cliff to the north, but down on the sands, somebody had set a white walled cabin, that I had seen from the top floor of the Folly. This would have been the Gingerbread House, with its thatched roof and its small garden out in front, if I had remembered. There was a window at each side of a shut door, but no latticed panes. The door itself was divided into two parts and both of them locked against us and a padlock nailed fast into the outside of the wood as well. There had been curtains at the window but they were faded and rotting. The glass was so dirty that it was difficult to see within. The flowers in the bed in front were choked with weeds three feet high. Even the thatch had been skeleton-picked in places by birds, as material for their nests.

"If you want to get in there's no problem," Ned Oakapple told us and rummaged out a penknife from one of his pockets.

"I don't know," I said, but Tinker did not want to go in. He raised his muzzle to the sky and howled, ran a little way back along the path and asked me with his eyes to leave the place be.

There was an old tattered man coming slowly down the path and it took Tinker's mind off his fears. He started his usual defensive barking to protect me from evil, but the man put him to flight with a flung stone. Discretion being the better part of valour, my champion moved a few yards away, but barking still, let the man come on down the path. He was what they called a "natural," a daffy, like I had been myself. He shuffled his body inside his clothes as if he was verminous and came over to us, sideways like a crab might walk.

"I wouldn't go in there, Missie, if I was you, you and your fine gentleman. Nobody don't come here no more at all, only myself and I ain't feared. There's ghosts walk this strand at night and inside the cottage too. She looks out the window to see if the hangman's coming to string her up."

Ned Oakapple told him to be off about his business, as he made short work of the padlock and the door lock with his penknife, but all the time, the old man hung about, shuffling his broken shoes in the sand and whining out his warnings.

"None in the house will come below here, only old Ben, and it's the best part of the whole coast. There was evil done here. Look how the tide runs fast. It cast her body up over there, by that pool and her fair hair all about her like a fan might be and seaweed for green ribbons. She was done with evil then, but maybe she weren't. She walks the cabin night times. Up at the house, they'll tell you the same."

I stood inside the cottage and searched my mind for memories. If anywhere was the Gingerbread House, this must be it, but it was nothing like it. It was a white-washed Irish cottage, gone to neglect and unloved, maybe haunted too. It would have made a perfect holiday cabin by the sea, with its one big room downstairs and another smaller one, a tiny corkscrew staircase up to three little rooms above. There was furniture here, but it was ruined by the damp. The table had the veneer rising an inch off its top and there was wood-worm, even in this salty atmosphere, worm that crumbled sawdust into small piles on the dirty stone floors. There was damp and decay and ghosts. Almost certainly there were ghosts here, if ever there were ghosts and no sound but the washing of the tide and the scrabbling of the pebbles on the beach.

"If you want to see something to put your heart in your

172

mouth, climb the cliff yonder, Missie. There's a place up there that was made by the Devil himself."

Tinker had found a rabbit and taken himself off at full speed and I wanted no more to do with the cabin. There was no doubt in my mind that this was no Gingerbread House. My nightmares were figments of my imagination, conjured up from reading about Hansel and Gretel. Where was the oven and the cage where the wicked witch had kept poor Hansel to fatten him for eating? Where was the climb of the holly-hocks up the white front, the dormer windows, the dark wood laths against the white front, the typical Grimm Brothers façade. The wood on the table, where a birthday feast might have been laid out, was past recognition.

"Walnut veneer," Ned Oakapple said. "It's a sin to leave a table like that mouldering down here, when there's folk's would give a good penny for it, but we'd best clear off and get the door fast again, for we're all guilty of breaking and entering and that's a felony for three respectable people and a dog to have perpetrated."

"Walnut veneer," I thought and imagined how the table might have looked set out with the iced cake with its seven candles, teddy bear and dolls in high chairs perhaps, but there had never been such a scene. I must put the dream out of my mind and it would go away.

"You shouldn't have gone in there," the ragged old man shouted after us as we walked up the path in search of Tinker.

"Sometimes, she's there, the little girl, and if you set eyes on her, you'll be dead within the year. The woman, that done it to her had no luck and she got what she deserved, but the Almighty don't miss what goes on. 'All wickedness is but little to the wickedness of a woman,' that's what the priest says. 'All wickedness is but little to the wickedness of a woman....' "

We stood at the top of the rise and looked round to see

173

what he had told us to search out on the cliff, but it was over-run with nettles and we could see nothing, but a plateau, abundant with thorn bushes and nettles and thistles. We turned away and made back towards the car and the old man told us we'd as like as not find the dog down a rabbit hole with a broken neck.

"And don't come back here no more," he called after us. "You've no right here and you're dead and gone and another woman in your place and you only come to try and frighten old Ben, but there ain't nothing to a dead woman, fast in her grave."

I sat beside Ned on the way home and Jonah shared the back with Tinker and presently Ned raised an eyebrow at me and I understood what he was asking me.

"Nothing," I answered him. "Not the blink of an eyelid or a twitch of a nerve. I don't know the place. I was never there, for if I had been, I'd never forget it. I'm not of any high and mighty descent and I'll settle for the Medical Hall for the rest of my life, and maybe we'll unlock the connecting doors after a bit."

Then I laughed and was in high spirits and would not tell Ned why, but my heart was singing with joy at the things Jonah had said to me. Maybe it was all a joke to him, but surely he had meant what he said? If he had been cruel enough to make a jest out of it, I wished I was Honor Corby, in her green grave somewhere out deep in the Atlantic, but I was not Honor Corby. I was Lesley Summer, a young girl of great imagination and given to dreaming dreams and seeing visions.

If Jonah had meant what he said, there was a future stretching out before me and I would run to it with open arms.

Zachary Myles had sent me to Ireland and he had known what he was doing. He had seen his son, Malachai happy in Ballyboy and perhaps he had seen Jonah maybe fixed in

174

England, some future date and all because of a will. It might be that Zachary Myles had been in some high place, where he could look forward down the years and if that was the way of it, he had done a very clever thing indeed.

Chapter Eight

"THROUGH THE DOOR"

So the years went by and the vacations, when Jonah came to stay at the Medical Hall, were the golden days, the days he went away were grey. There was an agony of the parting of farewell, as I watched the train creep out of the small station of Ballyboy, my face as white as death, my eyes aching with unshed tears. Then the turn back to the town, the squaring of the shoulders, the walk down the hill to Matthew and Aunt Ruth and the Square, to the bow-fronted windows with the coloured bottles, that had so entranced me, but which were no match for the colour, that Jonah had brought into my life.

Then he was through his final exam and must have a telegram sent from all of us and addressed with great formality to Dr. Jonah Rohan and after that the long months of waiting for the garnering of experience.

I was almost twenty the day I waited at the window to see his car drive across the Square. He had been doing a House job at a hospital—physician first, then surgeon. After that, he had been serving a term under a General Practitioner and he was not finished with that yet. There were another few months to go, till he came home for good. We were unofficially engaged, but it was most unofficial, for he was a casual young man. I wore his signet ring on my finger and Uncle Matt and Aunt Ruth Rohan and I never discussed it much. My mind was full of the thoughts of the lovely ladies with whom he must come in contact, beautiful, talented, lady doctors perhaps, who

176

knew their pedigrees . . . rich patients, nurses, sisters, film stars, for all I knew. I imagined that his letters were less regular, but always there was a good excuse. He had been up all night on a confinement. He had had to assist at an operation and everything had gone wrong from start to finish. He had been flaked out when it was over. Cottage hospitals were the devil and soon, they would build multi-storey giant hospitals with every facility under the one roof—and perhaps he was wrong about that, for where has the personal touch gone nowadays, with dreams realised?

We had not seen him for a year, when at last he came and I saw his car turn the corner by the Hotel and could not think this might be Jonah's car. Here was no vintage Bentley with the power strapped under the bonnet. It was a family model four seater, with two doors and it was sober black, sable like the Corby Hounds.

I stood at the window upstairs and watched him get out of the driving seat, for I had to get my emotions in check and not throw myself weeping into his arms and demand that he tell me personally that he still loved me.

This could not be the casual Jonah, this fine young man in dark clothes and a white shirt, college tie, polished shoes, grave face, yet underneath all the gravity, there was a sparkling quality still with the joy of home-coming. That day, there was a fowl in the oven and an apple pie and I had bullied poor Mary over the apple pie, as if she had never heard of such an exotic dish before.

"Will you let me be, Miss? Don't I know how to make the fork marks right by now after all your tuition in the way to do it? Go on above and watch for his Lordship's car. . . ."

I watched Jonah through the lace curtains that ran on big poles with knobs on the end, so that there was no fear of them slipping off.

God save us! He was even locking the car door with an

English law-keeping habit, when nobody ever locked a car in Ballyboy. There was a crease in his trousers and a shine to him and no patches to his elbows and the car was correctly parked in front of Medical Hall, not skew-whiff. He was walking in to meet Uncle Matt at the front door of the shop, standing back to look at the magician's bottles, shaking his head.

"God! It's good to be home. I couldn't believe it existed. I tried hard to get away but I haven't seen you since that day at the Senate House, when they gave me the degree. They excised fun and inserted responsibility. I didn't believe what you said, Uncle Matt, but it was true, but perhaps it's for the best."

"And where's my girl?"

It would never have done to dress up for such an occasion. He might have noticed it. I wore a clean white shop coat and beneath it, a black skirt and white blouse, silk stockings and court shoes, well polished, and I might have been waiting for my own degree. My hair had been brushed one hundred strokes and washed out first of all in rain water the day before and now it shone. It coiled up on top of my head and the band of gold encircled it and Tinker was at my heels with a red ribbon round his neck, which he totally disliked. Jonah relieved him of it in ten seconds and said that nobody should make a monkey out of an honest dog. Then he lifted his eyes to my face and stood there, saying nothing. After all, we had written with great regularity, but letters were dry paper. We had discussed modern advances in medicine and how the salmon were jumping the weir at Ballyboy and how his farewell party at the Hospital had been quite something, and there had been no time to write. He and I stood face to face now and each one assessing the other. Our words were unromantic for such a meeting of avowed lovers.

"So you haven't poisoned anybody yet?"

178

"Uncle Matt has seen to that. You've had more scope in your foreign field over the water. Have you made the mistake that creates the true doctor, or is it still to come?"

Then the Medical Hall melted away from our consciousness. We stood there in the tiled hall and the grandfather clock ticked away the fleeting seconds and he said nothing, only put out his hands and took my shoulders, looked at me from the top of the ebony rope down to the black court shoes and back up again, reached out to touch the coil of my hair, threw all decorum to the winds and grabbed me into his arms, held me so close that I could scarce breathe, kissed me on the temple and so to the cheek and so to the sealing-wax mouth, that was hungry for his lips.

We were aroused by Uncle Matt's voice at our side.

"Ruth will be getting impatient above. The fowl's in the oven and it's time to dish up. I can shut up shop here for it's half day."

Jonah had turned into a sensible young man and there was a perfection about him. He had lost his carelessness, but not his sense of humour. He had changed carelessness for propriety.

After the dinner was finished and the table cleared away, we moved grandly to the sitting room and here was no young man who chooses a wife with no thought of what father or mother or aunt or uncle will think. If there were more like him today, perhaps there might be less unhappiness.

He was awkward about it at first, but he addressed us as a family.

"You all know I'm planning to marry Honey. I have a few more months to serve out in England and then I'll have enough experience to take over the practice next door. Dr. Cane and I have kept in touch. The summer will be the best time to start. He's arranged to move out and I'll move in. He's going to live in a house on the river and fish all day. He'll

179

be there if I get stuck and Lesley will move in with me next door. I have the prospect of six hundred pounds a year or maybe more and I have the car. She and I haven't discussed whether she'll keep on her work here, but it's a matter for us all. Maybe, she still has hopes of getting her finals. It's time she had a try at it, if she wants a career, but God! What does it matter? When two people love each other like she and I love each other, we would be as happy in a cottage on the bog road with me footing the turf and her churning the butter."

It was all as out of date with today as it could possibly be, yet we were fashioned like that in those times and we thought nothing of it. Today, he and I might have eloped in his second year as a student and lived on grants over the lean years, till maybe we found other partners. That afternoon, he even produced a velvet box with an emerald ring and we all admired it and it fitted my finger and Aunt Ruth Rohan said she was glad it was not rubies, for rubies were for tears. Then he was gone back to England for his last stint and I was studying as never before, for soon I must present myself to the Pharmaceutical College for my final test.

Mrs. Ned Oakapple had kept up with some of it and least, she could hear me from the text book, to see if I knew the words.

Uncle Matt was satisfied with my practical work, but he was moving back out of the time on the calendar. He shook his head over all the new discoveries, and this was an age of discovery, when old drugs were being thrown overboard, perhaps they might find them again in a million years, when sheep grazed on the patch where King's College stood in Cambridge today.

I had a headache that night and no hope of ever getting letters after my name. Far rather, I would have set up house next door with Jonah and brought his babies up. I would have given all the money in my purse, though it was not a fortune, just to see him for five minutes and hear his voice. Mrs. Ned was tired too, angry at all the strange formulae, that "they" had produced at the last moment, and which she could in no way understand.

"You'll get through, Honey. Put your hand in God's hand and don't tell me again that God's hand doesn't know any longer how to gild a pill, or I'll box your ears for you. Why should a chemist have to make pills and tablets by hand, when you can get them down from the wholesalers' by the crateful for a few pounds?"

"Because it's a lost art, you daft woman!" Ned roared out from the fireplace. "Arts shouldn't be lost or the world will suffer. We'll get food packed in cardboard boxes soon that you just stick in the oven and they'll taste of cardboard too. One day, we'll live on tablets and maybe a drink that you stir in with water and it does you down the whole day, but they won't be the good happy times."

I left soon after that, when peace was restored and Mrs. Ned and I had talked a bit about the wedding and the choir and the music. We were to be married in Ballyboy Church and a great feastday was planned, if nobody had a baby at the last moment and called Jonah away. It was a fate that had almost befallen Dr. Cane in Ballyboy legend.

I walked down the street towards the Square and thought I smelt smoke. There was a chimney afire and it was past time, when people should be in bed. Uncle Matt and Aunt Ruth would be fast asleep by now and the lamp lit in the hall for me to take upstairs. Dr. Cane would be asleep too, dreaming of the fine fishing he would have in the river, instead of night calls and worries about whether a patient might live or die. In three months, Jonah was scheduled to move in and after the house was settled to our liking, I would walk up the aisle with Uncle Matt to give me away and Jonah and I would be "man and wife together."

There was smoke in the air. It came low down and hid the sky and I wondered if somebody had left a leaf fire alight. I could see nothing amiss, just the cloud and the smell of burning. Then I was at the corner of the Square and my heart stopped for five seconds and then bounded against my rib cage. The lamp in the hall always threw a ruby to me across the Square, by reflecting through the big glass bottle with the red liquid, but there was more redness to it tonight and a flickering. There was a smoke smell now, that would take no denying shake of the head. There was a dimness about the front window, where never had been anything but shining glass. There was a crackling and a singeing and a sudden shot as a bottle burst from the heat. There were containers of spirit and oil and inflammable stuff of every kind in there and the place was on fire. I went across the Square as fast as I could run and Tinker thought it a game and barked in front of me, hindered my progress, till I called him to get to heel. Then there was no key in my pocket. I had woollen mitts on and it took me a long time to get them off. How could I have forgotten that the key was in my handbag among a hoard of little tiny objects, that conspired against me ever to find it.

It was there somewhere, but there was no time to wait. I pulled on my mitt again and took off my shoe, smashed the glass of the door and put in a hand to reach for the lock. There was a whoosh as the air found the mouldering flame. The whole staircase blazed up like a blow lamp, yet I got my hand in to open the lock. The lower part of the stairs was blazing, but surely I could make the first landing? The linoleum was bubbling under my feet and the banisters burnt my mitt off and Tinker whined at my heels and here was the turn of the stairs. It was like an inferno. The landing had caught and the flames were ten feet in the air and the heat drove me back and back and back. Stair by stair, I gave up the struggle and

Tinker had run down ahead of me and was out in the street barking for help. I was shrieking out to Aunt Ruth Rohan and to Uncle Matt, screaming that there was fire, fire, fire and no time in the world left to them. I felt the tiles of the hall floor under my feet and in the light from the fire could see my blackened mitts, though I felt no pain. I must get to a telephone and call for help, but the Fire Brigade was not modern. It would take half an hour to get it on the scene. The men lived all over the town. The town water might be turned off, it sometimes was at night. I went into the dispensary and found the tap, turned it on, thanked God that the water was running. I looked round for some sort of a bucket and was in time to see the drum of surgical spirit go up like a bomb. My clothes were alight. I beat with my hands at them and backed away and backed away and the flames ran across my clothes like long-legged evil spiders. Then I was lying in the street outside the door wrapped in something and I thought I must be dead. There were people there, standing looking down at me and a Guard pushed them back and Tinker's nose was cold against my face and I thanked God for him, that he had come to the after life with me. His tongue licked at my hands and now I felt the long agony of fire that burnt them.

Then somebody lifted me and carried me and I wondered if it was Jonah, but did not know who Jonah was . . . only his name.

"Don't take her next door. It may catch too. Bring her across to my place. For God's sake let the dog come. He'll not be separated from her."

Then a voice close to my ear.

"It's all right, my lady. They've got the hoses on it now. Can't you smell the dampening down of it and see the way the steam's rising? Listen to the crackling of the flames and the way they can't beat the water, nor the courage of our boys when it comes to putting out a conflagration."

There was a long spell where I remembered nothing. It was darkness and cold for all that I lay on something soft and was covered with a blanket. There was a smoky smell to the blanket and I felt the coarseness of it and knew it belonged to the Tinker woman. I was so cold. My hands were burning, but I shivered with cold and I knew that all I wore was a pair of white pants soaked in salt water. My teeth chattered together with shock and soon, there was a fire poured into my mouth, that made me gasp.

"It's all right, Honey," somebody said and I couldn't trace the voice, only knew it was from long ago. "It's just the shock and you've got your hands scorched a bit, but nothing that won't mend as good as new. Aunt Ruth Rohan safe too. Thank God we remembered the dividing doors or at least Dr. Cane did. We got down his stairs without a single scorch mark and we're all safe and well and I thank God for His mercy."

I opened my eyes and looked up at him and could not remember who he was . . . a friend I knew from past or present, but it was all gone.

"Who are you?"

"Matt Rohan, your future father-in-law. Don't tell me you've forgotten the Medical Hall."

The Medical Hall with the bow-fronted windows and the big coloured bottles, the regimented ointment jars, the glass shelves.

"It is all gone?" I whispered and my lips were dry with the scorching and my mouth afire with brandy.

"The staircase is damaged and the hoses will have spoilt a deal of stock, but what harm is it, with all our lives saved? You were a brave girl to come up to the first landing after us. It's a miracle you escaped out of it, but why didn't you remember the dividing doors, after all the way you and Jonah talked about them?"

I shut my eyes and moved back to another land. This one

184

was a dim place and there was no making sense of it, only the feel of Patch sitting as close to me as he could get and the way the warm tongue would try to bring me back to him.

I wanted Jonah, yet I could not remember who Jonah was, or who any of them were. Yet in a way, I knew. It was a place of refuge I had found and slowly the dream of it came back to me and I wanted Jonah's arms about me instead of the gypsy's blanket, Jonah, who loved me, but how could he plan to marry a child of seven years old? I must be out of my mind. The sea had gone. There was no smell of it, only the smell of burning, no pebbled stones under my feet and the sea dragging me down and Patch was by my side and I had just seen him drown.

"I couldn't save you, Patch. I tried, but I couldn't save you."

It all went away but then I remembered it . . . every last bit of it. It all slotted into a picture and every part of it fitting into every other part.

Dr. Cane came and cut the mitts from my hands and I was in a bed between cool sheets. I felt a needle in my arm.

"You'll sleep now."

I kept my eyes shut and examined every piece of the completed picture and the things that had happened so many years ago were the brightest in colour. It all fitted, but there was no proof that it was not imagination. The drug took me out on the tide, but before I dropped into darkness, my hand found Tinker's head, or Patch's head. Were they not faithful Corby hounds, who would follow their mistress into death, and for now I must say nothing. I had learned the power of a silent tongue.

They would rebuild the staircase of the Medical Hall and it would stand proud one day soon, but there was time for me to go back down the years. Tonight was not the time to proclaim what I intended to do. Tonight was for the sleep

185

"the balm of hurt minds." Tomorrow was for the search for all the things I had lost along the way . . . and there were people who had taken me in once, with kindness in their hearts. Would they ever understand how I wanted my father. Tonight I had found him.

I hoped they would see that there was something that had to be done, before I picked up my life from the place it had been, when I walked into the Square and saw the red glow of the lamp in the hall shining through the glass bottle. . . .

I slept as deep as death. Then in the bright of the dawning, I opened my eyes in a strange room and for a minute, did not know who I was, nor what time it was, nor where I was, only that the sun had shone through a sash window with blinds that would run up and down. There were small wedges that you could put between the sashes on a windy night to keep silence against the elements and what they might do to old window frames. Slowly I remembered my completed picture. I sat up in bed and looked at my bandaged hands and my head was muzzy from sleep still. Slowly I went back over it all, the childhood days and the happiness. I remembered the awful thing that had happened and wondered if it was just another nightmare, for surely it could never have come about except in a dream from hell. Bit by bit, I traced it along the avenue of time, till I came to the blank wall, but now I had found the dividing door. I remembered so many small details that surely it could not be all nightmare? I knew the names . . . Patch, the dog, whose nose was never far from my heel, the dog with the noble pedigree, whose stone ancestors sat on the gates with one paw crossed over another and looked with disdain on the people passing by. I had gone to see Corby House and maybe it had impressed me so much that I had turned it all into a dream, that had turned into reality in my mind. "Gypsy Rosa Smith". The name jumped into my mind and I remembered the caravan and Midsummer Common, but I had known it in my second life too. I lay back in the pillows and snuggled down, shut my eyes and tried to sort out truth and reality and thought I had it all, every bit of it, in my consciousness at last, but where was the proof? There was only one way of finding that. I must retrace my steps and collect up the pieces of my life, I had lost along the way. In the meantime, there was silence for my tongue, for I had found the value of silence before. Then I slept and was awakened again by the jolly lady, who lived opposite the Medical Hall and who had a draper's shop. She was glad to see me better and she talked all about the fire and what had happened and I thanked her for taking me in. Mr. and Miss Rohan had gone to stay with Ned Oakapple and his wife and they were unhurt. Maybe I didn't understand such things, but the place had been fully covered by insurance. It was the staircase had taken the worst of it and Ned would soon put in another stairs. He was the man for the job too, for he'd find wood as old as the staircase had been, if he had to search the whole of the township for it.

She was a motherly woman and I felt gratitude for her kindness and her understanding. She fed me porage with brown sugar and the top of the milk and I remembered it from the old life, though she could have known nothing about that.

"If you don't eat up your porage, I'll put it down for Patch," somebody used to say, and I knew who had said it now. I knew that it had been left to Patch to uncover the jester in the bottom of the porage plate and how he had come to insist on that as his privilege.

Then breakfast was done and Dr. Cane was there and my hands re-bandaged and they would soon be as good as new.

"You're a brave lassie to have reached the landing," he said. "Only one as brave as yourself was Tinker, for he followed you every inch of the way. He scorched his fur coat but he'll be as good as new in no time at all, just as you'll be yourself."

187

Jonah came over on a hurried visit from England and his face anxious and drawn. If anything had happened to me, it would have been the end of everything. As for the Medical Hall, I was not to worry about it. Let Ned Oakapple do it and it will be better than it ever was.

When Jonah had gone back to his work in England, I found Aunt Ruth Rohan by herself in the Oakapple parlour and I had decided to confess to her.

"I'm going to run away again. I did it once before and I had nobody to tell about it then, but there are so many people now that I could tell, and I chose you."

She raised her eyebrows in surprise and then I told her that I had come through the dividing door. I knew who I was, but I had no proof of it. I was obstinate with her that I must find out by myself and I was going away, but I promised to come back as soon as I could.

She did not argue much with me. She was wise and I had picked her well.

"You know who your father is, but there's no proof and you want to find the proof yourself, before you break his heart again by telling him a thing that might be all imagination."

I nodded my head.

"I remembered it. I suppose it was the shock. I thought you and Uncle Matt were dead. It came back, the way a sea fog rolls in along the sand and blots out the sun. For a time, I couldn't decide which was past and which was now. I'm not sure enough yet. I've got to go back the way I came and look up each cross roads. I don't want to hurt people, who showed me such kindness."

I knelt at her feet and she gathered me into her arms and my face was against the silk of her blouse and making grey spots of tears against the white silk.

"There are things that must be done a certain way. You don't have to explain it to me, Honey. Come back when the time is right and we'll be waiting. I'll tell Jonah this is how you want to go about it, on your own and with no-one to tell you, you must not or should not. Just let me know one thing, for I'm a curious old pussy cat. Was it very bad?"

I looked at her, lifting my head up and my face tear wet.

"It was very bad, as bad as it could be. That's why I'm not sure it's real. If it was real, it was as bad and as wicked as any nightmare, but it's finished with and there was this place for me to find at last, and I can never tell you what it has meant to me."

She pulled herself together and very Betsy-Trotwood-fashion, questioned me about money and practical matters.

"I have enough saved."

"Well then, it can be precious little."

I wept afresh when she gave me a roll of bank notes, smelling of lavender that, she had stowed away in case of a rainy day. I would not spend any of it unless I must, but I took it to comfort her, that I would "have some means", and so I went, stealing out of the town on the noon train with nobody to see me off and Jonah still over in England, and writing loving letters to me.

I felt full of power as the train moved out of the small platform. I was like the examiner with the answer book. I had but to seek out the question and the answer was in my hand, but where to go first of all? Dublin was the same lovely city and the barges still linked their reflections along the river. Malt and coffee possessed the city and reminded me of that first day. I regretted that Jonah was not with me, for it is a lonely feeling to stand on a ship and watch a country fade out of sight. Where to start the unravelling? I had not yet decided and I turned the tangled ball over and over and looked at each loose end. There was the Orphan House. There was Zachary's grave. There was Midsummer Common in Cambridge with the crowds thronging the Fair, and the smell of the hot-frying fish and chips, the ozone of electricity, the shouts of the stall holders, the music from the gallopers.

I sat in the lounge on the B. and I. boat and decided to start off at the first town I remembered from my second life. Perhaps I might have unravelled it the other way round and gone to the Gingerbread House, but it was better this way. The journey was without mishap, only for the shuttling of my thoughts like a weaver's loom. I pushed back all memory of the Corby Hounds except for the one that lay couchant against my ankle, for I could never have left Tinker behind and broken his heart and my own.

"You must have a dog's ticket. You can't travel with a dog and no ticket," said the man on the train.

"The Station Master at Ballyboy said it didn't matter. He's such a small dog."

The English were a different race from the Irish. There were rules about dogs, that took it in their heads to be faithful and travel with their mistress, and I paid up. Tinker thanked my wrist with a lick of his tongue and got up on the seat beside me, for he knew his rights, now that his ticket was paid.

He and I travelled in very humble style, compared with the Bentley, but at last we reached the town where the Orphanage was. I still wrote to Betsey now and again, and I went to the address where she lived. The town had shrunk down to the size of a doll's village. It was but a step from the station to her cottage and there was nobody at home. It was all desolation and emptiness and cobwebs in the windows. A blowsy woman came out from the shack next door.

"They moved away three month back. He got fed up with working on the land and took his-self and his family off to Lunnon. It weren't a moonlight flit, for they was all paid up. That I do know."

I walked down the High Street with Tinker free at my heels

and very well-behaved. I would visit Mr. Barleydrop. I stopped short in astonishment, for his shop was gone. The road went straight through where his front window had been with the sweets ranged in jars. It joined a new by-pass at the corner.

"Mr. Barleydrop. Sweet shop? Never heard of it or him."

I got the same answer from half a dozen people and began to think I had wandered into another nightmare. Then suddenly I came on the church and the churchyard. Zachary's tomb was a point of stability and I looked for it and found it. There was the same long summer grass, where I had lain hidden like a leveret.

IN GRATEFUL MEMORY OF ZACHARY MYLES
DOCTOR OF THIS TOWN FOR FIFTY YEARS.
THE BELOVED PHYSICIAN
SUFFER THE LITTLE CHILDREN TO COME UNTO ME.

"There's more wrote under that," Mr. Barleydrop had said.

"Erected by his sorrowing son," I read and pushed down the encroaching grass. . . ."

"And by many of his parishioners, who were his patients and will never forget him. . . ."

I sat down in the long grass and Tinker hunted about in his usual search for snakes which always possessed him in unkempt fields. I called him to heel and reminded him that this was a place of mourning and he sat ten feet away with one paw crossed over the other and I looked up at a far newer tombstone. My eye read it idly and almost I heard Mr. Barleydrop along the years.

"I give the public six months and the forgetting begins and in no time at all, there's nobody who even recalls your name. If I was to die today, soon, no child in the whole village would recall poor old Barleydrop."

I heard my voice as distinctly as if I spoke the words aloud, as if they hung in the air still.

"I'll never forget you, Mr. Barleydrop. You don't forget people, so people won't forget you, for you're a good man."

Yet Tinker sat at the foot of his grave and I read the inscription that this place was sacred to the memory of John Barleydrop, late of this parish . . . and now he was dead and buried and a road ran where his shop had been.

I had started with the wrong end of thread to find the unravelling of the ball. At least, I might seek out Mrs. Creek or ask at the police station, to verify how I had come to the Orphanage. The authorities had called me "Lesley Summer", because I had been taken to the Magistrates and "Lesley Summer" spent summer in Cambridge and the feast on Midsummer Common and it all smacked of Oliver Twist and how he had come to be named in alphabetical order. Had it been by Mr. Bumble? My thoughts were tangled enough, but there must be some solution, as to the start of the thread for the unwinding. There had been a barrel organ. I had just to shut my eyes and there I was turning the handle in streets maybe, or in fair grounds with the man's cap down on the pavement at my feet . . . and this man I must find.

"There's a long long trail a-winding . . . into the land of my dreams, where the nightingales are singing and the white moon beams . . . The "long" and the "long night of waiting" skidded the cogs and the organ stuttered and it was clear in my ears, as when I had turned the handle over and over, with a blister on my fingers and with the slow chink of a coin. I must find this man, whom well I remembered. His fortunes were high sometimes and our fortunes moved with his and if there were many coins, there was the smell of drink on him and the woman I called "Mam" sad. I had put my arms about her sometimes, when he had struck her and I must find her. She would stand at a stall somewhere, with her face powdered against the tears, and the rifle up in her hands.

"Come on now, gents, try your skill at the rifle range! Knock down three of the jumping balls and you get a dolly for your sweetheart."

But the rifle had gone the way of all the money and we had had a dartboard and darts, that were screwed every way out of the true, so that a prize would be a miracle to win.

Mr. Barleydrop might have advised me. Had he not advised me before, but now there was only one service to pay to him, my poor Mr. Jelly Baby. There had been the crocodile walk and the way he would come out of his shop with the bag in his hand "to feed crocodiles" and there was nobody to remember him.

"I'll never forget you, Mr. Barleydrop. You don't forget people, so people won't forget you, for you're a good man."

I could count out the names of the ones that had been kind to me and here was one of the first and I had a duty. Zachary Myles had been kind to me down the generations, had been kind to so many.

I had noticed a garden in front of a cottage near the Church, that had been so filled with forget-me-nots, that were spilling over on to the pavement. Here was some small thing I could do and leave the rest till later. I went back and knocked on the cottage door and asked the old woman if I could take some roots for a grave.

"It's for old Mr. Barleydrop," I explained and she looked at me as if I were mad. "For Zachary Myles too. I want some to plant in the graves. . . ."

"Never heard of neither of them," she said and told me I could help myself to what I wanted, but I weren't to pull the roses, nor yet help myself to the fruit in the orchard, for that was likely what I was after. I thanked her and she softened to me and gave me an old piece of wood to use as a trowel.

"Though what a young gel the like of you wants to mess round with graves for, I don't know," she said and shut the door in my face.

I tidied the graves as best I could and set the forget-me-nots to breed and seed into the future and I was emotionally at a low ebb, not to say a bit earthy about the face and hands when Jonah found me.

I was on my knees by Zachary's grave when his voice above my head made me jump half out of my skin.

"What the hell do you think you're playing at? God knows if anybody should be planting flowers on that grave, I should. He's my relative and not yours. I've searched all over for you, after I had twisted Aunt Ruth's arm and got a tenth of the truth out of her."

It was very comforting to be in Jonah's arms again and his scolding soon stopped. He was like the mother who had thought her child lost for ever and had found it safe and sound.

"I've even turned up a few stones to find you," he told me. "If you're hoping to find Mrs. Creek and Miss Frith, don't waste your time. They're gone respectable, started a private school in a tin barn for the daughters of snob parents in the next town. They're all sweetness and light and nobody knows the past. There's no cane on the wall and not much knowledge in the air, only the prestige of not going to the village school."

I tried to explain about old Barleydrop and the way he taught me how people are forgotten, for I had a guilt about it.

"I sent him a Christmas card each year, but it was no payment for his love of mankind. They forget him."

"It's lucky for Mrs. Creek and Miss Frith that they've forgotten too," he said cynically. "Their misdeeds are gone with the wind."

"With the wind," he echoed in Miss Frith's voice and lifted my spirits. "Still they led me to the woman who had you in her care before the police took you. She was Gypsy Rosa Smith, and she was on Midsummer Fair."

194

I was tactful enough not to tell him that I had remembered it and I did not tell him what a deal of things were to be traced. I settled for a drive into Cambridge and tea with his old University lodging house-keeper, Mrs. Greenall. I was very happy that he had sought me out and found me and that he intended to stay with me "till I got all these foolish notions out of my head" and came back with him to Ireland. Mrs. Greenall's house had shrunk in size, but the tablecloth was just as white and there were buns from Fitzbillie's too, as sumptious a feast for two young lovers as anybody could wish. Then a long time after tea, she said goodbye to us and told us we would enjoy the Fair.

"You should go and get your fortunes told. The caravans are at the main entrance this year, but fortunes is not necessary with you two. You'll be happy ever after, if I know anything, knew it the day you went away in the Jesus boater and the nurse's cloak. You was meant for each other."

We drove to the car park and left the respectable car and it seemed far too staid and sensible for Jonah, after the Bentley, even after Ned Oakapple's Rolls Royce.

"I got Rosa Smith's name from the police station here . . . got a decent Desk Sergeant and put him in the picture and he told me about the case, remembered it, but he couldn't get any farther back. They never traced the Irish tinkers."

"Irish tinkers," I echoed like Miss Frith.

"Oh, yes. They were a decent enough crowd, on the round of the feasts and the fairs too, but they had no record of any name nor where they might be now. It's a long time ago."

He grinned at me and opened the door to let me out, locked it again, as carefully as any city doctor.

"Let's ask Rosa Smith—and I hope you realise how much I love you that I drop my whole career and come following you round the country—and for pity's sake, don't leave poor Tinker in the car. He's not to be parted from you, any more than I am."

We walked across the grass of Midsummer's Common with Tinker at heel very correctly and not chasing after the dogs belonging to the Fair people.

"I don't know what you're after, Honey. I daresay you'll tell me when you've a mind too. I know only a bit of what you said to Aunt Ruth, but I've made a guess at the rest of it."

I bit my lip and looked down at the way the grass had been driven down and walked over and ill-treated and how it had stood up well to its punishment.

"Maybe I don't want you to marry a girl, who doesn't know her own father?"

He stopped up short at that and grabbed my shoulders in a grip that made me wince.

"Your pedigree doesn't matter to me. I'm marrying you and I tell you here and now, that if you come from the scruff of creation, I'll still marry you. If it's an Irish tinker I have as a father-in-law, that suits me fine."

Here was the Fair and I remembered it, just as it was to-night with the summer's evening long light gone and the flares coming into their own. I had been here before and it was as familiar as the Medical Hall, as the Orphanage staircase, that I had scrubbed from top to bottom so many times. Here was the rattle of the china and the shouts from the men on the stalls, the Dutch auctions, the Boxing Booth, the music that assaulted the ear drum, the side shows with ladies scantily clothed, but more upholstered than any Victorian suite, beside the proprietor who tried to tempt his audience past the pay desk. Here was the Wall of Death, the motor bikes revving as if the performance was to start off at once and you must hurry, hurry, hurry. Here was the glory of the gallopers and the giant wheel that spun to the stars. Here was a sweet stall with rock and brandysnaps and chocolate and coconut ice and candy

196

floss and here the House of Ghosts, the Tunnel of Love, the Whip, the Swing Boats.

The actual sight and smell and feel of it were no more vivid than my memory, and I kept my ear open for the stutter of an old barrel-organ. Before I came to the caravan, I smelt the strawberries and the cherries from the stall, that stood beside it.

"Tell your fortune, lady. Bring the young gentleman with you and I'll tell you if he's the one for you."

She was older and more crusted with paint and the caravan was more full of gold china and tinsel bright tawdry things than I remembered, but well I knew the crystal ball and the round table with the velvet cloth to cover the crystal. I knew the whine of the coaxing voice, yet she had been kind to me, in her own fashion.

"Cross my palm with silver."

Here were the signs of the Zodiac too . . . the Ram, the Bull, the Heavenly twins. . . .

I put a pound down on the table and kept my hand on it, cut off her words, as if I had strangled her and was glad of Jonah at my shoulder. The light was dim on his face, for the caravan was gloomy in the corners to add to the mystery.

"You bought me for five shillings from an Irish tinker family. I was with you for a year or two maybe, touring the fairs, till you tried to teach me to steal. Then the police took us both into charge. They sent me to a kind of prison. Maybe you were put on probation, but I'm not holding it against you. I'm trying to find the tinker family. I'll see no harm comes to them or to you."

Her face went white under her rouge, so that her cheeks were the cheeks of a Dutch doll, painted with red circles. Her mouth hung open and she drew back from me as if I had hit her.

"I don't know what you're going on about. I'm an honest

woman, I am. I'll tell your fortune and let you get to hell out of here or you can get to hell without. It's all the same to me...."

She was getting a hysterical note to her voice, but she had fear in her eyes. I leaned over and put my hand on hers and she snatched it away from me.

"You were kind to me. You sewed red rosettes on my head band and you put rings round my scarf to make it pretty. I've nothing against you. I want to find an Irish tinker . . . you gave him money for me."

Her face did not believe me. Maybe I was the law, or maybe I was some evil thing, that had spirited itself up from the past.

"Their name was Daly," I told her. "A man and a woman and nine children. They had a stall with throwing darts at a board, a barrel organ."

"They ain't here no more. They don't travel the fairs no more. You'll never find that lot now. They're split up and gone away to the ends of the earth."

I was near enough to weeping, when Jonah took over from me. He told me to take Tinker out and go back to the car. Almost he pushed me through the door, so that I had no time to say goodbye to Rosa Smith. I saw him take out his wallet and then I stood ten feet from the door of the caravan and waited, with Tinker at my feet and passing people telling each other to look at the dog and the way he held his front paws.

Jonah did not come out of the closed door for five minutes and I took it into my head to explore every avenue of the Fair. Here was a chance I might never have again, of looking in every stall and booth for the man with the cloth cap or his wife or his children. The children would be grown up now. I might recognise one of them . . . Tomsie, Joe, Mary, Maeve, Timsy John, Bernadette. They called me Bridget. They had a poem that I knew well now, but then I had thought it meant me. It was Allingham about the fairies. . . .

> Up the airy mountain, down the rushy glen. . . .
> "They stole little Bridget
> For seven years long
> When she came down again
> All her friends were gone.
> They took her lightly back
> Between the night and morrow.
> They thought that she was fast asleep
> But she was dead with sorrow.
> They have kept her ever since
> Deep within the lake,
> On a bed of flag leaves,
> Watching till she wake. . . ."

I had been little Bridget Daly, and now I searched the Fair, trotting up one avenue and down another and Tinker very close against my heels with his tail tucked tight. I stopped sometimes to study the shadows in the naptha flares and once I asked a blowsy woman on a rifle range, if she knew where the Daly family had gone.

"Daly, never heard of none by that name."

"I'm Bridget Daly. I got parted from them. I'm trying to catch up with them."

"Well, you ain't going to catch up with them 'ere. Do you want a shot at the prizes or don't you . . . can't waste my time with you all night."

I shook my head and she leaned over and looked down at Tinker.

"That's a mighty pretty 'sooner' you've got there. Mind some of the lads don't lift him off you. He has the look of a rare rabbiting dog."

I went away and moved faster than before. I took care to

put the lead on Tinker. After I got out of her sight, I ran as fast as a hare and arrived across the grass to the car, tried to open the door and found it locked. I hung round and the Car Park man came up and asked me what I wanted. I was waiting for a friend, I told him, but he looked at me, as if he did not believe me.

"There's a lot of stuff been lifted off here."

Then Jonah was back and I was glad to see him. He told me that he should be shot for not having given me the car key and he opened the door and put me into my seat and Tinker jumped in after me.

"I'm sorry for being so long about it, but I've got what you wanted or at least some of it."

There was a flash lamp in the glove compartment and I saw the torn sheets of exercise book he was giving into my hand.

"Don't worry. We parted the best of friends and you'll likely never see her any more. She hoped we'd live long and die happy and there's a signed statement for you."

My eye caught the written word in his doctor's scrawl, a deal of writing.

"She couldn't speak much. She was what we call a natural, but she was a pretty little girl. I knew she'd draw the crowd, for she looked so well reared. . . ."

He glanced at me, where I sat at his side with Tinker's head on my knee.

"She bought you from a family called Daly, who had nine kids or thereabouts. They'd picked you up somewhere or another, because they'd lost a child and they thought the fates sent you instead."

"I know it, Jonah. I know it. . . . Will you wait ten minutes for me here and keep Tinker with you?"

I was out of the car and back to the Fair ground proper, back amid the shooting galleries and the Dodgems and the gallopers, the smell of the ozone in the air, the smell of fish

200

and chips, the smell of mint rock and hum-bugs and sweating humanity.

I found the blowsy woman with the shooting range again and I challenged her toe to toe across the shelf of her range. . . .

"It's you," she said.

It was a different me, and perhaps she knew it. Here was no simpleton, who could be fooled out of finding her people and I was set on finding them, if anybody was ever set on anything.

"You've come back again then?" the woman said and held the point-twenty-two, as if she meant to defend herself.

"I'm Bridget Daly. I told you I worked the fairs with my people and I've a mind to seek them out. If they're not on the fairs, then you know where they are. It's written all over your face, and they promised to come back for me. We missed each other with all the travelling about. Fair folks are like that, casual and careless, but they're kind and they help each other. I give you my Bible oath that no harm will come to the Dalys through me."

She looked at me very slowly, from the top of my head to the grass beneath my feet, as if she was a vacuum cleaner that sucked the soul out of me.

"God's honour?"

"God's honour! I want to find my people. I'm not the law."

"But they deserve the law. You was stole away. It's an open secret. Anybody on the Common would tell you, if they thought you wouldn't bring trouble. "Little Bridget", the Dalys called you. Their own kid was took and then there you was, mother naked or thereabouts, all wet out of the sea, and they thought you was *sent* . . . by the fairies, when you was lost from some other Tinker clan."

"Haven't I told you I'm Bridget Daly? I want to find my kin and they *are* my kin. How could I harm them? I loved

G*

them."

She looked sideways out of her eyes at me, asked me where the rabbiting dog had gone to and I told her that he was with my man. She gave in quite suddenly then, said that one tribe of diddycoys was the same as any other, but if it was the Dalys I liked, I was best with them.

"They don't work the fairs no more, the biggest part of them. Daly and Mam, they took the younger 'uns and they got hired for keeps, by a Farmer Parsons—for the picking and the harvest and that. Good workers they are and the farmer's glad of them. He loaned them a field outside the village, six miles north of here. Weston is the place and Parsons lives in Weston Farm. They're in a three acre field, camped snug enough. Picking straws, they're at, this week, straws . . . strawberries . . . to come in to the stall on the Common at the big gate, by the Four Lamps."

She looked at me out of fierce eagle's eyes and her hair was divided down the middle and drawn into a bun on the nape of her neck, so that she had a look about her of a woman who would not stop short of murder.

"What was the kids' Christian names?" she demanded, and I remembered back through the cobweb years.

"Tomsie-Joe and Mary and Maeve and little Shamus, Jane, Bernadette, Willie. . . ."

That seemed to clinch it, yet she threatened me with the point-twenty-two again and said that I was to see that no harm came to them through her loose mouth.

"Only good," I promised and dived between her stall and the next and vanished along the green avenues into the darkness of the parking lot, thereby finding Jonah again.

Tinker welcomed me as if I had been gone for ten years and sat on my lap with his head along my shoulder.

"We find a village called Weston and then we find a Tinker camp and it's six miles to the north of here. It's dark and it

202

may be difficult to locate and I don't know what will come out at the end of it."

"Happiness will come out at the end of it," Jonah smiled and took my shoulders between his hands again, and kissed me on the mouth. "Have I just not had my fortune read for me by Gypsy Rosa Smith and I'm to find happiness with a dark lady? If I have to wait till you've proved your birthright, then I'm willing to wait, but let us get on. I don't know if you might like to leave it till the morning, but I think we'd better get on. Let's find this village and the camp and see what we can catch from the night in the way of positive evidence."

He smiled at me and told me that it mattered nothing to him if I were Bridget Daly or any female woman un-named. It did not even matter one jot or tittle, if I really were a fairy changeling. One day and one day soon, I would be his wife and from that simple fact was no escape. Then we bumped out of the car park and went to find the village, that lay to the north.

Chapter Nine

THE FAITHFUL HEART

It was a night when the moon was full and the countryside silvered. It should have been easy enough to find the Fen village, but one village was the same as the next and they seemed to be stretched in a necklace, one after the other. The signposts did not help, for they guided us along to a point and then came a Y-bend and no signpost whatever to tell us which arm to take. We must have gone at least ten miles and been near it, once or twice, when at last we reached the village of Weston. There was nobody about. The roads were as empty as if the end of the world had come. We came to a cross-roads and turned to the right, drove slowly along between yellow brick houses and past the Parish Church. After that, the road became a lane and twisted and turned till we lost all sense of direction, but at least we passed a farm and hoped that it might belong to Farmer Parsons. It was a square house with a big barn to one side of it. There was no light in any window and we thought it wiser not the knock the owner up and ask for his identity or the whereabouts of a tinkers' encampment. Jonah drove more slowly and we scanned the fields at each side of the road. It was orchard land for the most part, but there were open fields too and acres of crops. In the dim light, we smelt strawberries and stopped the car to get out, saw a strawberry field, that, for all we knew, stretched to the horizon.

Another three hundred yards and we picked out the pin points of three open fires and closer still, caught wood smoke in our nostrils. There was a five barred gate and we looked through it and identified caravans. There were three of them, spaced round a disused railway carriage, that was set up on old sleepers. It probably acted as a central commune. There was an unreality about the whole scene, with figures that sat on one heel round the fires, each in a circle. They seemed like black cut-out silhouettes with no real life to them, but there were dogs, that barked and brought Tinker's ears erect, made the hackles on his shoulders bristle. I shut him back in the car and Jonah and I went to the gate. A rough voice from one of the men by the nearest fire called out to us not to pass the gate, "if we didn't want our throats tore out of our chests." The man got up and came towards us and Jonah laughed and brought the scene to life. Yet still, there was no friendship about the gypsy.

"What are ye after at this time of the night? Have ye lost yer way or what?"

The smell of the wild roses and the wood fires and the horses, that grazed nearby with spancelled legs, with straw thrown down for them to eat . . . the smell proved the memories that gathered in my head. The man had a storm lantern in his hand and he held it up to look at us. I saw his profile and his black curly hair and when he turned to look down at me there were twin reflections of the light in his eyes. I spoke to him in Irish and thought it as good a pass-word as "shibboleth" in the Bible.

"Don't tell me that one Daly doesn't know another, even if the years haven't run away from under us. I was gone when you came back for me and I'm grown up, the way you're grown up. It is Timsie-Joe you are or maybe Shamus? If you'll hold the light closer, you'll see it's Bridget Daly standing before you and her eyes glad to rest on you again."

They had hushed the dogs to listen and now they came back from the fires, yet slowly. They opened back the gate and drew us inside, gathered about us. It might have been a witches' meeting on Hallowe'en, with the fires burning in the background and the dogs whining and the horses whuffling through their nostrils. Then they were all there, talking at once and no sense coming out of them. They propelled us to the railway carriage and up three plank steps, turned the lamps bright and stood and stared at me.

"Glory be to God! It *is* little Bridget and her a woman grown. I thought never to see you any more till the Day of Judgement."

There was white in the black of Mam's hair, I noticed, as she held me close to her bosom. It was not the first time I had been held so, nor the twenty first. Did I not remember the ample breasts, like two down pillows for a weary head? Did I not recall the acrid, tangy, smokey smell of her, the way she dried my tears on the edge of the black shawl. Her hands were the same hard and calloused crab shells, but old kind and tender friends and her voice had the low, lilting, mournful, whining humility.

"There's been sin on my soul, night and day, for years, with the way I sold you to that woman on Midsummer Common. You were gone the next year and my heart broken on me."

She was speaking in Gaelic and I asked her to talk in English in case Jonah "hadn't the Irish in his mouth."

"It was a bad time, Bridget. We hadn't enough to feed ourselves and the children hungry. Rosa Smith had coin and I knew she'd feed you and look after you, dress you warm against the winter. She promised to give you back the next year when the Fair came to the Common in Cambridge. You went with her because you liked the bright rings on her kerchief and the bells on the dress."

They were all talking and excitement was running high amongst them. I looked round and tried to pick out the faces from childhood. They were adult strong gypsy faces now and

206

there were strangers amongst them, who might be wives and husbands. I remembered them, the Daly children, with faces as soft as maybe my own had been, but lean and hungry too, as my own had become. I had been with them for two years or more and they had thought me a good luck piece, sent by the fairies to replace the one who had died. They went over it now, talking animatedly. It was far west in Ireland near the Atlantic. They had turned their backs on the grave and made for England and then they had come on myself, all of a sudden, in the middle of a furzy lane, alone in the darkness of the night and cold as a corpse, with all my wits gone. They marvelled at the way my wits had come back to me with the years and said it was the will of God.

"You were with us a long time and always our luck ran well. We had a barrel organ and you were happy if we left you turn the handle. You were like a raggety angel with the sweetness in your face and people would throw down coin for you, enough to buy supper for us all."

I remembered what had parted us. It had rained in Cambridge the week of that last Fair. It had gone on raining from morning till night and the times had been hungry before that. Now we all starved and there had been this gypsy, who told fortunes. She had met me up as I wandered one of the paths and had taken me to her caravan, warm, dry, with no rain to beat down on us. The Dalys found me there and she had promised to care for me. It was not clear in my head now, but they filled in the gaps for me.

"She dressed you in a silk gown, with bells that jingled on the collar. She promised to keep you a year till we came again. She'd feed you well and treat you with kindness and she thought that you'd draw the customers in, for you were a pretty little dote. We gave her the silver things you'd had in your hand that first night, the gilt band too. You made us take back a bit of the band, or perhaps we took it from you ourselves, but if we did, it was only to bring us together again. It's not lucky to steal fairy gold . . . and you were a fairy child, if ever there was one. . . ."

The next year there was no gypsy fortune teller and I had disappeared with her. They could not know what I now knew, that she had taken me into one of the town stores and had tried to use me for her shop-lifting. She had picked up a scarf and tied it round my head, picked up a coat for my back and walked out of the front door. I recalled a policeman, tall in his helmet and the manager's office, but for all anybody knew, I was a child, without wits, dumb and educationally subnormal, not able to give an account of anything.

It is impossible to record the conversation we had that night, for we talked the hours away. We went on and on, around the subject, and in and out among the years. They could not understand how I had come to talk and to be so bright in myself now. "It was a miracle of God's, sure enough."

"I was lucky," I said. "I fell among friends."

I was back on the dark road with Mam's shawl about me and the thought of the Witch frightening all wisdom from my brain. She had been floating on the water, her arms out before her and her face submerged, but presently she might magic herself alive and come after me. Patch was drowned. The last fragment of my brain to remain clear had been the thought that Patch was dead and then I let that knowledge slip away with all the rest.

The dawn came early as it does in midsummer and the sun shot its first ray on something affixed like a knocker on the door of the railway carriage. I put down my mug of tea and got up to look at it from the creaking basket chair, where they had sat me down. I ran my finger over the crossed paws of a hound, in gold, screwed safely to the old door.

"You had that and the gilt band and the knife and the fork

and the spoon. We kept back that bit to bind us together, so that we'd find each other, but 'tis not good luck to hold on to fairy gold, as we tolt you. You'd better have it this minute and take it with you, if you're set on going."

Timsie-Joe had a beard as black as a raven and a smile as white as the blossom in a May hedge. He took out a villainous knife and unscrewed the gold paws from the door with great care.

"It's brung us great luck, Bridget. We have fine work here and not always moving on and moving on. We work for the farmer and one crop follows the next. Then there's trees to be felled and hedges cut, ditches cleaned. There is work for as many more again as us and he's a decent man. We have food in our mouths, and meat once a day, and a place to lay our heads at night and horses and fine caravans. It was yourself that brung us the good fortune, little Bridget."

It lay warm against my hand and I could see the slots, where the side arms had fitted into it. It was the centre piece of the jewellery that Ned Oakapple had described, right enough, and more proof to my armoury of proof, yet one had to be certain. One had to amass proof upon proof upon proof, for there were big issues at stake and hearts that must not be broken with false hope.

I must go with my man, I told them, for the sun had risen and it was "not fitting that a girl spend a whole night with her man and they not yet wed." I would come back again and soon. I would only bring good to them and never evil. I thanked them for the love they had given to me.

God help them! There was not one of them could read or write, they had no wireless to listen to—and a newspaper would be as dumb to them as blank paper. How could they know what they had done in taking me in, when I was lost in darkness, and always they had offered me kindness.

"We called you Bridget. Maybe we were calling you out

of your name?"

"My name is Honey," I told them and asked down God's blessings on them and so we parted.

Half a mile away at the cross-roads, Jonah stopped the car and turned to me.

"What the hell was that all about? I held my peace, but maybe, you'd put me in the picture. I'm a patient man."

I took the gold band from my head and slotted the side bits into the crossed paws, put the complete head-band back in position.

"He called me 'Honey'. He always called me 'Honey'.

The Witch called me "Schneeweisschen" and the tinkers called me little Bridget. The Magistrates called me Lesley Summer, because it was summer on Midsummer Common and the Fair was on. Maybe it wasn't on, but I was associated with it and with the gypsy. I think I know what my name really is at last and I'll tell you about it, but I'd like to tell you in my own way, if only you'll have patience with me. I must be certain beyond any doubt, no matter what it is, you'll marry me and I'll be your wife and that's the happiest part of my story."

"But it's like a Chinese puzzle. There's no understanding it. You're not one of the Daly gypsies, but you might well be. They found you. They took you away and adopted you and it was all very unofficial. You might have been another gypsy child, but they didn't think what your mother might have thought of the abduction of her daughter . . . and where did you come by the gold head-band . . . and the cutlery? Why did they all think you were out of your senses?"

"I was out of my senses with shock."

I turned to face him and put my hand on his arm.

"I came over here to find the end of a thread and I thought I might unravel something, but there's more to it and I'd be glad if you'd come back to Ireland with me now. I know that you'd probably rather cut my head off, for you must be sick of the whole performance, but it is an important thing to both of us. I promise you. I have to do what I have to do in the right way. There might be great unhappiness if I put one foot wrong. Oh, Lord, Jonah! I don't know whether I'm right about it even now and if I'm not, then I'd be causing such pain. . . ."

He looked at me in silence for a long time and then he told me he would play it my way. I smiled at him and reached into the back of the car for a rug.

"We'll sleep for a few hours then, for surely it's not impossible to spend a night with one's man without sin? Tinker will witness our propriety."

He took me into his arms and Tinker lay like a fox fur along my shoulder.

"What does it matter what clan of gypsies you belong to?" he whispered to me. "They can steal the eye teeth out of my head and welcome in exchange, but how could people think you were daft and dumb and illiterate all those years? You've got an I.Q. as tall as Nelson's Pillar."

He kissed me gently and lovingly, but after a while he went on thinking out loud.

"The more I hear, the more I think that Zachary Myles had a hand in this. I've never had any doubt that he made me abduct you from the Orphanage that day. It was a mad act, completely impulsive and I'm not given to impulse. Zachary painted a picture in my mind what would happen to you, if I left you there, in the interval before the police moved in. That Matron could strike as quick as an asp. There was no time for magistrates' orders and no time for the signing of forms about taking children into care, yet I took you into care and it's turned out well and will turn out better still, and just for now, rest your head on my shoulder and close your eyes. Tinker will just have to move over a bit. Tomorrow is going to

211

be a better day and you'll maybe start telling me some of it, some of this unravelled tangle of yours."

So we drove up to Holyhead and crossed in two to three hours and went straight to the Vale of the Shannon next day, and all the long journey, I refrained from telling him what I thought was the whole story. I was not sure how it was going to end and there was a delicacy about it, which would need much understanding on his part.

I pointed the route of the car and he was surprised when I did not turn for Ballyboy but went straight on to the Shannon, then on again to the climb to the house with the Corby Hounds.

"This is the beginning of the story," I told him and still he was patient with me, especially when we did not even pause at the gate lodge, but swept past the Folly and down to the cove by the sea, to the white washed cabin. He pulled up the car and asked me if we were not trespassing and I told him no, but that there had been a deal of trespassing in the past. Tinker had got out and was nosing round in the long-neglected grass, looking for snakes, scratching at the door of the cabin, as if there were rats within and maybe there were.

It was all gone to neglect and the walls wanted the white-wash brush over them. The painted sills had rotted and the thatch had been pilfered for birds' nests. The rain had leaked down trails of grey tears along the white walls, like the trails I had left on Aunt Ruth Rohan's white silk blouse one day.

The grass was three feet high and full of poppies, full of summer-weed-flowers, that had choken the hollyhocks and the daisies and the delphiniums. Only the red bachelors' buttons were impudent in the border of the plot before the windows and the London Pride had run rampant.

There was a patience about Jonah or maybe a pride, as hardy as the London Pride, that refused to be choked by weeds. He had determined not to beg any more of the answer

212

out of me and for the most part of the journey I had been a poor companion, trying to gather my memories about me like a tattered garment.

We walked down towards the tide's edge to sit on a flat rock and I told him that the time had come for me to start my ancient mariner's story. He grunted to himself that it had taken long enough, and I thought he was not very pleased with me, but if I had to do it my way, then do it my way I must.

"Only first, promise me that you love me and will marry me," he said and there was a sweet interlude when I did just that, with doubts growing up my mind like Jack-in-the-Bean-Stalks, that when he heard the whole of it, there would be no desire in him to have anything to do with me.

Tinker was bored with it all and he had tired of searching for snakes and had gone to sleep at my feet, blinking a bright eye now and again to make sure there were no wicked robbers or cut-purse thieves about.

I started at what I thought must be the beginning and I went right on.

There had been a man hereabouts a long time ago, I told him, a happy man with a loving wife. After a while, they had a little daughter and they seemed all set to live happily ever after.

"It sounds like one of your wood-cutters who lived in the middle of the forest," he remarked and I told him indeed there was a flavour of it.

Unhappily the wife had died and the man was desolate. He had an infant daughter but no mother for her, yet he was happy enough and she was his one treasured possession and as she grew up, he loved her more and more. Then one day, he took it into his head that it might be better if she had a woman's hand to guide her. There were women who helped him with her upbringing, but he wanted a superior sort of person to teach her and he got a governess, an "Au Pair" from the Swiss-German border.

Jonah was impatient with me all of a sudden. He accused me of playing histrionic games with him and I knew it was no game I played.

"Oh, come on now, you're the child and you're no wood-cutter's child. Wood-cutters don't have German Au Pair governesses."

"Jonah, I love you. Put up with it a bit longer. It's so important to me and to you and to somebody else."

"You're talking about yourself and you were well-to-do, and presently you'll tell me the German woman married your father and stole your inheritance. I don't care a damn for your inheritance."

"I was the girl, Jonah, and he loved me and she hated me, yet she pretended not to hate me, pretended that she would be a loving second mother and presently, became a second mother, and was such a loving person, that I called her the 'Witch'. It must have been a matter of inheritance. I daresay I was heiress to his belongings, but she was not in her right mind. I heard the people of the house say she was mad and indeed, I think she was, and every day, she taught me German and told me Grimm's fairy stories and told me of the Gingerbread House and the way Hanzel and Gretel had been caught there, how their father and stepmother tried to lose them in the forest. My father had given me this cottage in the cove and it was a lovely happy place. It shows what a spoilt child I was, for it was my play house and I was proud of it. It was different then, with flowers and fresh paint and the moss growing on the thatch, and such furniture inside, like the Seven Dwarfs might have had. She called it the Gingerbread House and she put a spell on it by that, in my mind at any rate, and every maid in the house was ranged against her on my side, but there was nobody who measured her wickedness, nobody who imagined that what happened, could ever happen."

I got to my feet and paced up and down for a while and again he tried to interrupt me and I begged him to wait.

"I was spoilt rotten. I don't deny it, but I was a child. I had no defence. I see it now. She was fair in the hair with a face cut from perfect flawless marble, not a line on it, a broken-English voice, and a way of getting out the whisky when he was lonely with the grief for my mother."

"Oh, God, Jonah, I remember it in dribs and drabs and it comes to me in the night and the sweat stands on my brow. I can speak German fairly well and I know all about Snow White and Rapunzel and Rumpelstiltskin, but there was no softness between her and me, only a pinching and a slapping and the proper way a little girl must behave."

"I had a dog called Patch and she hated him too, said it was unhygienic that a dog should sleep by his mistress's bed and Patch guarded me and bit her once, when she slapped me. I think that was when she started to plan the nightmare, that happened on my seventh birthday. I had pulled myself back into a shell. We lived a secret life, Patch and I, with walks by the sea and with hunts after rabbits, but he never caught anything and I didn't want him to. Then it was my seventh birthday and there was to be great celebration. There was a cake with seven candles and there was to be a big party in the house, but first there was a picnic in the cove. I didn't want to go, but I couldn't think of an excuse. If I did, she over-ruled it."

"She had made the cake with her own hands and she gushed over me with too much false sweetness. There were dolls to bring and my teddy bear and Patch, and it was not necessary for any of the women of the house to come. They must pack up a hamper with the good things. She would see to it all."

I walked up the sands to the house and remembered it with

such colour that it was all there again, with the biscuit-coloured wicker hamper, with plates and the settings and the white cloth and the cake and the candles in little sockets and Patch very attentive to the cake, with his head on one side.

"I was to lay the circular mahogany table. I knew it was very kind of her to be so interested in me. If Father had been there, my heart might have been lighter, but he was away till evening. I set out the silver things, one place setting for each doll and the cake dominant above it all and I looked in the mirror and she smiled at me."

"Have you seen the well of treacle, Honor?" she asked. "Maybe we could get some treacle for our tea."

"She led me to the hole in the top of the cliff, that backed the cottage and I knew well that it was a hole into deep sea and no treacle well, but her broken English went on in my ear."

"Often about Elsie and Lacie and Tillie have I read to you, who lived in the bottom of a treacle well. Up here it's like Alice in Wonderland. Come on the high place and look down. You can smell the treacle."

I walked up the rough path and Jonah followed me, his face grim, his mind wondering if mine had gone straying again.

"On the high crag behind the cottage was this deep pit, three feet across that pitched straight down into the tide and the sea had been running high that afternoon. Her ash blonde hair was silver in the sunlight and her smile as false as only a child might detect."

"Lean over and see if you can smell the treacle," she said.

"I mumbled ungraciously that it was a hole that drowned anybody that went near it. I'd been warned against it a hundred times. Then like a conjurer, she produced a rabbit out of her pocket. It was Patch's toy rabbit and he was very devoted to it. She must have taken it from his basket at home

216

and brought it along on purpose, but on purpose for what?"

"Come Patch! Here is your baby. Come and catch him. Run, run, run and do not let him run away."

"She shook it in front of him hither and thither and he went wild with barking, all his commonsense scattered. She threw the rabbit down the flue in the cliff and the next moment, Patch was gone. I went to the edge and knelt down, peered after him and knew that by now, he would be fighting for his life in the swirling tide. I turned to see her coming for me. At last she was the Witch in all reality. Almost I could see the long nails and the talon fingers, as she came at a run to push me after Patch. I had only time to fling myself sideways, burrowing down into the grass and she was over my head. There was a hollow splash far below and I knew she had been caught in her own wickedness."

"It was awful, Jonah. I ran down to the sand and there was Patch far out and trying to swim. He was frightened and he held himself too straight in the water and he swam away from the shore. I must have taken off my clothes. I don't remember doing it, but it would have been madness to have walked into the sea with a full skirt hampering my legs, my petticoat. I flung them down in the water for all I cared, shouted to Patch to come back to me, screamed that I would swim out to him. All the time, I could see her face in my mind, white with fury and hate and her hands clawed to push me to my death. Then I was in the water and the waves were rolling me upside down and about. At the top of a high roller, I saw her farther out again, on her face with her head under water, her hands out-thrust and floating too and Patch had seen me and had turned around. Almost I reached him. Oh, Jonah! he was as like Tinker here as two peas in a pod and I loved him and there was no time to get to him, for he was sinking lower and lower, and the waves washing over his face. Then I couldn't see his frightened eyes. I couldn't see

217

the Witch. The current took me and carried me and threw me and there was a darkness and a smothering and then nothing, but an ache in my head and lights that flashed. I was on a rock by a sandy beach and I did not know who I was. I was utterly lost and it was night and I was almost naked . . . cold. I lay for a long time. I don't know how long, I was very sick. When I felt better I got up and began to walk and after a while, I trotted along the sandy lane and I was crying. I don't know if it happened, Jonah, but I think it did, but I may have dreamt it. I had been setting the table when she called me and still I gripped the place setting in my hand and the gilt band was in my hair. Then there was a horse that came clip-clop, and there was talking, and the smell of smoke and a black shawl with a fringe to it and it was warm. The woman was crying, because she had had a baby die, a little girl, not long born. They had buried her by a cross-roads and put a wreath of hedge flowers on the grave and they were drunk, the man and the woman, yet her shawl was warm and if I belonged to the fairies, it didn't matter. Two to one, I was one of the Smith brood, who had got herself lost and frightened to death, but that did not matter, one more mouth?"

"It was bad luck for them in the green island and they would turn back to England where the coin was good. They'd play the Fairs again and maybe set up a stall—a shooting range, a few darts boards, didn't cost a hat of money. At any rate, hadn't they the old barrel organ? It would bring in the price of some food for the children."

"So I travelled with the Daly brood, in the camouflage of their children and one raggety child would be hard to pick from ten. I didn't speak and I had lost my wits, lost my memory, except for the dreams that came in the night-time. So we trekked slowly across Ireland and over the sea to England and round the fair-grounds for one year and another—

and maybe another, to the fortune teller's caravan, and so to the police, to the Female Orphan House."

Jonah was looking at me in amazement. I had crouched down on the grass and Tinker was guarding by my side, close in against me, for he knew my every mood and he knew that my mind was troubled.

"You're telling me—you're trying to tell me—you've been trying not to tell me for the last day or so, but it's obvious. . . ."

"Nothing is obvious Jonah, only that I love you and you love me."

I stood up and took his shoulders in my hands, tip-toed to kiss him and thought it might be the last kiss between him and me. I put my finger on his lips to beg for silence.

"Don't say anything more. I'm not sure of anything. For all I know, it may all have been a nightmare between the night and the light. Just come with me. Put your hand in mine. There's a path I know, or think I know."

I turned left down the cliff and around the cove a bit, then up an incline, where there was room for us to walk side by side and Tinker barked, with a joy in the sound of it, and ran ahead of us, excited suddenly, jumping along as if he went on springs, looking back at my face now and again—running on, surer of the way than I was, for it turned and twisted and went between hedges, after it achieved the top of the next rise. The sun made the smell of the wild flowers as sweet as my love for Jonah, yet soon I might be without it. It was a walk that would have given great pleasure on any other day, for there were little hazel groves and small dells of wild orchids and the grass was moss soft under our feet, and golden with butter-cups.

Once or twice, Jonah tried to ask me what I was about, but always I shook my head and knew that again I had chosen the weapon of silence as armour. Then there was a coppice that led out to a great expanse of grass and four hundred yards

219

away was the mansion with its plinth of four steps to the front door for elegance and the door standing wide open to the stranger. Tinker stopped up short, his ears erect, his flanks quivering. He made a small whimpering, whining sound. He was like a dog carved in jet, so still he stood, only for the nerve trembling of his sides. Then he barked, not once, but in a hysteria, as if he were on the trail of a hundred hares and they within six feet of his nose. He glanced back at me for permission to go and I gave it with a wave of my hand, yet I did not clearly know what I had given him permission to do or where to go. He was off like a shot from a cross-bow. He stretched himself out at full gallop across the green grass, a sable hound on vert, if ever there was one.

A dog had come out of the front door and was looking down from the eminence of the four great steps, proclaiming the presence of an intruder with furious barking. Tinker stopped when he got to the foot of the steps. Then he sank to his belly and went slowly up from one step to the next, all barking stopped, and with a humility about him. The other dog was stiff-legged and wary. Then they recognised one another. It could be nothing else. The hostility between them was away like mists before the sun. They touched noses, licked ears, jumped up with paws about each other's necks, sprang this way and that.

There was a tall yew hedge that ran out from the north wing of the house and I drew Jonah into the shadow of it. Then a man came out from the front door to see why the dog had barked and my heart turned over within my chest. His hair was greying but I remembered it, when he had been as dark as my own hair was now. He did not see us, for his attention was caught up in the two dogs, who were wild with delight, one in the other.

They raced and chased up and down the grey steps, like black notes in a symphony of praise, notes that trilled up an

220

octave and down again. They sprang from top to bottom of the steps and then out across the wide expanse of green, that reached for the sun. Flying like birds, they went, shoulder to shoulder, from the top of one bank to the next with no effort in the world. Four hundred yards they raced at top speed and then back again, so alike that there was no telling one from the other. Yet there was no barking now, no sound but the cooing of the doves from the dove cote in the stable yard. I knew that the doves were white and that their tails fanned out in grace, that they were so lazy with kindness that they would never leave home as I had done.

At last, I looked with all my attention at the one I loved, the one who had called me "Honey". The yew hedge was close enough to the foot of the steps for us to hear what he called to the dogs.

"I told you he'd come back again . . . told you that the beggar woman stole him. He's too fly not to escape and come back, weren't you his woman and pups you had to him?"

I remembered the rasp of his beard against my face and how he had given me such love that few daughters could have known. Tinker was a Corby Hound. He had been stolen, as I had been stolen and it was only coincidence that had brought us home together, for there was no mistaking that I had come home too. There was no room for doubt any more. I stepped out from the shadow of the hedge and the man saw me and he forgot his delight in the dogs in a moment. He looked down at me as if he would draw the soul out of me and his face was carved in the marble of shock.

"Constance," he said, but that was my mother's name and then I saw the knowledge swaying in his brain that Constance was dead and long gone down the years.

"I'm Honey."

I went to him up the steps with all the humility that Tinker had shown and he met me in two strides, grabbed me into his

221

arms. I felt his fingers find the band in my hair.

His voice was muttering against the top of my head in thanks to God that I had come back.

"I knew that you weren't gone for ever. I've felt it all these years, known that if I had faith enough, you'd be found."

"Honey," he said and again "Honey", and his beard was the old scrub against the softness of my cheek and my tears wetting his face and mine. Then Tinker thought to come and jump up and make a great fuss about his master, for after all, had not he come home too?

"It was a beggar woman came to the back door. When she went, the dog had disappeared and I knew she'd had him, but we couldn't trace her."

I began to tell him what had happened to me and maybe it was a longish time, before we remembered Jonah. He was standing at the foot of the steps and very much put out with me and I shall never lay blame on him for it.

"I'd like you to meet Jonah Rohan, Father . . . Dr. Rohan. We're engaged to be married."

"So it's out now? You're Miss Honor Corby and a great heiress?" Jonah said rudely. "There's no doubt about it, for you carry the proof on your head and in my pockets but we've gone the long way about finding out your identity, haven't we?"

My father stretched out a hand in welcome, but Jonah shook his head and the sun glinted off his fair hair.

"Oh, no, it won't do," he said. "It won't do at all."

He was furious with me. It had been the last kiss I had just given him down by the sea. Well, I knew it.

"We're promised to each other," I told my father haltingly and he tightened his arm about me.

"Oh, no we're not," said Jonah, balling his fists on his hips, his arms akimbo. "I was engaged to a penniless gypsy lass with no family and God only knows what heritage. I want

222

nothing of Miss Honor Corby, heiress to Corby House, born with a gold spoon in her mouth, if ever anybody was."

He walked along at the base of the steps till he came opposite us, regarded us both with defiance.

"I'm sorry, but I'm only a new-fledged doctor and I haven't a penny piece in the world. My hands are empty and I'm not marrying any great lady now or ever. I bid you goodday. It was grand while it lasted, but it's over now, with all the dreams of the Gingerbread House and the Jesus boater and the nurse's cape . . . all the fun we had and the way the sun never went in, while we were together."

He spun on his heel and the anger on him still, though I thought that maybe he was not far from tears and trying to hide it. He went walking away down the avenue and his car lay in the other direction and he had even forgotten that.

I ran down the steps after him with a dog on either side of me, barking in sympathy. I shouted after Jonah like a tinker woman.

"You can't go away like that. We love each other. It's just not fair. You told me you'd marry me, even if I were the lowest tinker in the world. You can't leave me because I'm somebody else. I'm the same person I always was. I'll die, if you go. Do you hear me? I'll die."

He stopped, but he still kept his back to me and I sank down on the last step and wept in my despair.

"You said it didn't matter if I was the scruff, or the scruff of creation. You know you did, and there are so many people we have to see after, Betsey and the Daly family and we have to mind Uncle Matt and Aunt Ruth Rohan . . . and the Oakapples. . . ."

There was a great shout of laughter above my head and I looked up at my father, recalled in the old days how I used to think he was like God and indeed I thought it still. He was certainly god-like in his wisdom and judgement. His laughter

223

spread over the green lawns, reached for the skies and off towards the blue sea. It caught Jonah in a net and held him fast.

"It's no good, Jonah Rohan. You'd just as well turn round and come back. I've known this lassie from a long time ago. She's as faithful as one of her own Corby Hounds. If you run to the ends of the earth, you'll find no escape from her love, or from your own."

Jonah started to walk back to me, slowly at first and then more quickly, his hands coming out towards me, his body casting a long shadow, yet there was no shadow between him and me down the years that were waiting at our feet.

THE END